BARGHEST BRAWL

BARGHEST BRAWL

THE ORIGIN STORY OF MONSTERS™ BOOK FOUR

MARTHA CARR

MICHAEL ANDERLE

DON'T MISS OUR NEW RELEASES

Join the LMBPN email list to be notified of new releases and special promotions (which happen often) by following this link:

http://lmbpn.com/email/

This book is a work of fiction. All of the characters, organizations, and events portrayed in this novel are either products of the author's imagination or are used fictitiously. Sometimes both.

Copyright © 2023 LMBPN Publishing
Cover Art by Jake @ J Caleb Design
http://jcalebdesign.com / jcalebdesign@gmail.com
Cover copyright © LMBPN Publishing
A Michael Anderle Production

LMBPN Publishing supports the right to free expression and the value of copyright. The purpose of copyright is to encourage writers and artists to produce the creative works that enrich our culture.

The distribution of this book without permission is a theft of the author's intellectual property. If you would like permission to use material from the book (other than for review purposes), please contact support@lmbpn.com. Thank you for your support of the author's rights.

LMBPN Publishing
PMB 196, 2540 South Maryland Pkwy
Las Vegas, NV 89109

Version 1.00, April 2023
ebook ISBN: 979-8-88541-164-6
Print ISBN: 979-8-88878-313-9

THE BARGHEST BRAWL TEAM

Thanks to our JIT Readers

Dorothy Lloyd
Jackey Hankard-Brodie
Diane L. Smith
Jan Hunnicutt

Editor

SkyFyre Editing Team

CHAPTER ONE

In the living room of her little bungalow of exile on the Ambrosius Clan estate, Greta Ambrosius drew a deep breath and prepared herself for the hard conversation she was about to have with two of her grandchildren. It might have been *the* hardest conversation, but that was neither here nor there. For the last twenty years, she'd known this was inevitable.

There really was no time like the present.

"It's a bit more complicated." She looked between Halsey and Brigham with grim determination. "Family history they never taught you in school but definitely should have. Looks like it's time to change that."

Although Halsey felt Brigham's confused stare plastered to her face, she couldn't take her eyes off their grandmother sitting across from them in the armchair to the right of the fireplace.

We've been through hell and back to do our jobs. To fight for the Ambrosius Clan militia and hunt monsters and do what nobody else can do, only to find out half of what we've been told is a complete lie. Maybe even everything I believed about who and what we are as elementals. Now Meemaw thinks it's the right time to hash it out?

White-hot anger curdled in the pit of Halsey's stomach as Greta's living room filled with a tense silence nobody seemed particularly keen on breaking.

That wasn't going to fly. She'd raced out here, dragging Brigham along because he was too stubborn to let her disappear, to finally get her answers. Real ones this time.

Doesn't mean I have to be happy about it. Or that I have to sit here and patiently wait until somebody else feels like talking.

"A bit more complicated, huh?" Halsey sat up straighter and cocked her head, glaring at her grandmother. "Even more complicated than a complete stranger telling me to go figure out who the hell I am before he'll even sit down to talk to me? Or how about the fact that the Order of Skrár knows all about the things somebody else *really* should've told us a long time ago? Because that's complicated enough as it is."

Greta nodded slowly, her jaw muscles clenching as she let herself sit with her granddaughter's anger. "I'm fully aware of that, kid. Trust me."

"Sorry." Halsey sat back against the couch cushions and folded her arms. "I'm having a hard time trusting much of anything right now."

"Hal," Brigham muttered, now casting her a sidelong look of disapproval. "If you want her to talk, give her a chance to talk."

"Oh, so it's all up to *me* now, is it?"

"That's not what I'm saying."

"Right, because nobody around here ever says what

they actually mean." When she whipped her head toward her cousin, she found more than disapproval in his expression. Now there was an underlying pall of extreme discomfort. The kind neither of them was used to experiencing. Not at the same time, not together, and certainly not here at their Meemaw's house.

The shock of seeing that discomfort all over Brigham's face made her pause long enough for her cousin to fix her with a remarkably sad, pleading look as he lowered his voice. "Come on, Hal…"

She vigorously shook her head and pointed at him. "Don't talk to me like that. Like this is all my fault, or *I'm* the one who should've figured out by now why everyone's been lying to me about everything."

"It's *not* everyone."

"No, only the one person I thought I could trust to lead me in the right direction when I actually needed some goddamn help!" Halsey was well aware she'd lumped her best friend turned mission partner in with the rest of the Ambrosius family, who had apparently been keeping more than a few secrets from their best team of monster hunters. The tiny flicker of hurt moving across Brigham's eyebrows only made it clearer. Now that she was finally starting to say what *she* really meant, she didn't think she could stop this flood of emotional outbursts.

Halsey pointed at Greta but kept yelling at her cousin. "I came to Meemaw for help *weeks* ago, and she told me to go talk to the *living records*. The Order of Skrár. Then we went off to kill an unkillable chimera, so I could finally sit down with someone who might have some answers, and the asshole sent me right back here! What else am I supposed to think, huh?"

"That's not fair." He sat up straighter on the couch and gestured toward Greta. "She *just* said she'd tell us what we wanna know. What *you* burst in here demanding to know—"

She cut him off with a bitter laugh. *"Demanding?"*

"You're blaming Meemaw for everything without even listening to what she has to say." Brigham's grimace of frustration and disbelief as he shook his head almost cut through his cousin's all-consuming anger. "Did it ever occur to you that maybe the way you react to stuff like this is the reason nobody wants to tell you anything?"

That little revelation from her cousin stopped Halsey in her tracks. She stared at him, unable to think of anything to say as her lips parted in surprise.

He really went there.

Brigham seemed to immediately realize he might have taken it too far with that overly heated statement. He clamped his mouth shut, blinked quickly, and held Halsey's gaze. Now both Ambrosius cousins had loosed a few of their own personal truths that would be impossible to take back.

Before either of them had the chance to either directly address the growing conflict between them or try to gloss over it yet again so they could move on, Greta picked that moment to intervene for all their sakes.

"She's right, Brigham."

He whipped his head back toward their grandmother and gaped at her. "Even if she is, she can't talk to you like that."

Greta calmly lifted a hand to stop him and dipped her head. "Emotions run hot in this family. We all know this. Believe me, what's already been said in this living room today doesn't come anywhere close to what's been shouted at me over the years when emotions run hot. Yeah, that does include from my own children." A tiny smile flickered at the corners of her mouth as she held her grandson's gaze. "I'm not nearly as fragile as they'd have you believe."

Halsey couldn't help but snort, which got her a quick sidelong look from Brigham. Fortunately, though, he didn't use it as another excuse to jump all over her.

She'd already figured out years ago that the Greta Ambrosius the rest of the family viewed as physically weak, mentally frail, and even verifiably crazy, was anything but. Brigham had recently been brought into the loop about this before the cousins had journeyed back out to Ireland for a private investigation of their own, but apparently, he still needed more time to get used to the truth.

We all do. And we're all dealing with different truths at the same time.

"So," Greta started again, her smile growing as she looked between her feuding grandchildren. "How about we pop a few ice cubes into everybody's piping-hot anger cups and agree to keep my living room a neutral zone for now? What d'ya say?"

Halsey inhaled deeply, feeling herself calming down already, and offered her grandmother a small, noncommittal shrug.

Brigham blinked at Greta a few times, almost looked at

his cousin for clarification, then shook his head. "Meemaw, I have no idea what that means."

"A truce," Halsey muttered without looking at him. "Fresh start. Do-over. Whatever you wanna call it."

Greta pointed at her with an expression of mock seriousness that didn't quite ring true. "No more yelling at me, or each other, or yourselves. That's a very important quality of neutrality, don't forget."

"No yelling," Halsey added in the same flat, bored tone, though she couldn't help a tiny smile.

She's good at this. She's always been good at this. So what did she do to make the entire Council feel like it was a good idea to get rid of the best arbitrator we have?

Turning her thoughts to that particular mystery in and of itself was enough to deflate Halsey's agitation. For now, anyway. If Greta Ambrosius said she would explain the family history Halsey and Brigham were "never taught in school," that was exactly what the woman would do.

Not without a few assurances first, though.

With a knowing smile, Greta leaned forward in her armchair and spread her arms. "I'm going to need verbal confirmation before we can get to all the deep diving. Or as much of a verbal confirmation as you're capable of dishing out at the moment. Brigham, the phrase 'cat got your tongue' has never looked so blissfully sincere on anyone else."

Only then did he seem to realize what their grandmother was trying to weasel out of him using humor, lightheartedness, and her signature eccentricity. After gaping at the woman for a moment longer, Brigham cleared his throat and nodded. "Yeah. Clean slate. No yelling. That's cool."

Before Greta switched her gaze from one grandchild to the next, Halsey was already offering a verbal response so everyone could stay on the same page. "Sounds good to me."

"Peachy." The woman's gaze fell instead to the copper orb of alchemized magical sand her granddaughter had been clenching in her hand since bursting into her house. Greta nodded at it and clicked her tongue. "I'm gonna need you to do something else with that hodgepodge firecracker you've got in a death grip, girl."

"What, this?" Frowning, Halsey held up the orb and was once again surprised that Brigham slightly flinched away from it as she did.

Their grandmother's only response was to raise an eyebrow and keep staring at the orb.

Brigham sighed, then muttered, "That's not gonna do anything."

"What's that, boy?" Greta cupped a hand around her ear and leaned toward him. "I said no yelling, but incoherent murmuring wasn't part of the deal. Speak up."

After casting Halsey another quick look that made her feel like her cousin was actually afraid of her now, Brigham stuck a thumb out toward the orb in her lap and shrugged. "Doesn't matter where she puts the weird little ball, Meemaw. You could lock it up in a different room, and Hal could still get her hands on that thing if she really wanted."

For the first time since Halsey had barged furiously through the front door of her grandmother's house with Brigham close on her heels, Greta actually looked surprised. She stared at her grandson for a moment as if *he* were the one who'd suddenly and inexplicably developed an ability to manipulate a special kind of unknown element. One that could rip apart an invincible chimera into three different animal pieces, no less.

Then she guffawed, threw herself backward into her armchair, and slapped her hands on her knees. "Well, I know *that*."

"Wait, you do?"

"I don't wanna have to look at the thing while we're talking," Greta continued, ignoring the baffled look on her grandson's face. "It's incredibly distracting."

"Fine." Without a jacket or a bag beside her, Halsey plunged the orb into the crack between the couch cushions.

Brigham sucked in a sharp breath but didn't say anything. He did, however, lean away from the bulging little hole between the cushions when his cousin finally jerked her hand back out, and it seemed like he wouldn't be able to quit staring for quite some time.

"How's that?" Halsey asked flatly.

Greta studied the spot on her living room couch occupied by one of the most powerful magical weapons they'd ever seen, which none of them understood in the least. Then she clicked her tongue and shrugged. "Sure. Why not? Now shut up, both of you. You wanted the full shish kebab on this one, so I'm gonna give you the full shish kebab. But it's a real pain in the ass to have to stop what I'm doing because one of you felt like coughing up a smartass remark. Got it?"

Neither of her grandchildren said a word.

"Good. Now give me a minute. I need to figure out the best place to start." Dropping her forearms heavily on her chair's armrests and dropping her head back against the cushion, Greta stared at her living room ceiling and popped her lips in silent contemplation.

Correctly assuming this was a good opportunity to say something, Brigham leaned toward his cousin and murmured, "Shish kebab. Was that a dig on Turkey, or do you think it's just…you know…"

Halsey pressed her lips firmly together to keep from laughing before she could finish the sentence for him. "Just Meemaw being Meemaw? I'd say it's a little of both."

He nodded curtly, frowning as if it was what he'd been thinking all along. Then he remembered the gold orb she'd stuffed between the couch cushions. Immediately, Brigham leaned as far away as he could get from the strange, alchemized ball turned magical weapon. He leaned against the couch's other armrest to act like this was all another normal day at Meemaw's.

At least it feels a lot more like normal now than it did five minutes ago. I guess I might've come on strong there in the beginning. Maybe…

Taking a deep breath, Halsey let her cousin have a moment to collect himself and focused on their grandmother instead. Greta still stared at the ceiling, her lips pouting in deep thought while she drummed her fingers on the armrests.

Any second now, she's gonna start talking, and we'll finally get some answers. They better be good ones 'cause I've waited way too long to hear the truth.

CHAPTER TWO

"I guess the beginning's as good a place to start as any," Greta mused. "Not for *me*, obviously. I guess not even the beginning for either of you, but that's irrelevant."

Halsey and Brigham exchanged the kind of quick sidelong glance they'd been exchanging for as long as either of them could remember. Fortunately, they both managed to hold in their laughter and any other clarifying questions they might have asked under different circumstances. Yet they'd promised to keep their mouths shut while Greta spun the tale that desperately needed to be told.

That single look, though, made Halsey feel a whole lot better about the state of her relationship with her cousin, best friend, and mission partner.

Maybe this isn't too broken to fix. Hopefully, that doesn't change after we've heard what the family never wanted us to hear.

Finally finished with her diligently silent deliberation, Greta clapped her hands together and shifted in her armchair to get as comfortable as she'd get during a rare storytelling session like this one. Then she centered her gaze somewhere halfway between her grandchildren's faces and began.

"This must've been...oh, what? Twenty years ago? Damn, it feels like so much longer than that. How old are you two? Twenty-three and twenty-four? Yeah? Good. Well, unless the laws of math have suddenly changed and nobody told me, I'm going with twenty years.

"The two of you were running around in pull-ups. Yeah, Brigham. Your mom would never admit it, but I do mean *both* of you."

Halsey couldn't help but snigger, which got her a scathing look from her cousin before their grandmother continued and really got invested in her own story.

"Of course, *I* was twenty years younger too. If either of you has to ask how old that actually was, you can keep wondering on your own damn time. I know I look amazing." With one hand, Greta patted the underside of her straight, thick, silvery-gray bob, then continued. "I was still on the Council, too, believe it or not. Sat in your Uncle Arthur's seat at the head of the table, as it were. I was still one hundred percent active in the field. Come to think of it, that was probably the first sign something in our family was about to walk the plank and fall overboard head-first."

When the woman paused again for a lot longer than seemed necessary, Halsey wondered if her grandmother was waiting for either of her grandchildren to ask a question at this point.

Nope. She said no talking and no questions. She only needs more time to find the right stop on memory lane. If I were her, I probably wouldn't have thought about all this in a long time, either. On purpose.

With the promise of everything yet to be revealed, the Ambrosius cousins exhibited a surprising amount of patience for their grandmother's sake and remained perfectly quiet.

Then Greta clicked her tongue and released a contemplative little hum. "I wasn't paying attention to those kinds of useless signs at the time, though." She thumped a fist on the armrest and grinned. "I was fighting monsters. All over the place. Two missions a week, minimum, and they never took me longer than forty-eight hours. I'm sure you've figured this out by now, but being extraordinary at what we do happens to run in our blood. Take that however you want. *I* was living life to the fullest, and I had no idea my last hunt was shaping up to actually *be* my last hunt until way after the fact. Thank you, hindsight, and all that crap."

Halsey pressed her lips together and forced herself not to interrupt the oddly disjointed flow of her grandmother's thoughts expressed aloud. *I hope she gets to the point sometime today.*

"Anyhoo…" Greta shook her head, then chuckled wryly. "That very last mission of mine, which I had no idea would truly be my last, had me hauling my own ass out to Greece after one major asshole of a minotaur. Big ol' bastard, too. Almost ten feet tall without the horns, four feet across the shoulders, and had a pair of hooves like you wouldn't believe. I had to forget everything we all know about minotaurs that day 'cause I *didn't* find him where he was supposed to be. You better believe that sonofabitch turned Metsovo traffic into a maze of its own."

A brilliant smile broke across the woman's face as she turned toward her grandchildren, eyes wide and expectant as if she were waiting for a very specific kind of reaction from them.

Halsey was too focused on paying attention to every little detail of her grandmother's story, hoping the information she'd been seeking for months would reveal itself in the tiny details of the Ambrosius Clan matriarch's words.

Brigham couldn't get over hearing the sweet, smiling, cookies-and-milk-giving Meemaw he'd grown up with cursing like a sailor as she recounted her monster-hunting days.

"Turned Metsovo traffic into a *maze*," Greta repeated. When the reactions she was hoping for didn't immediately present themselves, her smile faded into a dull, deadpan disappointment. "That was a joke. Seriously, are either of you paying attention? Obviously not. Well, forget it. I've had tougher crowds."

Before either of her grandchildren could intervene with either an apology or an acknowledgment of the joke, the woman soldiered on with her story.

"Since we're getting down to brass pickles here, I went after this thing myself because the minotaur was terrorizing the little town of Metsovo day and night. Storming up the steep cobbled streets, bashing in the windows and doors of breezy little cottages built into the cliffside. You get the picture.

"Craziest thing of all, this particular bovine bastard was damn well intent not on the actual people there but on the *temples*. You know the kind. White stone. Architectural columns. Marble statues of all the Greek gods and goddesses, and what have you." Greta waved away the mental image. "I never put much stock in all that deity nonsense. Of course, that's easy to do when *we're* the ones with magic. We know where all the demons, angels, ETs, and whatever the hell else folks wanna call these things come from. 'Cause we're the ones chasing 'em across the globe and putting 'em in the ground."

Halsey blinked slowly and tried to look like she was patiently waiting for the rest of her grandmother's story to reveal itself. Except now she was starting to get annoyed all over again.

I swear, we're gonna have serious problems if she starts telling us all the red tape I keep running into is because of world religions...

"You might be asking yourselves why the hell any of this matters, right?" Greta pointed at her grandchildren and wagged a finger between them. "Well, it damn well matters, and I'll tell you why. That minotaur I chased down in Greece twenty-some years ago was the first monster *not* doing what the damn things have always been doing and are supposed to *keep* doing. To top it all off—"

"Wait, twenty years ago?" Brigham interjected, oblivious to the semi-dirty looks being shot his way by both Halsey and Greta. "Are you saying this whole thing..."

"Yeah, kid. I am." Greta tilted her head and raised her eyebrows in classic Meemaw-warning fashion. "I also told you to keep your mouth shut and your hands to yourself until I'm done 'cause we got a lotta ground to cover and only so much oxygen to go around. Got it?"

Thoroughly berated, he clamped his mouth shut and

nodded. He frowned at his empty hands as if he couldn't figure out whether he'd actually done anything that warranted such a scolding.

Halsey pressed her lips together and dipped her head to hide another smile.

This version of Meemaw is still new to him. If he's not used to it at the end of this little chat, he probably never will be. I hope she can cut down on the crazy talk and get to the point before we all run out of patience.

The fact that Greta had declared her willingness to "bare all" was probably the only thing keeping the Ambrosius cousins in their seats right now. Especially because the woman had only touched on the first incredibly important fact.

All the werewolves acting against their nature the first time Halsey and Brigham were sent to Ireland to take care of them weren't actually the first. Apparently, it was Meemaw's giant minotaur. Twenty years ago.

After another long moment of staring at her grandson, Greta was finally satisfied enough with her warning to continue the story.

"I won't bore you with all the details 'cause they're weird as shit. I had to get creative that day. Nothing your Meemaw couldn't handle, of course, but we're not putting *my* hunting skills under a microscope, are we? No. The important thing is I took the minotaur down, threw myself a little ouzo party with the locals afterward, then came right back home to our happy little family plot outside Lufton, Texas, with a whole different mission in mind. Specifically, to find out why the hell that single, big-ass, hard motherfucker of a monster wouldn't do what every other minotaur has done over the centuries and was so damn hard to kill."

Greta looked at Halsey and fiercely held her granddaughter's gaze. "You might even say I tried to blaze the trail *for* you, kiddo. Didn't know it at the time, but hindsight is always a fifty-fifty chance you were wrong then and are still wrong now."

It took a lot of concentration and willpower for Halsey to refrain from trying to correct her grandmother's misuse of the common modern saying or asking what the heck that was supposed to mean. The facts would work themselves out eventually. Yet when she shot Brigham a quick sidelong glance, she found her cousin leaning back against the cushions at the opposite end of the couch, frowning with his eyes closed and his lips moving as he tried to puzzle out the woman's odd use of an incorrect phrase for himself.

"So what does one of the best Ambrosius Clan monster hunters at the time do with this new and illuminating info?" Greta cheerily asked as she dived right back into her story. She pounded a fist on her chair's armrest again before pointing at Halsey. "We all know the ending to *that* story, don't we? She comes back home, dives into a few ancient records nobody's bothered to look at for decades and maybe even generations because nobody gives a shit. We're all too busy hunting down the monsters that have been acting the same way for as long as any of us can remember.

"Trust me. Those records my decrepit husk of a brother still cares for were a lot easier to get ahold of back then. A lot changes in twenty years, doesn't it? Damn. Feels like so much longer. I know I already said that, but it bears repeating."

The woman drew a deep breath, closed her eyes briefly, then nodded. "Unlike *your* short-lived hullaballoo in the Clan library looking for answers, girl, *I* actually found something. A piece of history overlooked by pretty much every Ambrosius elemental because, again, who wants to pore over history when they've got monsters to kill? Nobody. Not even Charlemagne. Then again, my brother started growing down and in a hell of a lot sooner than the rest of us, am I right?"

Greta snorted at her grandchildren, both of whom stared back at her with blank cluelessness. "That was another joke. Guess you had to be there. And we're moving on."

It took her a moment to remember what she'd been saying before she'd started cracking jokes at the expense of her only brother. Who was now the oldest living Ambrosius elemental and self-proclaimed protector of all knowledge and histories magically preserved within the Ambrosius Clan library. When Greta finally got her brain back on track, she cleared her throat and nodded.

"The minotaur was weird as hell. I'll give you that. However, the record I found in *our* library when I got back from the confusing little tumble with the man-bull was even stranger.

"It was an eye-witness account written down by one of our very own ancestors. Cedric Ambrosius. I don't feel like doing the math on this right now, and that's not even one of my skills, but the man conveniently remembered to *date* his account. I like to think it was for posterity and all that.

Which, you know, is what he *should* have done. I'm getting ahead of myself, though.

"This was prime reading, too, you know? The kind where no detail was forgotten, no fill-in-the-blanks left up to the imagination. Apparently, way back in the year 953 A.D., there were a hell of a lot more elementals running around than there are now."

Halsey's pulse quickened as she realized this was what she'd been looking for, and now it was what she would wait the rest of the damn day and night to hear from her grandmother's lips if she had to.

"Not sure which part of that is more interesting," Greta mused as she gazed across the living room, tugging on one earlobe in thought. "Again, not the point. The real kicker is what this Cedric wrote down in his little Age-of-Iron diary.

"As the story goes, in his own words, Cedric and a bunch of his buddies were walking around along the western coast of Ireland together, yucking it up, drinking ale, having a grand ol' time. A good half-dozen of them. All from *different* elemental families, if you can believe it."

Halsey swallowed thickly and tried not to let her excitement get the better of her. *Six different elemental families? We know there were a bunch of us before the great war and the Ice Age we created to lock the Blood Matriarch away at the bottom of the ocean. But this is like two million years later, and now there are only three families left. What happened to the rest of them?*

"I know it's shocking to even consider," Greta continued, jolting her granddaughter from her private musing because it felt like the woman was reading Halsey's mind. Even though that was impossible.

When Halsey flicked her gaze quickly up toward her grandmother's face, she found Greta's bright blue eyes focused intently on her before the woman gave her a slow, knowing nod.

"Six different elemental families running around together as a gang of best friends without a care in the world. Makes you wonder what in the fiery blue hell happened to the rest of 'em, doesn't it? Not to mention who knows how many other families were alive and kicking back in the cheery Age of Iron."

With a casual shrug, Greta stopped tugging on her earlobe and folded her arms instead. "Unfortunately—or fortunately, whichever perspective floats your socks off—Cedric only talked about the five buddies of his that day in Ireland. Ambrosius, of course. There was a Havalon there with him, believe it or not. Also a Grendier. Somebody from the Grispin Clan, and the other two…"

She paused, wrinkling her nose and grimacing in concentration, then puffed out a sigh. "Hell, I can't remember the other names. Doesn't matter anyway."

Brigham gaped at her, his eyes bulging and his jaw dropping open. "Doesn't matter? There were other—"

"Hush, you." Greta pointed another warning finger at him. "Or you can go wait outside with the garden gnomes, and your cousin can fill you in on the details afterward. They're not as friendly as the name suggests."

Frowning, he nestled farther into the corner of the couch, folded his arms, and shot Halsey one of those curious, questioning looks.

The garden gnomes. He's definitely gonna ask about that later.

She tried not to laugh as she focused on giving their grandmother as much of her attention as she could. If Greta Ambrosius didn't feel like she was being *really* listened to, she wouldn't take the time to finish anything she'd planned to say. With good reason, too.

For at least the last twenty years, Greta Ambrosius had historically been silenced, talked over, accused, exiled, berated, labeled an insane woman, and subsequently shoved to the back of the Council's mind. Most of it had happened before Halsey was old enough to be aware of anything behind the scenes, but she'd also watched the same story play itself out more than once in the last few months alone.

Today, if her grandmother said anything, it would be with the understanding that she wouldn't put up with the same treatment from Halsey and Brigham as she'd been getting from her own children for years.

I hope he understands that part and keeps his mouth shut until we get to the Q-and-A.

Whether or not Greta had been thinking along the same lines, she didn't immediately dive back into her story again after yet another interruption. Instead, she fixed a warm, kind, knowing smile on Brigham and waited for him to look up at her after he'd been thoroughly put back in his place, which he clearly hadn't understood until now.

At least, Halsey hoped he understood now.

When he looked back up at their Meemaw and found her gazing at him with grandmotherly kindness, a tiny smile bloomed on his lips, and he nodded.

The second he did, the look instantly disappeared from Greta's face. She leaned back in her armchair again, crossed one ankle over the opposite knee, and dropped her forearms on the armrests. Then she gazed around her living room as if she were looking at a different time and place and finally continued.

"The only detail Cedric didn't particularly cover in this fun little entry of his was what all those elementals were doing together in Ireland and why. I'm sure those pieces of the puzzle will pop out of the shadows eventually. If they end up being remotely useful, of course. Maybe they won't. Who knows?

"Can't blame the guy for failing to set the scene the way we would've liked it to be set, though. If *I'd* been in his shoes, or leather sandals or furry boots, or whatever the hell they wore back then, I'd probably find the where and why of my little elemental party about as relevant as a fart in the wind, too."

Brigham snorted but remembered to keep his mouth shut.

"Makes sense all six of those happy-go-lucky elementals didn't have much attention to spare on anything else," Greta added, her blue eyes glinting in the warm overhead lights of her living room as she prepared to drop the final realization on her grandchildren. "Our ancestor and his good ol' boys found their proof way back when. Maybe sooner than they knew what to do with it, but still.

"That proof, kids, was in the enormous Viking longship they found shipwrecked on the coast of Ireland."

CHAPTER THREE

Vikings?

Halsey's mind spun with all the different pieces her grandmother had tossed up into the air like historical confetti.

That's it. That's the missing piece I should've been able to find on my own. If I hadn't been banned from the Clan library, anyway.

In Greta's few seconds of theatric pause, Halsey weaved together more threads from the past than she'd been able to manage since the day she and Brigham found the silver coffin on a white sandy beach beneath the cliffs.

Vikings spoke Old Norse, didn't they? At least in 953 A.D. They had to. Plus, the silverback alpha said something to me in Old Norse before he—

She couldn't quite finish the thought. Not now.

After her last trip to Ireland, she still didn't feel like she'd had enough time to process what had really happened that night in the woods when she'd hunted down the silverback werewolf alpha who'd actually *wanted* to be hunted. The werewolf who'd held back from attacking her outright, who'd spoken to her in a thickly foreign accent. Who'd forced her hand and the blade of her axe into his own chest because the man within the monster had been so desperate to escape.

The same man who had given Halsey his name as she'd delivered the final blow and who'd *thanked* her for the act of taking his life.

No one else that night had given it a second thought. The killing part, at least. She still hadn't told anyone the alpha werewolf had spoken to her as both man *and* beast. As far as she knew, no other elemental monster hunter alive in the world today had even a sliver of a problem when it came to disposing of the monsters they hunted. Halsey's overwhelming distaste for the act and her refusal to take a life, even a monstrous one, had dictated her every move in the field since her first mission.

Halsey didn't kill monsters.

Now, in only the last few weeks, she had two under her belt.

The chimera was different. That thing was literally unstoppable. Until I went with the absolute last resort and found out it was actually a monster-killing bomb...

She shot a furtive glance down at the bulge between the couch cushions where she'd temporarily buried the copper orb of alchemized sand that definitely wasn't *only* sand.

No matter which way she looked at it, killing the chimera in Turkey was justified. Distasteful, yes, but justified. Halsey and Brigham had faced the real, imminent threat of death when they'd gone up against the nearly unstoppable beast, and in the end, it had come down to nothing more than survival. A fight to the death, yes.

The silverback werewolf alpha in Ireland, though…

The beast had forced the blade of her axe into its own chest, and the man had thanked her for it. In the same breath, he'd delivered his final request to remember the name of Rolfr Magnusson before offering one final mystery in a language as dead and forgotten as the six elementals who'd stumbled upon a Viking longship shipwrecked off the coast of Ireland.

That was something entirely different, and Halsey didn't know if she would ever fully manage to convince herself what she'd done truly had been the *right* thing to do.

Now, she had an incredibly strong hunch she was about to find out what the alpha had meant by his near-death ramblings about trying to fix an ancient mistake.

About not being able to bear his monstrous life now that he knew *she* was back.

That's the ship. The Mother of Monsters was there. That's the missing piece!

Halsey was so caught up in reworking the facts, both new and old, she was unaware her grandmother had stopped talking and hadn't bothered to pick the story back up.

Then Greta cleared her throat, ripping Halsey from the churning vortex her mind had become and back into the present.

The young elemental jerked her head up to stare at her grandmother with wide eyes.

"Oh, I can see those wheels turning *now*, girl." Greta fixed her with a slowly growing smile tinged with a surprisingly feral-looking excitement. "Care to share with the rest of the class?"

Brigham scoffed. "Oh yeah? So *she* gets to talk in the middle of things, but *I* get threatened with garden gnomes."

Greta raised an eyebrow at him. "Well, she didn't interrupt me, Brigham. This particular pause in my story was intentional."

"Uh-huh." Folding his arms, he looked between his amused grandmother and his startled-looking cousin, then huffed a wry laugh. "I see how it is."

"I don't think you see nearly as much as you give yourself credit for, my boy." With a light chuckle, Greta spread her arms and continued staring at Halsey while still addressing Brigham. "That's not your fault. You've been thoroughly primed *not* to see certain things, like the rest of this family. Take, for instance, the look on your cousin's face right now."

Brigham slowly turned his head toward Halsey and studied her profile, still leaning into the couch's armrest and away from his mission partner as if she might leap after him at any second. Or explode. "Probably just trapped gas."

Greta threw her head back and howled with laughter, which startled both of her grandchildren this time.

Halsey shot her cousin a glance and managed a tiny smile. "Nice."

"Well, she's telling me to read your face, and that's the only thing I'm seeing right now. Remember that time you thought you had appendicitis?"

"And you stayed up with me all night to make sure I didn't die if I turned out to be right."

Brigham pointed at her and smirked. "You were wrong. I rest my case."

"Halsey." The sudden seriousness in their grandmother's voice made them both instantly look up at her again in wary expectation. Greta tilted her head and held Halsey's gaze firmly. "I did ask if there was anything you wanted to share."

Halsey swallowed and shook her head. "No. Not yet, anyway."

"Fair enough."

"There's no way that's the end of your story." Now that she'd come down from her momentary mind-trip in the clouds, Halsey sat back against the couch, folded her arms, and fixed her grandmother with the same knowing, half-amused stare. "So keep talking."

Greta thrust a finger toward her. "That is the kind of *knowing* our family's lost so much of over the years. Buried under all this other bullshit. Which is exactly why we find ourselves in this hellhole situation."

"What does that have to do with a ship?" Brigham asked, then immediately shut his mouth with a muffled click when he realized he'd already been told too many times to keep his thoughts, questions, and hands to himself.

Their grandmother chuckled. "I'm gonna let that one slide, kid. Can't expect anyone to race off across the starting line if there's nobody there shouting, 'One, two, three, go!'"

With absolutely no idea what that was supposed to mean, Brigham shrugged and nodded as if he'd been on the same page with his wildly eccentric grandmother all along.

"The ship itself has nothing to do with anything." Greta's smile faded as she dipped back into storytelling mode. "It's what Cedric and his elemental friends found *on* the ship. Probably didn't seem like much to them at the time. Or at least not as big of a deal as it's become over the centuries. But for us? For us, it changes *everything*."

She waited a moment longer to let the full weight of the statement sink in. Then, with a sigh, she dropped her head against the armchair and gazed at the ceiling. "Time does funny things, doesn't it? I haven't looked at that little sliver of history in such a long time. The details get muddled in the ol' noggin, obviously. Plus, Cedric was so eloquent in the way he described such a harrowing discovery. Hard to imagine we have something of a poet in our ancestral line, isn't it? I'll try to do it justice, though."

Halsey shifted slightly on her side of the couch and forced herself not to look away from her grandmother or to open her mouth and prompt the rest of the story with a bunch of questions she'd literally refused to ask.

She's stalling. Which means we're getting down to something major now, aren't we?

"Well." Greta smacked her lips and splayed her hands along the slightly fraying upholstery of her armchair. "Fuck it. The art of verbal mastery has never been my strong suit. Some people find it endearing, actually. Like your Pappy. Hot, holy hell, would he have loved to see this the way it was written… Another lifetime, I suppose.

"Yet Cedric knew what he was doing. He described the Viking longship with stunning *aplomb*. Once he and his buddies got close enough to figure out what it was, of course."

She briefly narrowed her eyes as if she were calling up the imagery all over again and plastering it in the forefront of her mind. "They'd never seen anything like it, of course. That ship had been a warzone. The site of a gruesome battle, unlike anything those six elementals had ever witnessed. Blood everywhere. A few body parts, sure. Hair. Nails. Shredded clothing and empty boots. That wasn't all of it, though.

"There were things on the ship that had no business being on any ship at all, let alone a vessel built and manned by some of the period's greatest warriors on land or at sea. What kinds of things? Yeah, that's the real kicker, isn't it?"

Looking between her grandchildren to heighten the suspense, Greta raised her eyebrows and lowered her voice. "Teeth ripped right out of jaws. The long, sharp, deadly kind. Canines. Fangs. Splintered claws that looked like they'd been severed from a bear paw on the deck. Toss in a few broken horns, a splattering of brightly colored scales, and a heap of feathers that crumbled to dust in their hands when Cedric and his buddies went in for a more thorough investigation."

"Holy shit..." Brigham whispered.

"Exactly." Greta didn't look to Halsey for a similar reaction. Maybe because she was too invested in spelling out Cedric's gruesome account, or maybe because she could already accurately guess what her granddaughter was thinking.

For Halsey, the revelation was nothing new, mind-blowing, impossible. She'd always assumed something like this had happened. Since the moment she'd found the magically climate-controlled records in the Clan library that jumped from boring accounts of everyday elemental life to the Ambrosius Clan's first missions as if they'd always been hunting monsters, Halsey had known something was off. Something like this was bound to show up eventually. Though she couldn't possibly have guessed it would turn up here in her Meemaw's house, discussing a missing record over a thousand years old that chronicled a monstrous slaughter aboard a Viking longship.

Maybe even the *missing record.*

The thought occurred to her a split second before Greta dived back into her retelling of their ancestor's account.

"Of course, our ragtag team of chummy elemental explorers had no clue *what* they were looking at. They only knew it was weird as hell and certainly didn't belong in their previously held assumptions of the way the world worked. *Our* world, if you know what I mean."

Greta searched Halsey and Brigham's faces again, then pursed her lips. "So. They had a longship built *not* to crash, crashed up on the beaches of Ireland, covered in blood and gore and…pieces that technically weren't supposed to exist. Because technically, up until the shipwreck, I guess they *didn't* exist.

"Then they had a giant bastard of a ship pummeled to bits from the inside out. It wasn't only all the blood and guts. The hull was ripped up and slashed and splintered from stem to stern. Giant, blistering bits of wood hauled up and tossed around and cracked apart like they weighed nothing. Big ol' slashes, like claw marks, across everything. Charred holes in the wood. A few little splotches of what our dear ol' Cedric described as 'a disassembling of the very wood itself, as if it had never existed in those exact holes along the deck.' Or something like that, however he said it.

"If the dude had known what *we* know about all the different ways a monster can fuck your shit up, he would've called those holes acid burns. You know, like from a pissed-off basilisk or hydra." She paused, scanned the ceiling in thought again, and shrugged. "Maybe even a Mongolian Death Worm if we're getting *really* technical."

This time, when it looked like her grandmother was about to lose track of her story by thinking out loud like this, Halsey tried to steer everything back on course by clearing her throat and folding her hands in her lap.

Apparently, seeing her granddaughter take on the authentic-looking, if not terribly convincing, role of good little student pulled Greta back to the point of her tale. She chuckled, straightened in the armchair, and mimicked Halsey's posture perfectly. "Uh-huh. Acid-schmacid, right? Well, either way, the good ol' elemental boys from way back clearly couldn't put two and two together on any of the longship's monstrous leftover clues. Most likely because 'two and two' didn't exist yet. Until this point in the story, of course."

Brigham slowly shifted along the couch's armrest to find a more comfortable position for the storytelling session that was clearly taking a lot more time than he'd expected. He exhaled a long, heavy sigh as if he were only now fully committing to the time and diligent attention this little sit-down required.

Halsey knew better.

She's losing him. Fast. Am I the only one in the family who can look past the crazy talk to pull out what Meemaw's actually saying?

Though her cousin returned his full attention to their grandmother, he slowly rubbed the back of his neck now and couldn't manage to hide a small grimace of confusion, irritation, and impatience all rolled up into one.

Just a bit longer, cuz. She's almost at the punchline. I can feel it. If he still doesn't get it when she's done, I guess I'll have to explain it in Brigham-speak. Wouldn't be the first time.

That thought almost made her laugh, but she squashed her amusement back down into a tight ball and managed to turn it into a small, muffled snort.

"Sure. It's funny. Hilarious, even." Greta narrowed her eyes at Halsey and slowly nodded. "If you're the kinda person who pops their boat off with all the little funnies before the big, bad hammer actually comes down. By all means…"

Pressing her lips together, Halsey dipped her head to momentarily avoid her grandmother's gaze. Otherwise, she'd burst out laughing and interrupt the woman's story all over again. *Okay, I guess Brigham's not totally alone now. I have absolutely no idea what any of that was supposed to mean.*

With Greta Ambrosius, it was always hard to tell how much of her eclectic rambling was performative, an intentional attempt to manipulate specific responses from those around her. Because some of it was due to her being an eighty-one-year-old woman who'd seen the entire world, fought a lifetime of monsters, and was now paying the price within her own family for being herself. Whatever was going on inside the woman's mind, she offered her grandchildren another knowing smile that hinted at more wordplay and mind games to come.

Greta continued. "A literal boatful of monsters would be enough to make anyone seriously question their own worldview. Maybe even rethink a few major life choices, and who are we to judge? The clues didn't stop with slash-and-hack blood and guts and an obliterated vessel that couldn't have been destroyed by any weapon or ability known to man at that point in time. Not even Cedric and his friends, elementals with *magic*, had seen something so horrific. They certainly wouldn't have used their own power to create such a chaotic, messy, gut-churning scene. At least, I hope not.

"And yes, there's still more. There's *always* more, isn't there? For this special ancestor of ours, the *more* was a man." Greta raised her eyebrows as she gazed at them, looking like a mischievous adult telling ghost stories to a bunch of kids around a campfire.

"Only one man left. Dead, of course. If he'd survived that beastly massacre during the voyage, we'd be hearing a very different story right now. But we're not. One dead man with a slash across his belly and covered in dried blood. Cedric and his buddies voted on an educated guess and came up with a unanimous three days. That's it."

She lifted three fingers beside her face for emphasis. "Three days since this mystery man's death. According to the wealth of forensic-investigation resources at their disposal at the time, they also guessed he'd been slashed across the belly by a sword and left to bleed out on the deck. Makes sense when his body was surrounded by the classic weapons we've all come to know and love. Daggers. Broadswords. Longbows. Also, don't forget the treasure."

At the mention of treasure, Brigham perked up a little, his attention on the story reinvigorated.

Of course. Viking ships and a monster bloodbath weren't enough. Halsey barely shook her head and forced herself not to look at her cousin. *But* treasure... *That's clearly the good stuff.*

"Heaps of it," Greta added, once again throwing in the right comment with the right amount of intrigue to make it seem as if she could read minds. "Everything strewn around the man on his deathbed. Or death-*seat*, since he was propped upright against the center mast. Didn't look all that interested in the treasure, or at least he hadn't been when he'd died.

"The way Cedric wrote it all down, it looked like the dude had been ripped away from some other fight on some other battlefield and miraculously plopped right down into the middle of all the carnage on the longship. Casually sitting there without a care in the world. Except for the dying part, obviously. Yet it looked a hell of a lot like this one remaining fella couldn't have cared less about the treasure or all the blood, guts, shed skin, and claw marks around him. Simply your average eighth-century Joe caught up in the mess of a furious skirmish that ran his longship straight onto the shores of Ireland."

After finishing that wonderful bit of oral storytelling, Greta paused to gauge the reactions of her audience.

At this point, Halsey and Brigham were practically on the edge of their seats, hanging on a thread of anticipation before it broke into the revelatory final piece their

Meemaw was sure to deliver. Yet instead of diving back into the twice-recounted tale head-first, Greta sighed heavily and blinked as if waking up from a lovely little catnap. "Any questions?"

"That's it?" Brigham blurted.

"Ha. It's a good thing I didn't give you a limited number of questions beforehand, kid. You would've totally wasted the first one."

He frowned and leaned farther over his lap, nodding for her to continue. "So there's more."

"Of *course* there's more." Greta snorted. "I may be kooky around the edges, Brigham, but I'm not a sadist." Clicking her tongue in disapproval, she pursed her lips in mock insult and shook her head. "It's like you don't even know who you're talking to."

"Sorry." Even Brigham seemed surprised by how quickly and easily he'd backed down. Then he tried to backtrack enough to pull out the rest of what they'd come to hear. "They found something else on the ship, right? Come on. There had to be something else."

"I just said there was more. Good grieving bologna. You kids these days have such a warped capacity for retaining information, I swear..." Greta slammed her hands onto the armrests and pushed herself to her feet. "You start to think you got a couple of real good ones on your hands."

"Whoa, whoa," Brigham practically shouted before remembering they were all inside, and nothing around them was anywhere near close to life-threatening. So far. "What are you doing?"

She blinked at him in confusion, then blandly gestured

toward the empty chair behind her. "Well, I *was* getting up. Now I'm leaving."

"*What?*" Halsey shrieked before starting to push herself up off the couch. "Meemaw, you can't—"

"Would you *relax* already?" Greta shouted. Her grandchildren instantly froze, neither of them quite sure what to do in this particular situation.

There's no way. Halsey gritted her teeth. *No fucking way she'd drag us through all that to drop everything now and walk out...*

Her grandmother pointed at her in warning. "I absolutely *can*, by the way. You're in *my* house. My rules. My timeline. I can do whatever the hell I want."

The boiling anger that had fueled Halsey's mad dash across the Ambrosius estate property on the back of a sputtering ATV returned with full force, and she fully stood from the couch in an attempt to stand down her own grandmother. "I came here for answers." She spoke evenly, fighting not to scream at the woman the way she wanted to. "*You* said you would tell us everything."

Still sitting on the couch, Brigham cleared his throat, but his cousin was far too invested in her righteous anger to pay much attention to anything else.

"Spewing out half a story about someone *else's* story that doesn't even mean anything yet sure as hell isn't *everything*," Halsey continued. "I'm not leaving until you're finished revealing every secret and digging up every lie and letting every family skeleton out of the closet. You owe us that."

Greta had already stopped short in her intended path across the living room, and now she stared at her granddaughter with a mixture of amusement and approval. "Oh, is *that* all?"

"Hal…" Brigham murmured, his voice even quieter now.

It was all too easy to keep ignoring him in lieu of holding their grandmother's full attention and hopefully getting her point across in the way she intended. "No more, no less."

For a moment, the Ambrosius women merely stared at each other from across the living room. Then the knowing smile on Greta's lips flickered, and she shrugged. "Yeah, that's what I expected. Try to see things from my perspective for a second, huh? The two of you have been sitting there all snuggly and cozy on my couch for however long you've been here. With your mouths *closed*. At least for most of it.

"I, on the other hand, have been running my mouth nonstop like it's paying the bills. So sit down, wrangle all that pent-up rage into something more manageable you can chew on, and let your Meemaw do her thing. Now, who else wants some goddamn lemonade?"

CHAPTER FOUR

Halsey stood stock-still in front of the couch with her fists clenched, staring at the spot where her grandmother had been standing before delivering her declaration of thirst. Now that Greta was gone to rummage around in the kitchen, all the anger and resentment Halsey had let build up again over the last few minutes had absolutely nowhere to go. Because, apparently, she'd jumped to yet another incorrect conclusion that the last person in her family she'd thought she could trust was shutting her out.

Brigham had finally had enough of trying to be subtle. "Hal!"

"*What?*" she snapped and whirled toward him, ready for a fight with something. *Anything.* Since that was what she'd been building up to.

Her cousin stabbed a finger at the couch cushions and widened his eyes. "Your personal magic bomb's about to go off again."

Confused, Halsey dropped her gaze to the couch cushions and the bulging space between them where she'd buried the gold sand-orb. The same golden light that had erupted before she'd decided to use it against the chimera flickered from deep within the couch, growing brighter by the second.

"Shit."

"Yeah."

She plopped down onto the couch again and slowly reached for the pinched gap between the cushions. "Why didn't you say something?"

"Well, I *tried*..." Brigham leaned as far away from the glowing part of the couch as he could, but the armrest at his back prevented him from escaping. "Except trying to get between you and literally anything while that creepy ball of who-knows-what starts up another light show would make me suicidal. Which I'm definitely not."

"What do you mean 'getting between me and anything?'" Taking a deep breath, she slid her hand into the crack between the cushions and gingerly fished around for the orb. "It's not like we brought a monster in here for me to fight off later."

"I don't know, cuz." He cringed, slid one foot across the rug, and braced himself to leap to his feet while staring at her hand thrust between the cushions. "Watching you and Meemaw go at it like this is almost the same thing..."

"What?" The second Halsey looked up at her cousin in disapproval, a stronger pulse of gold light flashed from within the cushions. "We weren't *going at it*, Brigham. She only told half a story and was basically leading us on the whole time with—"

"Jesus, Hal. Turn it off!" Brigham leapt to his feet, grabbing the couch's armrest with both hands to swivel sideways around it until he stood on the other side, not daring to put his back to the unknown magic his cousin controlled. The magic that had cleaved the chimera apart from the inside out.

At his terrified shout, Halsey quickly looked back down at her hand stuffed between the couch cushions and the flashing pulses of gold light growing faster and stronger from below.

"It's fine," she murmured as her fingers finally found the cold, smoothly rounded surface of the orb. A twinge of the thing's alchemized magic raced up her arm with the same kind of warm, quivering energy she'd felt right before using it as a last-ditch effort against the chimera.

"That's not what fine looks like," Brigham replied breathlessly, unable to look away from the source of the light and the magic he didn't understand but had seen enough of to thoroughly fear. "You said you could control that thing."

"I can."

"Then why's it still doing *that*?"

Taking a deep breath, Halsey pulled the orb out from between the couch cushions and squinted against the sudden golden glare filling the living room. Her cousin flinched away from the thing, though his fingers dug into the couch's armrest so fiercely he seemed unable to let go of it at this point. Then she exhaled slowly and focused on the orb.

He's right, though. I could control it out in the middle of nowhere in Turkey when it was only us and an unkillable monster. Away from anyone else who could get hurt or anything else I could destroy...

The orb erupted with a violent pulse of light before emitting the same low, buzzing whine she'd somehow *understood* before using the orb against the chimera.

Brigham hissed and crouched behind the side of the couch.

Cut it out, Halsey. Don't think about death and destruction. Damn it, come on. This is totally the wrong place and the wrong time!

Gritting her teeth, she focused on calming her breath again, along with her anger and frustration over everything she hadn't been able to control and still couldn't.

The strange magic within the copper orb wasn't one of them.

You made the damn thing. So make it do what you want. Turn it off...

This kind of visualization was a whole different approach Halsey still hadn't gotten used to. Completely different from the feeling of reaching out and connecting with the life force of whatever natural thing around her responded to her elemental magic. It took so much more concentration, so much more effort, especially because she was sitting in her grandmother's living room with absolutely no threat in sight.

It shouldn't be this hard. A frustrated growl escaped her as the orb kept flashing and buzzing in her hand, and she doubled down on trying to make the magic inside it respond to her commands. *Turn the hell off!*

"Well, this is disappointing," Greta blurted from the entrance into the living room.

Her grandmother's unexpected reappearance startled Halsey, and all her concentration was immediately ripped away from the gold orb in her hand. She sucked in a sharp breath, bracing herself for the inevitable lurch of exploding magic she wasn't sure she'd be able to contain this time.

Instead, the pulsing light around the orb sputtered and went out. The buzzing drone cut out, and the tingling warmth racing up her arm disappeared without a trace.

It was over.

Seriously? That's all it took?

For a split second, Halsey and Brigham both stared warily at the orb. Then she turned on the couch to look over her shoulder at their grandmother standing in the living room's entryway.

Greta held a serving tray with three full glasses of iced lemonade and an almost-full pitcher. She merely raised an eyebrow at the orb in Halsey's hand that now looked like a cold, dark, metallic toy. "After everything, I would've thought you'd at least wait for me to join you before showing off a few new tricks."

"Meemaw, I can explain… Wait, what?" Halsey blinked dumbly at the woman and didn't bother to turn around again toward Brigham when he released a massive, growling sigh. "You're not—"

"Terrified like him?" Greta nodded toward Brigham and snorted. "Furious? Disappointed? Ready to throw you out of my cozy little house and tell you not to come back until you figure your shit out? Is that what you were expecting?"

"I…" Halsey had absolutely no idea what to say to that because now it was perfectly clear how quickly and easily she'd fallen into her old pattern of assuming the worst. Or assuming anyone else in her family would automatically assume the worst of *her* without letting her explain her side of things.

Still, this wasn't the rest of her family or any of the Ambrosius elementals sitting on the Clan Council. This was her grandmother.

Even if Halsey had momentarily forgotten it, Greta certainly hadn't.

"Please, girl." With a wry laugh, the woman left the entryway and walked casually into the living room with her tray of drinks. Ice cubes clinked away against the glass. "Insulted, maybe, sure. I thought we'd gotten past the point of you trying to hide things from me."

"We have."

"Oh yeah?" Stopping between the couch and the two armchairs, Greta bent slightly to gently set the tray down on the coffee table. "You think so?"

"Sorry." Halsey readjusted her grip on the gold orb, her fingers aching after having held the thing so tightly, even for such a short amount of time. Then she lowered the orb into her lap and tried to hide it beneath both her hands.

"Don't apologize to *me*, girl. I'll get over it." After grabbing one of the tall, thin glasses of lemonade, Greta raised it in the general direction of the couch as she headed toward her armchair again. "You might wanna check on *him*, though. Looks like somebody hit a sore spot or something."

Brigham straightened behind the side of the couch, finally managed to pry his clawed hands away from the armrest, and cleared his throat. "I'm fine."

"Uh-huh." Their grandmother raised her glass toward

him in a silent toast as she lowered herself into her armchair again. Then she sipped her coveted lemonade and sighed in contentment. "Might as well open the floor again for any questions, concerns, or, you know... Burning desires." When she met her grandchildren's eyes, she found only blank stares aimed back at her. "Or explanations, if you feel like it."

Halsey and Brigham finally managed to look at each other, though he paid special attention to *not* lowering his gaze toward the gold orb in her lap, only mostly hidden by her hands.

Nope. We're not getting sidetracked that *easily.*

Pressing her lips together in grim determination, Halsey turned back toward her grandmother and shook her head. "I think it's better to focus on one thing at a time."

"Like my unfinished story you think I so abruptly cut off right in the middle." Greta clicked her tongue and rolled her eyes before muttering, "Like we're all incapable of picking back up where we left off after a nice little break."

"I wouldn't exactly call this a *nice little break*, Meemaw. We're not in school."

"Hmm. You sure about that?"

Neither one of the Ambrosius cousins knew quite how to respond to that because it wasn't quite clear exactly what Greta was getting at with a question like that. Whether or not the woman eventually chose to explain her thoughts and motives was another unknown at this point.

She did say they should've taught us all this in school. Militia training. That little bit of history is useful, yeah, but what does this have to do with our personal *history? With* mine?

Halsey and Brigham watched their grandmother with wary expectation as the woman casually sat back in her armchair and sipped her lemonade, letting out cheery little hums of enjoyment.

Surprisingly, Brigham was the first one to try to get things moving forward again. "Meemaw."

"Hmm?" Greta looked up at him with a dreamily happy smile.

"The story," he prompted, both looking and sounding incredibly uncomfortable with having taken on the role usually played out by his cousin. Halsey was the go-getter. Brigham was the one who helped her put all the pieces together afterward. Yet neither one of them had nearly enough pieces to piece anything together at this point.

It also probably didn't help that he still hadn't gotten used to this different version of his grandmother. The version of her that swore, barked interruptions, went on long tangents that made no sense before getting to the point, and strung the Ambrosius Clan's best two-man monster-hunting team along for a game of How Long Can I Hold Your Attention.

At least, Halsey assumed that was her cousin's current problem as she watched her cousin's eyebrows flicker in and out of a frown. Even his smile looked more like a grimace.

Maybe it wasn't such a good idea to let him follow me here. This is all way too weirdly new for him. If she drops another massive reality bomb on us today, he might not be able to handle it.

She instantly realized how much her brain was trying to trick her into isolating herself and her grandmother together through all of this. Again.

Brigham was her best friend, her mission partner, the one person who'd been there for her through absolutely everything, not as an instructor or a caregiver or a commander but as her equal. After everything they'd been through in the last few months, he still hadn't given up.

No, he can handle this like he handles everything else. We both can. As long as Meemaw gets to the freaking point already.

When their grandmother didn't respond to Brigham's gentle prodding, he turned his grimace onto Halsey and offered a tiny shrug. He didn't have to say anything to get his point across. *Help.*

She couldn't help but nod back at him before returning her attention to their eccentric grandmother, who now acted ignorant to everything these two young elementals sitting in her living room were trying to accomplish.

Halsey sat back against the couch cushions, being sure to slide the gold orb between her thighs this time and cover it with one hand while she slung her other arm over the armrest. "Are you trying to down the whole pitcher first, or can we get back to it?"

Greta froze, her head dipped forward and her glass barely removed from her lips after her last sip. Halsey felt her cousin's disbelieving stare on her, but she'd fully committed with the last biting little statement and couldn't back down now.

They needed this. Whatever their grandmother was finally willing to tell them about the past, it was crucial. For their present and, more importantly, for their future.

The stunned silence seemed to stretch on forever until Greta nearly choked on her mouthful of lemonade. For a moment, the woman looked like she was struggling to swallow or breath or both, then she finally managed to recover herself and threw her head back to roar with laughter.

The bellowing sound echoed around the living room and made Brigham jolt in his seat on the far side of the couch.

Halsey didn't move, but now she knew a smile was absolutely warranted.

Greta simply kept laughing.

Well, at least I got her to quit pretending this is a regular trip to grandma's house for hugs and lemonade. Any time now, Meemaw. Let's go.

Once the woman finally recovered from her explosive amusement and managed to get her gasping breath back under control, she leaned sideways in her overlarge armchair, propped her elbow up on the armrest with the weeping glass of ice-cold lemonade in her hand, and grinned at Halsey. "I swear, girl. Every time you stop by, I end up more and more convinced time travel might actually be possible."

Brigham almost choked on nothing. "Please tell me that's not the punchline of this weird history lesson."

She chuckled. "That *would* be a hell of a turn, wouldn't it?" His blank expression bordering on horror made her laugh again. "Not *real* time travel, kid. More like..." Greta turned her bright, glistening, blue-eyed gaze back onto Halsey, and her smile widened. "...gazing into a mirror."

Brigham looked between them, opened his mouth to

say something that didn't quite make it out, then shifted on the couch. "You mean because everyone thinks Hal's just like you?"

"More like they're afraid of it." Greta nodded slowly, though she didn't remove her gaze from her only grandchild with whom she had this special type of connection. "I like what I see in this reflection more every day, though."

Halsey returned a small, proud smile that broke through her pursed lips.

Okay, here we go. Now we're about to get to the good stuff.

After another long moment of silence, Brigham was starting to feel left out of this secret little circle between the two women in the room. Not knowing how else to handle it, he puffed out a sigh and slumped back against the couch cushions, fully relaxed and too confused to care about how confused he was right now. "So, about that longship…"

"Yeah. About that." Greta finally turned her smile onto him next, then gestured toward the tray on the coffee table with drink in hand. "It's rude to refuse hospitality like this. Even from your Meemaw. Drink your lemonade, then we'll get to it."

Huffing out a laugh, Brigham stood from the couch in a bent-over stoop to grab the other two glasses off the tray. Then he handed one to Halsey, returned to his seat, and took a small sip to humor the eccentric old woman he hardly recognized anymore.

"Oh, shit." He pulled the glass away from his mouth to stare at it with wide eyes. "This is *way* better than Chick-fil-A's."

Greta tilted her head and raised her glass toward the

couch again with a knowing smile. "Believe it or not, kid, your Meemaw knows what she's doing. A little lemonade always helps the lemons go down."

Halsey snorted at her cousin's baffled frown, then drank.

CHAPTER FIVE

"Where were we?"

"Dead man and treasure on a ripped-up Viking longship," Halsey offered with a curt nod.

"Ah. That's right." Greta grinned and gazed up at the living room ceiling. "Along with our great-great-great-great-whatever Cedric crafting so many educated guesses with all his other elemental buddies."

"Did they figure out what actually happened?" Brigham asked.

"Well, that's the million-dollar question, isn't it? What could've *possibly* caused such a horrific tragedy and left only one human body behind as evidence? What kind of *monster* would've been capable of causing such magnificent damage with so much carnage in its wake?" Greta smirked and swirled her lemonade around in her glass with the gentle clinking of ice cubes.

"Very subtle," Halsey murmured.

"Monster." Brigham sank into himself a little, and now he looked downright disappointed. "You're saying there was a monster *on* the ship? That it…what? Destroyed every part of the boat and tossed the entire crew overboard before scrambling off to who knows where but left a single guy behind with all his treasure? Come on."

"*I'm* not saying anything," Greta replied with a coy, one-shouldered shrug. "Cedric and the other elementals at the shipwreck sure had a thing or two to say about it, though. Especially when we consider the final super-fun little nugget they found with the body."

Halsey scrunched up her face. "The treasure?"

Her grandmother clicked her tongue in annoyance. "What is this, Selective Hearing Day? No, I'm talking about… Oh." All the irritation disappeared from her features now that she realized the real issue. "Guess I got way too thirsty before getting to that part, so of *course* you have no idea about that."

"About *what*?" the cousins urged at the exact same time in the exact same tone.

"Well, listen to you two." Greta sniggered and spread her arms. "About the ritual scroll hanging out with all the blood-splattered treasure and the dead body. A ritual scroll of *blood magic.*"

At those words, a surge of cold awareness flooded through Halsey's entire body. Then an instant flush of understanding replaced the cold with heat, more anger, and a touch of self-righteousness she couldn't help.

This changed everything.

"I knew it," she whispered.

Brigham leaned away from her and scoffed. "Knew what?"

"Don't flatter yourself, girl." Greta waved off her granddaughter's comment and sniggered again. "Go nurture your budding mind-tricks somewhere else. You had no damn clue what I was about to say."

"I meant about the monsters," Halsey clarified with a hint of annoyance. "The ship. The Blood Matriarch already having been summoned once to create monsters. It *did* happen, and the firsthand account from Cedric is exactly the proof we needed!" She turned toward Brigham with wide eyes and a growing smile of realization. "Legend soup, my ass."

Greta choked on her lemonade again. "What was that, now?"

"Nothing," Brigham muttered offhandedly, though most of his focus was centered on frowning back at his cousin's excitement. "I still think you're getting ahead of yourself here."

"How the hell am I doing that?"

"Hal, just because there was some kinda blood-magic ritual scroll on a boat with a dead guy over a thousand years ago doesn't prove anything. For all we know, the scroll could've been part of the plunder."

She choked back a laugh. "The what?"

"You know, all the treasure. Vikings did that, didn't they? Sailed all over, stormed into towns and villages, took people's stuff, then booked it back across the ocean on their big-ass boats—"

"You keep calling it a boat," Greta muttered.

"Ship. Whatever."

"It was *there*, Brigham." Halsey stabbed a finger into her opposite palm to accentuate each new point, unaware she was no longer thoroughly covering up the top of the gold sphere shoved between her thighs. "A blood-magic scroll was on *that* longship, at *that* specific time, shipwrecked on the coast of Ireland for *our* ancestors to see. And the ship had been torn to shreds. By monsters."

"Again, we don't have proof of *that*, either."

"Oh, come on. Are you gonna sit there and tell me there's another viable explanation for this insanely coincidental combination of factors? Way back in 953 A.D.? Are you kidding me?"

Brigham raised a finger and opened his mouth for a biting retort that never came. "No. I don't have any explanation for all those things coming together at the same time—"

"Well, then, there ya go!"

"That's the *point*, Hal. We don't actually have hard proof or verifiable evidence of *anything* from back then. Not when it comes to monsters on Viking ships and dead guys in a pile of treasure plus blood magic."

Halsey stared blankly at him for a moment, then snorted. "Are you hearing yourself right now? 'Cause what you said sounds *exactly* like the kinda thing we've been going up against every day for the last two months."

"No. This is different."

"How? Huh?" Tucking her legs up beneath her on the couch in her excitement, Halsey scooted slightly closer to her cousin across the cushions and leaned in. "How is ripping apart an indestructible chimera with a golden ball of magic neither one of us has ever seen before any more normal or even *believable* than a ritual scroll being read out loud on a Viking longship in 953 A.D. to summon the

Mother of Monsters from her prison at the bottom of the ocean?"

As if from somewhere very far away, Greta hummed and slowly sipped on her lemonade, enjoying the enlightening little exchange between her grandchildren.

Neither of them noticed anything their grandmother did now. They had once again fallen into their lifelong pattern. Halsey plowing full steam ahead with an outrageous idea, or the occasional battle axe, and Brigham coming behind her with all his logic, reason, and an incredibly valuable ability to poke holes in damn near anything.

Yet his ability fell short when he couldn't come up with an answer. In a tiny corner at the back of his mind, Brigham knew his cousin was right. The rest of him wasn't quite ready to believe everything he'd thought about history, magic, monsters, and the elementals hunting them hadn't been the whole truth and nothing *but* the truth.

So he heaved a growling, agitated sigh and shrugged. "It's not. They're both pretty fucking insane…"

"Yes!" Halsey pounded a fist into her other hand and grinned, practically bouncing on the couch cushion. "I knew it! This is *exactly* the kinda thing we've been looking for—"

"Wait, wait. Hold on a sec." Now that he'd had more time to cover every possible angle, the floodgates of potential plot holes and what-ifs had finally opened in his mind. "Okay, first of all, how do we even know it was actually a blood-magic ritual on the scroll?"

"Oh, sure. Cedric had a *fantastic* reason for making something like that up."

"That's not…no." Brigham clenched his eyes shut and shook his head. "How did *he* know? Sure, our Clan library has maybe a few tiny things on blood runes, and there's probably a whole lot more stashed away with the Order of Skrár in…wherever they keep their stuff."

"Oh, without a *doubt*," Greta chimed in with a chuckle.

"Okay, great." He tried to nod her way, but it ended up looking like a giant head-twitch with more of his concentration centered on making his point. "What I'm saying is we have a lot more resources now. Libraries. Records. Whether or not you and I know everything there is to know about all of those resources, they're obviously still *available* to us and probably any other elementals who wanna get their hands on more knowledge. Yeah, even blood-magic knowledge. I seriously doubt Cedric and anyone else back in history with him had the same kind of access, though."

"All right. Now you need to make up your mind." Halsey folded her arms and tilted her head as if he'd actually done something to deserve that look.

He *hated* the feeling of her giving him that look.

"What?" Brigham stared right back at his cousin, though he really wanted to tell her to quit looking at him like that because it gave him the creeps. "My mind *is* made up."

"Yeah, *you* think so. But you gotta pick one, man. Either we have way more resources and know so much more about the past than people in the actual past, or we have no way of confirming anything from way back when and can't actually draw our own conclusions. You can't have it both ways."

For a moment, that one actually stumped him. "Fine, but this is hearsay on top of hearsay, Hal. It's weird that another elemental, one of *our* ancestors, apparently wrote this novel-length journal entry about something *he* didn't understand, with a whole lotta conjecture on top of it. I'm asking how Cedric even knew what blood runes were in the first place."

Before Halsey could think of a reply, argumentative or not, Greta stood and stepped to the coffee table. "Probably the same way your partner recognized a few blood runes on a few ogre hands when nobody else would've thought twice about it. Especially seeing as those runes were nowhere *close* to where they belong."

With mouths agape, the cousins dropped their "brainstorming session" and turned toward their grandmother. She didn't look at either of them as she lifted the pitcher dripping with condensation and slowly poured herself another ice-cold glass of lemonade.

"How's that, exactly?" Halsey asked, though her voice had suddenly lost all its strength and now made her sound like a terrified little girl. Which was, of course, something she hadn't been in a very long time and the last thing she ever wanted to be again.

"Yeah," Brigham murmured with a stiff nod. "What she said."

Greta set down the pitcher, had a nice, long sip of her drink, then replied as casually as if she were giving them her lemonade recipe. "It's in our blood. Plain and simple."

"Um..." Halsey chuckled and looked at her cousin again, not expecting him to understand more than she did but not having anything better to do, either. He was clearly just as clueless and confused. "No, it's not."

"What she said," Brigham repeated.

The armchair creaked as Greta settled herself gingerly back down into it, taking care more for the sake of her incredibly full glass than her aging body. For this eighty-one-year-old Ambrosius woman, aching joints and wobbly legs still had a long way to go before catching up to her. Then she took another long sip and sighed. "You two are so caught up in your stupid argument about a whole shitload of nothing. It's like you gave up on using your heads."

"Meemaw..."

"We're *elementals*, kid. Descendants of the hardcore, badass magical heroes who gave their lives to take down the Blood Matriarch and end the great war. Of course, they also sacrificed an insanely large portion of this planet's lifeforms in the process, but that's apparently irrelevant. You should hear some of these normies running around calling themselves *scientists*. They think the Ice Age was a *good* thing as a result of *natural causes*. Who am I to argue?"

"We know all that," Brigham murmured. "Pretty sure it doesn't explain how recognizing blood *runes* is in *our* blood. Unless you put something stronger than lemonade in this lemonade." He looked down at the drink he'd been holding this whole time and gave it a tentative sniff.

"And *I'm* pretty sure you've been drinking your mama's Kool-Aid," Greta quipped.

"Her what?"

"Unless that lemonade's too strong for you, and you *accidentally* said I can't tell the difference between blood magic and our own."

Oh, shit. Halsey froze in her seat and stared at the fireplace mantle above her grandmother's head and to the right because it wasn't the woman's face and also didn't make it insanely obvious that she'd immediately looked away. *She's pissed.*

Brigham slowly turned his head toward his cousin, his entire face a white sheet of numb befuddlement. "Hal, what the hell's going on? My mom's never made Kool-Aid in her life..."

"Oh, for the love of all the moldy socks in my basement." Greta closed her eyes and pinched the bridge of her nose, shaking her head.

Fortunately, Brigham didn't say a word about this private riverside bungalow not even *having* a basement. Whether or not he'd picked up on the disparity, Halsey sure as hell wouldn't bring it up, either.

Now she's stepping right into her crazy-old-Meemaw shoes. Which is exactly why she's so pissed.

"Halsey," Greta murmured, still pinching the bridge of her nose. "Help a little ol' lady out here, huh? Of all my children's spawn, I never thought Gracelyn's *youngest* son would need the fucking alphabet spelled out for him. If *I'm* the one who has to do it, I will give myself an aneurism."

"What the hell?" Brigham whispered, terrified by the idea that something he'd done had upset his dear, sweet Meemaw so much.

His dear, sweet Meemaw lifted her head, opened her eyes, and stared directly at him. "On purpose."

"Okay, well...don't do that." Halsey shot her grandmother a condescending look that only made Greta shrug before nestling back in her armchair. Then she pointed at her cousin. "You, don't take any of that personally. At least try not to, anyway."

Brigham's mouth hung open as he slowly shook his head and stared off into space located somewhere to the left of his cousin's face. "My brain is so screwed up right now. I think it's safer not to try anything."

"Well, then listen." Halsey shot her grandmother one final glance and was only slightly surprised to see the woman had recovered from her short-lived bout of having been so deeply insulted by her own flesh and blood. Again.

Now, another tiny smile flickered at the corners of her mouth as she stared intently at Halsey and took another long sip of lemonade.

Uh-huh. You sit there and keep smiling, Meemaw. This is exactly what you wanted to happen.

Because in the split-second of a look from Greta, Halsey fully realized what was happening. In a matter of minutes and a small handful of nonsensically aggressive comments, the woman had managed to get the two younger monster hunters back on the same page together as a team. By painting herself as the lunatic outsider who needed to be handled more gently than everyone else in the family.

Now Halsey could explain what Greta had actually said beneath all the jumbled, confusing nonsense, and Brigham was once again open to hearing her out.

Yep. I'm officially convinced. Crazy and brilliant are the same thing.

Puffing out a quick sigh, Halsey studied her cousin's still-blank expression and nodded curtly. "She's talking about the history *between* us."

Brigham blinked and managed to meet her gaze again. "Wait, I thought you and I were good..."

Greta sniggered.

Halsey ignored the sound and her immediate gut-reaction to laugh at him too. "No, not you and me. Elementals and blood humans."

"Um...huh?"

"Right, well, here's how I see it. If I've got it all wrong, we both know Meemaw's gonna step in and correct me anyway, so I don't need to remind her of her options."

That got Brigham to smile again. At least his facial muscles went through the motions, even if the consciousness behind them hadn't yet caught up. Color seeped back into his cheeks too, so it was a good start.

Halsey continued. "For the entire history of our bloodline and *way* further back than the extent of normal human history, there have been elementals. *And* there have been blood humans. That was the whole point of the great war, right? We've always been fighting them, and they've always been fighting us. We're...connected that way, I guess. All of the elementals to all of the blood humans. The magic's in our blood like it's in theirs. The monsters created through blood magic can't help doing what they do. Like *we* can't help our elemental magic and the fact that it makes *us* monster hunters."

"Took the words right out of my mouth," Greta mused. "If they'd been there in the first place."

"We killed all the blood humans," Brigham interjected with a confused frown, completing ignoring his grandmother's asides. "Not *us*, obviously. Our ancestors. The ones who pooled together and used every bit of magic they had to lock the Matriarch up at the bottom of the ocean. The Ice Age they created wiped every blood human off the map. That's why there *aren't* any now, Hal. They all died."

Raising her eyebrows, she gestured toward Greta and tilted her head. "Obviously not."

"No. That's not… It's totally impossible."

Greta released a massive sigh. "Herein lies the ultimate struggle within *our own family* for the last twenty years." Both of her grandchildren turned toward her in expectation, and she shrugged. "We all thought it was impossible, kid. The Council still does, for the most part. Sure, a big ol' bagful of severed ogre hands with blood runes stamped on them goes a long way to convince them there's a hell of a problem right now with this world's monsters. But we're going *further* back here. You understand?"

Brigham looked so lost that Halsey felt compelled to step in and help him out again. "Our ancestors took out the Blood Matriarch for sure. We know she's been gone for millions of years, or all this craziness with monsters would've been happening a long time ago. Who knows? Maybe even all the elementals and normal humans would've been totally wiped out by now. That's not the point, though."

"Doesn't seem like there *is* a point to all this, Hal." Her cousin clicked his tongue through the side of his mouth and looked at her the way he'd looked at her right before she'd decided to call that emergency Clan meeting first thing after coming back from their first mission in Ireland. The look was full of pity, disappointment, and cringe-like disapproval of whatever Halsey Ambrosius was about to do next.

It was the same look she'd received from every member of the Ambrosius Clan Council during that meeting, including her dad.

How can he still be in denial about all this? After everything we've seen? We're sitting down with the woman who used to be the head of this entire militia, and he still doesn't want to open his eyes...

Yet she wouldn't give up on him. Not now. Brigham was her best friend and her partner, and right now, he was the only other person who was capable of physically being with her during missions while they uncovered their family's secrets. He was the only one who could back her up when she figured out exactly what was going on here, the way he'd always had her back.

"The great war didn't wipe out all the blood humans," she insisted, holding Brigham's gaze. *"That's* the point."

"Come on, Hal…"

"Just shut up and listen, okay?" Halsey managed not to snap at him quite as harshly as she had over the last few days, but she still couldn't keep all the frustration from her voice. It was enough to make him shut his mouth, at least, and he frowned at her with at least a little willingness to keep listening. "If all the blood humans were killed way back then, there would've been no one around to keep up their traditions. Blood magic and blood runes would've been just as extinct as all the blood humans we've always thought were wiped out. Hell, monsters wouldn't even exist *now* like they existed way back then before the great war."

Brigham didn't say another word as his cousin paused to take a breath and rearrange her thoughts. If Halsey had been more aware of his response, she would have sincerely appreciated it.

Now she was on a roll as all the pieces of this ancient puzzle started to fit together in her mind, and she couldn't stop. Laying it all out in the open was as much for her cousin's benefit as it was for her own.

"Our ancestors, the ones who survived the great war and the Ice Age, the ones who went south afterward to start new lives and continue their own elemental bloodlines, *they* all thought they'd succeeded. With the Mother of Monsters buried in the Circle of Creation at the bottom of the ocean, with no blood humans left to free her and no monsters left to do her bidding, I totally get how it could seem like we totally won. Our ancestors back then *weren't* fighting monsters, right? They were living it up with elemental magic, generation after generation, with no real purpose for it.

"Then suddenly there *were* monsters. In 953 A.D. I looked through those records myself, Brigham. There's a whole bunch of them from before that year, and nobody talks about monsters even a little. It's all about crop yields and who married who and who had a bunch of kids and who traded land with some normie shareholder or whatever."

Brigham wrinkled his nose and opened his mouth to respond, but Halsey didn't give him the chance.

"Then the next record in line goes right to fighting monsters. That's it. Like the monsters suddenly appeared overnight, out of thin air, and the Ambrosius Clan hopped into action to go hunt them down like there was never a two-million-year break in what we've all been *born* to do.

"I know it's a hell of a gap between historical records of our own family, sure. Even *I* thought I was going crazy when I found that little hole in the records. Come on, we all know Charlemagne would've given himself a stroke if he knew anything was missing from the library."

Greta sniggered at that, which made Halsey shoot her grandmother a quick sidelong glance before she pointed at the woman again. "But it's not a mystery anymore. *Meemaw* took the missing record. The one she told us about. That's the missing link. The first time I came here to talk to her about gaps in the records' timeline, she even admitted taking it right out of the climate-controlled—"

"Hold up." Brigham raised an open hand toward her, grimacing in a mix of reluctance and complete bafflement. "You already talked to Meemaw about all this?"

"Well…" *Shit*.

CHAPTER SIX

Halsey bit her lower lip and rapidly considered her options. She'd been keeping a lot of things from her cousin. Now, in her attempt to explain to him how all this worked and what this missing record meant for the future of every elemental on the planet, she'd let one of those delicately omitted lies slip through the cracks. She couldn't cover it up with another lie because Greta was sitting right there, watching the whole thing.

"Yeah," she finally conceded with a sigh. "We've already talked about this. A little."

Without moving a single muscle beyond his eyeballs, Brigham looked from his partner to their grandmother, then asked, "When?"

"A few months ago."

"You didn't think it was a good idea to *tell* me that?"

"Brigham, you were out with The Burger throwing ugly rocks at wyverns, and I was stuck here on a mandatory suspension for a month!" She hadn't intended to start yelling again, but having to explain everything to him was getting under her skin. "I was here alone. I was trying to figure everything out. *Alone.* Everyone thought I'd gone off the deep end, including you."

"No, I didn't—"

"Oh, come on." Halsey rolled her eyes and scoffed. "You didn't believe anything I was saying at that first emergency meeting, like everyone else. Which got you pancaked against a tree by ogres you and Cadence were totally unprepared to face. *Because* nobody believed me."

He didn't have a good argument to spit back. For a moment, it seemed like Brigham would back down and let her get back to the historical revelations that proved what the entire Clan faced in the very near future. *If* he quit running around in circles and let her get to that part.

Slowly, Brigham lifted a finger and pointed at Greta again as he held his cousin's gaze. "You came here to talk about missing records and information that Cadence and I should've had before that fucked-up mission. Without me. You didn't tell me about that."

She responded with a half-hearted shrug. "It wasn't exactly at the top of my list while you were lying in a hospital bed. My bad."

"I've been back in the field for a month now, Hal. *With* you. You still didn't mention it, which kinda feels like you're going behind my back."

That made her pause. The last thing she wanted was to make him feel like that, but it was all true. She *had* been going behind his back because he hadn't trusted her enough from the beginning to back up what she knew in her bones was the truth, and she didn't want her best friend turning against her like nearly everyone else in their family.

She couldn't say that out loud to him now. It wasn't the only lie.

I can't start digging into werewolf alphas talking to me and begging for death. He'll totally freak if I say anything about trying to meet with Halil Aydem before Brigham even heard the guy's name. So suck it up and admit to this one, Halsey. You can figure out the rest later.

"Neither one of us had any idea what was going on back then, okay?" She tried to smooth over the situation enough to move on to their grandmother's important discovery. "That was before the ogres, so I still didn't have any proof. I didn't want you to think I was nuts like everybody else did because I came here to talk to Meemaw about missing monster history." She shrugged and hoped her little confession was enough for now. "I'm sorry."

Brigham studied her face for a moment longer, his gaze roaming across her features like he was trying to peer into her mind and double-check the facts.

Halsey's cheeks heated, and she forced herself not to look away. *That's what guilty people do. I'm not guilty. Right now, I'm just...strategically keeping a few things to myself until the right time to share them. Or until I screw up again and spit out the truth by mistake...*

Finally, Brigham cocked his head in concession and looked away from her. "Fine. Just...don't pull that shit anymore, okay? I'm here with you."

"I know." Suddenly aware again of their grandmother

sitting right there on the other side of the living room, Halsey laughed dryly and tilted her head toward Greta as if the woman couldn't actually hear everything they were saying. "That last little chat with Meemaw was useless, anyway. It's not like you were missing much."

Greta snorted. "I told you exactly what happened to that missing record you were so desperate to get your hands on."

"Yeah, and that's *all* you said about it besides the fact that you're the one who ripped it out of there." Halsey couldn't help but smile at her grandmother now, which was made even easier by Greta's constant knowing smile fixed on both her grandchildren as they worked out their differences. Or at least one of them, anyway.

"*You* took the missing record?" Brigham asked.

Greta clicked her tongue. "I really thought you were listening this time, kid."

"What? I'm always—" He cut himself off, having figured out by now it was no use arguing with this version of his grandmother, which seemed to be the true version. "Why didn't you tell her about Cedric's whole Viking ship adventure the first time she asked?"

"The first time isn't always the *right* time," Greta replied, her knowing smile unwavering as she nodded toward Halsey. "A lot's happened since then, and today felt like the right time."

"Because now we know what to do with it," Halsey added. "That scroll Meemaw took from the library? Cedric's story? It answers so many questions. Maybe even most of them, if we can find out where the Mother of Monsters is and—"

"Whoa, whoa, whoa." Brigham shook his head and flopped an arm over the couch's armrest again. "You went from missing records from forever ago to finding the Mother of Monsters right now. Like, in *our* lifetime."

She fixed him with a blank look. "So?"

"So I'm hoping you can fill in *that* giant gap, Hal. 'Cause trust me, I wanna believe you. I wanna get on board, but I'm not gonna jump up and be all gung-ho about going after the *Blood Matriarch* without something more to go on. You get that, right?"

"Of course." Another wry chuckle escaped her before she realized her brain had hopped from one giant revelation to the next, and she'd expected her cousin to follow along like he always did. Yet this wasn't a monster hunt or the Ambrosius cousins planning a bit of entertainment on their time off.

This was bigger. This was about getting him to understand what no one else in their entire family was willing to even consider, let alone understand enough to take action on it.

"I'm not trying to go after the Mother of Monsters right now, cuz," she reassured him. "At least not right now. But this record of Cedric and the other elementals finding the ship? That fills in the blanks. Maybe we can use it to find the Matriarch when we need to."

Brigham shook his head. "I still don't get it."

"Okay, then...back to the library records, I guess." Halsey scrunched up her face as she tried to gather her thoughts back onto the same train of thought she'd been riding until her little slipup confession had derailed the whole thing. "Bottom line before anything else is this.

Before Cedric's story, monsters didn't exist. There's no record of them in anything our Clan library has, and I'm pretty sure we have everything an Ambrosius elemental has ever written. Then *after* Cedric's account of the shipwreck, all the records of Ambrosius elementals doing anything and everything included monster hunting."

He still stared at her so vapidly that she was sure she hadn't hit the mark, so she added, "It's like if the Ancient Egyptians went from riding in chariots to racing around in Ferraris overnight. *Something* had to intervene and change the status quo."

"I know what it means, Hal. I'm trying to look at it all from your perspective, but it's not…" Brigham scrunched up his face in aggravation. "It doesn't add up. Anything could've happened between Cedric and the other elementals finding the ship and them going out to fight monsters. You're *assuming* the monsters were there, but we don't actually know. Cedric didn't even know—"

"Well, of course he did," Greta interjected, once more interrupting her grandchildren's debate. This time, they didn't summarily ignore her inserted comment.

"How?" Brigham asked.

Halsey cocked her head. "Yeah, you seem weirdly sure about that, Meemaw."

"And you're not? It was right there in…" Greta froze, popped her lips, then raised her lemonade glass in another silent toast as she chuckled. "I forgot to add that fun little detail, too, didn't I?"

Halsey and Brigham only had to keep staring at her for the woman to realize that was what had happened.

"Oh, come on." Greta rolled her eyes before taking another long sip of her drink. "So I got a little off track."

"A *little*?"

"Don't look at me like that, girl. It's not like you don't recognize the feeling. The two of you were so caught up in your own thing. I didn't have the heart to cut it short 'cause I wasn't done with *my* end of it."

"That's the whole reason we're *here*!" Brigham snapped.

His grandmother only looked marginally taken aback by his outburst before snorting. "Don't get all pissed at *me*, kid. *You're* the one who needs somebody to spell the whole thing out for you."

"Yeah, because you guys keep talking about this missing link like it proves anything, but it's only a bunch of—"

"Not when Cedric and his pals were interrupted in their search through the longship. By a real-life, scary-as-shit monster, right in their faces." Greta's pert look almost dared him to argue with her again. Brigham's mouth popped open, but he didn't say anything else.

"They actually fought monsters?" Halsey asked softly. "On the beach?"

"On the *ship*." Greta took another long drink of her lemonade, reveling in the next wave of sudden anticipation she'd created with yet another mind-bending revelation. "It was only the one. According to Cedric, anyway. Of course, since we can't actually go back in time to find our own cold, hard *evidence*, maybe it's not even worth discussing at this point."

"No, wait," Brigham blurted. "If Cedric wrote an actual account of monsters on the ship—"

"Mons*ter*," his grandmother interrupted, lifting one finger.

"Whatever. If they saw something there that actually connects the blood-magic ritual scroll to monsters, we can't really…" He wrinkled his nose, even more frustrated after his previous argument had been almost completely debunked. "I mean, it's not…"

"Not as impossible as you thought?" Halsey suggested.

He didn't look at her, but he shrugged and gestured toward Greta. "That's what he saw, right? Or at least what he claimed he saw."

"Well, it was more detailed than that." Greta shifted in her chair and took up her storytelling position once more, her forearm resting on the armrest and the ice clinking around in her glass as she swirled her lemonade. "The way Cedric told it, he and his entire group of overly curious elemental friends didn't have any more time to thoroughly inspect the rest of the ship because, yes, they were interrupted. By a monster."

Halsey and Brigham waited intently, hanging on their grandmother's every word.

Greta leaned slightly forward in her armchair and lowered her voice for added mysterious effect. "A werewolf, actually. One very large, very mean-looking werewolf *alpha* with a stripe of silvery fur along the creature's back."

Halsey swallowed thickly and turned her head to meet Brigham's gaze. Her cousin's eyes were wide, clear, and full of awareness. *Yep. Now we're on the same page.*

"The thing was on some kinda mission, by the sounds of things," Greta continued, oblivious to the look shared between them. "Cedric and the rest of the gang were on their toes enough to make sure none of them got seriously hurt in the process. Apparently, all the werewolf wanted was to chase them off the destroyed ship before ripping up whatever was left. Including the scroll of blood magic, so no, we don't have a copy of *that* one lying around somewhere. All thanks to an alpha werewolf in 953 A.D.

"Of course, our Ambrosius back then didn't call the thing a werewolf in his account. Or an alpha. How could he, when that was literally the first werewolf anyone had seen in nearly two and a half million years? It's hard to miss the picture when he called it, 'a massive beast over seven feet tall, standing on two legs like a man but covered in fur and armed with razor-sharp fangs protruding from a wolf-like snout.' And don't forget the claws." She raised a clawed hand and wiggled her fingers. "I'm not sure he got all the details a hundred percent right. Silverback, sure. 'Lines of silver tipping the creature's monstrous claws?' I don't know. That sounds fishy to me."

"The claw marks," Halsey whispered.

Brigham stared blankly across the room. "Holy fucking shit."

Greta sniggered. "You know, I think that's exactly what *I* said when I read the whole story."

"There's only one alpha," Brigham added, slowly turning his head toward Halsey again but unable to stop staring blankly at the empty space in the middle of the living room. "For every monster. That's the one you..."

"He was a *Viking*." Halsey didn't want to think about killing the silverback alpha with her own two hands and the blade of her throwing axe, even if it had technically been self-defense in the end. Yet the man who'd died at her hand, half in her arms and half beneath her with the blade of her weapon buried in his chest, had given her more clues than she'd known what to do with at the time.

Not only had Rolfr Magnusson thanked her for the deed before muttering something in Old Norse that Halsey still hadn't found the time to translate, but he'd offered a warning too. Whether or not the man had fully understood how elemental monster hunters worked and what the Ambrosius Clan, or any Clan, was capable of against those of his kind, he'd told her exactly what she needed to know.

"He tried to stop her," she murmured.

"What's that?" Greta asked before taking another sip of her lemonade. "Also, what's all this about claw marks? That's pretty much the *only* thing any werewolf leaves behind, other than a slew of dead bodies or more turned werewolves. A few slashes aren't all that interesting, really."

"They are if they're on the lid of a silver coffin that washed up on the beaches of Moher, Ireland," Brigham added breathlessly. He sounded far away, both to his own ears and to Halsey's.

She felt like she might pass out. Or start screaming and throwing things. Or maybe cease to exist altogether.

Rolfr Magnusson was the silverback alpha from the ship. The claw marks across the lid were his. *This whole time, I thought they were from some monster trying to* open *the stupid thing, but he was trying to close it back up.*

"It already happened," she murmured, trying not to let the magnitude of what they were piecing together overwhelm her. "Now we *know* this isn't the first time the Blood Matriarch's been released since the great war."

"What?" Brigham swung his gaze toward her face, though his eyes looked glassy. Probably because he was still coming to terms with the realization that everything he'd previously thought impossible was all starting to make incredible sense. With or without proof, the results were impossible to ignore.

Halsey counted off the selling points of her slightly adjusted theory on her fingers. "No monsters before the ship. Monsters *after* the ship. Destroyed ship that looked like it had been ripped apart by all kinds of monsters. Only one human still aboard, dead and surrounded by treasure plus *blood magic* written down on a scroll. Plus, the silverback alpha with silver claws who didn't actually attack Cedric and the other elementals but went to work destroying the evidence instead."

"Hal, you totally lost me again…"

"No, I didn't. You figured it out too. The silver Cedric saw on the alpha's claws was from the lid of the silver coffin. Werewolf slashes. The alpha was *there* the night we found it, Brigham. Calling the other werewolves back. Calling them *away* from the beach, the coffin, and probably from the Mother of Monsters. Shit, how close did we come to her that night without even knowing it? Where did she *go*?"

"Doesn't sound to me like *trying to stop her*," Greta interjected. "Who's 'he'?"

"The werewolf alpha." Halsey drew a deep breath as her head kept reeling. "We thought the claw marks were from some werewolf trying to get in and open the thing right before we found it. I think they came from the alpha *closing* the lid instead. He was trying to stop her."

"You sound awfully certain about that, kid."

I am. Except I can't spill the beans on a talking werewolf and the man inside it giving me his name and explaining why I had to be the one to free him from hundreds of years as the first monster of his kind...

"It's a hunch," she demurred. "A strong one."

"Uh-huh." Pursing her lips, Greta squinted a little, glanced quickly at Brigham, then figured she'd drop the subject and let her granddaughter handle the truth in whatever way she deemed best.

Meemaw already knows about the alpha. This isn't about the fact that he talked to me or begged me to kill him, though. Right now, it's about him being on the ship the first time the Mother of Monsters was pulled from the sea. All the bedtime stories Meemaw used to tell us as kids are actually real.

"All the other clues point to the same thing," Halsey added quickly and was immediately grateful her quick thinking helped cover up the fact that she still wasn't being entirely honest with her mission partner. "Plus, the alpha tore up the blood-magic scroll, right? Because he didn't want anyone else to get their hands on it."

"Wait, so you're saying someone on the *ship* used the scroll?" Brigham asked. "To...what? Summon the Mother of Monsters up from the bottom of the ocean?"

"There's literally no other way to interpret the story," Greta replied calmly. "This was obviously the day monsters as we know them re-entered the world."

"So, who was it?"

"Use your imagination, kid." The woman frowned at her grandson, then sniggered. "It could've been any one of those Vikings."

"Viking blood humans." He scoffed. "This keeps getting worse."

"If they were only screwing around with it, sure," Halsey added thoughtfully. "Maybe blood-magic runes were a lot more readable back then, you know? Like Icelandic or Old Norse. I mean, people in Iceland still have their mother language. Old Norse doesn't exist anymore *now*, but back then?"

She shrugged and tossed the train of thought aside. "It doesn't matter *who* read the blood-magic ritual out loud. What matters is the scroll still existed, and not in a vacuum, either. It came from somewhere. Which means someone was protecting the knowledge of blood humans and their magic. That's what pulled the Matriarch up the first time."

Greta made a noncommittal hum. "It could've been the monk." Then she shrugged and raised her lemonade glass to her lips again.

This time, Halsey fully turned her body on the couch to face her grandmother head-on. "What monk?"

"Oh, for crying out loud, girl! The only one there. Dead man with a giant slash in his—" Greta froze, then glanced at her lemonade in confusion and distaste before letting out another small chuckle. "Whoops. It's all blended together up here more than I thought."

She tapped her temple, then gazed at the ceiling to help with her memory recall. "Cedric said the body they found looked like the man could've been some kind of monk in life. Benedictine, maybe. Gregorian? Alexandrian? Or whatever. Sounds like I'm spouting random people's names. Not that the elemental search party knew much about monks way up in or around Scandinavia, and neither do I, but still. I like to think of our dead human as *the* monk."

Brigham stared at her, then raised his eyebrows and nodded. "Great. Any other super important details you can pull out of thin air for us?"

"Ooh, look who's got a little venom back in his stinger." Greta chuckled and raised her glass toward him in a silent, ice-clinking toast. "Seeing as the last time I saw this story penned in our Cedric's loving hand was twenty years ago, I'd say I did a damn fine job recalling all the important bits. Clearly, you have higher expectations of me."

He sighed and shook his head, ripping himself from his frustration a lot more easily and quickly than Halsey ever managed. "Sorry, Meemaw. I just—"

"You had your whole worldview turned topsy-turvy and dumped right back down onto your head. I get it. Takes time to get used to, but I can tell you right now you sure as hell aren't in Kansas anymore, kid. If you're still trying to pretend you are, I'd say you need to get your head checked."

Brigham grimaced like he'd been served a massive bowl of creamed corn. "I don't wanna think about Kansas right now. Or ever."

"Well, why the hell not?"

Halsey fought to keep back a laugh as she replied, "Wyverns."

"Huh. Oh, *those* wyverns." Greta grinned at her grandson. "The ones you and Owen had to stone out of the damn trees, right?"

"Meemaw, I said I don't wanna talk about it."

The woman tossed her head back and had a good laugh at that. Her laughter snuffed out abruptly, then she pointed at Brigham and winked. "You still know what I'm saying."

"Yeah, I know what you're saying." He pointed back at her and tried to smile, though the grimace of distaste at the mention of Kansas hadn't quite yet run its course. "Hal was right."

CHAPTER SEVEN

"Wait, what?" Halsey gaped at him and felt like an idiot for not having anything else to say.

"This whole time. Since we found the coffin." Her cousin shook his head and finally looked up at her.

The grimace was gone. So was the anger and confusion and drive to keep poking holes in her theory about the Mother of Monsters and blood humans still in the world and everything they thought they knew about their family and their purpose being covered in so many lies they didn't know where to begin. Now he only looked sorry and sad.

Damn it. If I'm waiting for the right time to spill all my secrets, this would be it.

Instead, the only thing she could manage to say to him was, "That actually means more than you know to hear."

"Yeah, I bet. After everything the Council's done and the way they've been treating you over all this." He nodded at their grandmother next. "The way they've been treating *both* of you."

"Aw, that's sweet." Greta shot him another wink, then

stood from her armchair to pour her third glass of lemonade.

Halsey's insides squirmed. *Really? He's gonna keep going with all the incredible things he's saying and actually admit he was wrong? Now I feel like the worst mission partner ever. I have to tell him.*

When she glanced at Greta, it seemed like her grandmother had the exact same thought. Or maybe Halsey's mind wanted to trick her into thinking that.

"Listen, Brigham. I know you have my back. You always have. So you don't need to—"

"Of course I do." He spread his arms, gazing at her with such sincerity that she wanted to leap off the couch and run from the room. "I've always had your back in the *field*. Always will, and that's a given. With the rest of it, though? All this running around looking for clues and proof and stuff? I didn't actually believe any of what you've been saying or that any of this could even be possible."

"Well, now you know it is. I'm glad we're on the same page there."

"I didn't believe *in* you," he continued with even more pleading in his eyes. "That made me a shitty best friend, no matter how you look at it."

"I promise you've never been a shitty friend," she murmured, trying to smile back at her cousin as the guilt and discomfort kept growing in the pit of her stomach. *Just tell him, you idiot.* She drew a deep breath to continue. "There's something I have to—"

"Whatever you have to say isn't gonna change my mind, cuz." Brigham shrugged, seemingly pleased by her gracious reaction to him admitting he'd been wrong for months now. "You laid it all out for me. You both did. Is it still gonna be a hell of a struggle to get the Council to see what *we* see? Yeah. We both know you were never gonna stop trying to convince them until you actually got them to see all this, though. I want you to know I'm not stopping either."

"That...means a lot." Halsey's gut clenched as she realized she was quickly running out of time to tell her cousin the truth without overriding his genuinely heartfelt confession with her crappy one. "Hey, while we're on the subject of putting everything out in the open..."

"Yeah, I know." Brigham's eyes widened as he leaned slightly toward her on the couch, though an entire cushion remained between them. Then he released a self-conscious chuckle and shrugged. "Neither one of us is good at this kinda thing, but...well, desperate times and all that, right? So I'll say it."

"Brigham, that's not what I—"

"I'm so sorry, Hal."

The urge to spill her guts right there in their grandmother's living room, which had been growing stronger and tighter this whole time, deflated inside her like a popped balloon.

Fuck.

"Thanks," she muttered because not saying anything at that moment would have been even worse than holding back everything he deserved to hear.

Then her cousin smiled and perked up before pointing at her. "From here on out, the only time I'm ever gonna try to poke holes in your theories is when you *ask* for it. Promise."

"Okay." Halsey couldn't think of anything else to say that wouldn't make her sound more ridiculous than she did right now. "Sounds like a plan…"

"You'll have to bear with me," Brigham continued with a glimmer of his usual playful smirk now returning. "You both know logic and reason have been my MO for, like, forever. I'm not saying I'm gonna give that up a hundred percent now."

"Yeah, definitely don't do that." She glanced at Greta now, who sat in her armchair, smirking and watching the whole thing as she drank her lemonade.

Yep. She's gonna bring this up later to remind me what a shitty move I made lying to him in the first place.

"With *you*, cuz, I'm giving it up." Brigham raised his right hand like he was about to swear on the bible of monster hunting and nodded. "Even when I don't know what the hell you're talking about. Even when you can't even explain it. If you tell me you know something, you're sure, or you *just feel it*, or whatever, I'm all over it."

Halsey chuckled weakly. "Hey, no need to get down on one knee and swear your fealty over a sword or anything."

He snorted. "*That* would be dope. But I'm serious, Hal. I've been screwing up big time since we got back from Ireland. The first time, I mean. I'm just… Well, honestly, I feel shitty about it. I'm kinda secretly hoping you're not gonna put in for a new partner or something."

Despite feeling awful for not having used this opportunity to clear the air between them, Halsey laughed. "And try to get someone else up to speed on all the impossible legends coming to life before we have to go out and fight another war all over again? Please."

"Ha. Yeah, I thought so."

"Besides," she continued, "I'm pretty sure Meemaw would totally close her doors to any more of these *illuminating stories* if I brought someone totally new into the picture. We got a decent thing going, cuz. Let's just...focus on that, okay?"

She knew she was digging an even deeper hole for herself, but Brigham was being such a great sport about the whole thing. She couldn't justify breaking the still-unshared news to him right now. Not anymore.

Plus, Brigham Ambrosius apologized about as much as Halsey did. Each of them had an impressive track record of being right in each of their areas of expertise, and the need to admit any wrongdoing and actually apologize for it hadn't come up for either of them very often, especially since they'd graduated and had set off for real missions as official Ambrosius Clan militia operatives. For the most part, neither one of them had ever had much to apologize *for*.

Now he's got me beat on that one. I'll have to find the perfect time later. If there even is *a good time later with us facing screwy monsters and the Blood Matriarch walking around again in the flesh. Also, if we make it out alive...*

Brigham sniffed, then inhaled deeply and nodded. "Yeah, you're right. Stay positive, huh? Focus on what we *know* we've got going for us, and the rest'll just...work itself out. Like it always does." His reassuring smile flickered a little, and Halsey didn't miss the quick, furtive glance he shot at the copper orb still resting in her lap, now fully uncovered.

He did, however, quickly cover up the wary gaze and

instead turned his attention onto Greta. "So we got all that mushy crap out of the way."

His grandmother tilted her head with a gentle smile. "I'm as much a fan of the mushy crap as the next grandma. Just don't expect it to come from *me*."

"No, of course not," Halsey cut in. She could already see it in the way Brigham faced their grandmother now, squinting at her with a thoughtful smile. He was ready to move on and get back to the whole reason they'd barged through her front door.

"You can't tell us not to expect a few more answers from you." Brigham folded his arms and failed at trying to look stern and commanding. Most of that was because of his goofy grin, now fully returned. "Nice try, derailing us from the part of the conversation that actually matters."

"I had nothing to do with it." Greta shrugged. "Plus, I wouldn't necessarily say the last five minutes *didn't matter...*"

"You know what I mean." Brigham stared at their grandmother as if he could force the woman back on track with the big familial reveals by gazing at her intently enough. "We covered Cedric's missing record and what it *actually* means. Other than the fact that at least one of your bedtime stories turned out to be a real historical event, anyway. You still haven't gotten the part about what it has to do with *our* family."

Greta blinked at him in surprise. "You *do* remember the part about Cedric being an Ambrosius, don't you?"

"He's talking about all the other family history you said they should've taught us," Halsey clarified, though she had a feeling their grandmother was already acutely aware of what Brigham had meant. "The secrets everyone's been keeping from us."

"Yeah." Her cousin pointed at her without looking away from Greta. "'Cause there's no way Cedric's story about a Viking ship and a dead monk is the only one."

"Well, you're probably right." Their grandmother slowly sipped at her lemonade again, then pulled away to stare at the glass when she was finished and smacked her lips.

She didn't say anything else.

Sure, she'll tell us everything we wanna know. As long as we keep asking the right questions. Typical.

When Halsey looked at her cousin, she found the exact same realization on Brigham's face. He raised his eyebrows in question, and she shrugged with a gesture toward their grandmother. Which, of course, they both knew meant she was giving him the floor to keep working Greta Ambrosius for all the long-lost secrets she was worth.

"So you found Cedric's fun little monster story in the records twenty years ago," he reiterated.

Greta dipped her head in acknowledgment. "So you're back on the paying-attention track."

"So why doesn't the rest of the family know about it?"

That question caught their grandmother's attention, which came in the form of Greta choking on her next sip of lemonade and lurching forward in her armchair in an effort not to spray her mouthful all over the living room. When she finally recovered, she stared right into her nearly empty glass and scoffed. "Well, *you two* were hardly old enough to read that account for yourselves. I'd say the same thing applies to the rest of your generation and everyone else who hadn't even been born yet."

Brigham scrunched up his face and shook his head. "What?"

"Oh, does the phrase 'the rest of the family' suddenly not apply to all your cousins?"

The complete bafflement overtaking Brigham's previous confidence made it perfectly clear Halsey had to jump in for more clarification.

Apparently, Meemaw's in one of her insanely literal moods.

"That's her way of saying we're not the only ones who know about the missing record."

"Wait, what?" Brigham turned his confusion onto Halsey. "I was talking about the Council. Do *they* know?"

"Not all of them," Greta murmured.

"What, so you called a private meeting with *half* the Council and figured it'd be fun to leave the other half in the dark?"

The woman flicked her gaze up from her lemonade glass to fix Brigham with a piercing gaze as she slowly sat back in her armchair again. "The Council of today and the Council of twenty years ago are two very different things, kid. That includes more than the Ambrosius elementals sitting in those seven gods-be-damned chairs."

Halsey was acutely aware of the change in her grandmother's mood. It was the first response with bite Greta had given today, even compared to her grandmother's ridiculous statements that anyone could easily have taken as personal insults. Yet the flash of anger and resentment behind the woman's eyes said more than anything Greta could have put into words.

Once again, Halsey had to jump in before things got twisted up and flipped inside-out. Now that they were here, there was no way the three of them wouldn't see this conversation to the end.

Not if I want a meeting with Aydem.

"You showed them," she stated gently, hoping it would bring her grandmother back into the present. It worked, though now both Greta and Brigham looked confused by Halsey's out-of-context statement.

"I show a lot of people a lot of things, girl. That's not insinuating anything." Greta snorted. "You'll have to be more—"

"Cedric's account of him and all those other elementals finding the ship in Ireland." Halsey nodded at her grandmother and waited for her cousin to put together the pieces on his own. She knew he was capable of it. Hopefully, Brigham wouldn't need any more coaching after the giant revelation he'd finally managed to wrap his head around. "You took it to the Council twenty years ago, didn't you?"

For a moment, it looked like her grandmother would remain clueless about the whole thing. Then a tiny smile flickered at the corner of her mouth.

The implications finally sank in for Brigham, and he sank back against the couch cushions with a heavy sigh. "Oh, shit…"

"Quite." Greta wiggled her eyebrows at him, then swirled what was left of her drink around and around in her glass some more. "Though at that point, I brought it to the *rest* of the Council. The six other Ambrosius elementals I trusted implicitly. Those I believed would stand beside me when they realized what we'd all been too blind and too busily overzealous to see."

"Because you were the Council head," Brigham murmured.

"We don't need to hash *that* out all over again." She dismissed the comment with a flippant wave, then stared off across the living room with a pinched expression halfway between a nostalgic smile and a grimace of disgust. "But yeah. You pinned the tail right on the seven-headed donkey. I brought the *rest* of the Council everything I'd found in our library and everything I'd seen with my own eyes.

"I'd thought my story of how weirdly hard it was to bring down that big-ass bastard of a minotaur would be enough to get their attention. Not to mention the unorthodox methods I had to use to get the job done. I'm *way* past the cutoff date for militia performance reviews, so we're not getting into that."

Brigham released a halting, uncertain giggle, which only made his grandmother smirk before she dived back into her tale.

"It does stand to reason, doesn't it, kid? The Ambrosius Clan's Council head went out on her own to take down a monster and came back with news of something very different and very wrong bubbling beneath the surface of what we've always known about monsters and how to hunt them. You'd think those responsible for the safety, wellbeing, training, and assignment of an entire *militia* would be willing to look at all the possibilities. But no." Greta thumped her empty fist on the armrest and hissed. "Turns out they'd rather sit up in their tower with their heads up each other's asses than consider the prospect of anything around them actually changing."

With a snort, Brigham tried to cover his smile with a hand and muttered, "*That's* an image I didn't need."

"It was also the first time I'd gone directly to my own Council with something I knew was important and found them staring at me in pity and disbelief and something I'd say comes dangerously close to loathing. 'Oh, look at her. The poor old woman doesn't know what she's talking about. She's losing her mind. She's going senile. Keep humoring her, and it'll all go away.'" With a frustrated hiss, Greta shook her head. "It damn well *didn't* go away. I can tell you that right now."

"Even when you showed them the scroll you found with another *Ambrosius* detailing how monsters actually came back into the world?" Halsey asked.

"Please." Fixing her granddaughter with a look of mock consternation, the woman jerked her head toward Brigham and added, "We all saw how much effort it took to get *this* one to see the truth for himself. Nearly half an hour of watching it stare him in the face, but the on-switch got sticky there for a minute, didn't it?"

Brigham sniggered again, then realized she'd been talking about him and his ability to see all the connections Halsey and Greta had both already made. Then he frowned and pulled his head back in mock insult. "Hey…"

"It's a statement of facts, kid." Greta waved him off. "Don't worry. I already know you're a smart cookie with a relatively good head on his shoulders. Even *after* being chucked through the woods like an ogre's hacky sack. So you've got nothing to prove and nothing to convince me of. Trust me."

While he tried to puzzle meaning from his grandmother's latest odd statement, Halsey took the opportunity to keep the conversation moving forward. "The Council wanted to write the whole thing off as another coincidence."

"Not only that, girl. A few of them called it *irrelevant*. Then there was something else. Who was it? Wallace, probably. The man was adamant about Cedric's entire account being... Oh, what did he say? 'A scintillating but summarily worthless piece of storytelling through creative fiction and nothing more.'"

"Right. Like Charlemagne would ever keep *fiction* in the Clan library."

"Well, if he'd known about *this*, I'm sure he would've hopped right onto Wallace's buzzkill train and thrown the scroll right out with that week's trash." Greta shrugged. "I didn't have the time or the patience to bash my head against the wall trying to convince *my own family* we had a serious problem on our hands. One with the potential to get even bigger and uglier if we didn't start investigating and cataloging the other things that would prove we haven't been paying attention *for centuries*. So I didn't bother."

"Wait, just like that?" Brigham asked. "You were too impatient, so you said screw it and didn't even try?"

She slowly turned to look at him head-on again, then broke into a crooked smile. "Don't put words into my mouth. We both know I'm way more efficiently stubborn than *that*. Also stubbornly efficient, now that I think about it."

"You said—"

"I said I didn't have the time or the patience to play

teacher to six other members of our family whose only *real* job is to teach everyone else and their spawn. The right way. Which they've failed to do this whole damn time, and I know I'm not selling weapons to the armory!" She thumped her fist down on the armrest again, her shout echoing through the sudden silence of the living room.

Brigham wrinkled his nose. "You mean 'preaching to the choir.'"

"Don't try to correct me like you have any idea what's inside my head, boy. I know what I said, and it was exactly what I meant." With a snort, Greta rolled her eyes, then pointed at Brigham as she fixed Halsey with a conspiratorial frown. "Is he always like this?"

"I mean…"

"Actually," Brigham cut in, "it's usually the other way around."

"Oh. Good. Then you know how annoying it is." After flashing her grandson a tight grin that was nowhere close to the kind of smile grandmothers were known for handing out, Greta slumped back like a pouting toddler and grunted. She scanned the opposite wall of the living room behind the couch and her grandchildren's heads. "What was I saying?"

"Um…" Brigham clicked his tongue. "Selling weapons to the armory?"

"That's right. We could say I gave up on the Council when I figured out how snug and cozy they all were, wrapped up in their blindness and their fear of anything that might've rocked the boat to one side or the other. How stupid they were for it."

The woman paused and tittered. She leaned sideways

and fixed her grandchildren with a different kind of grin that didn't make either of them feel like they'd stepped into a horror movie. This time, Greta looked like her regular, weirdly playful, mischievous self again. At least to Halsey, anyway. "You're forgetting who I was back then. Which is totally understandable, by the way. I don't expect either of you to keep your best memories of me from when you were still in diapers. So I'll only say that being the head of the Ambrosius Clan Council sure as shit had its benefits. Certain…privileges, if you will."

She paused again, apparently for added effect, but now even Halsey couldn't figure out what her fun little hint was supposed to mean.

"Meemaw." Halsey chuckled and hoped her grandmother wouldn't keep taking so many things so personally. Which was strange to see in a woman who, for Halsey's entire life, had acted like she didn't give a damn about much of anything. "We can't actually read your mind."

Greta's loud, derisive snort suggested what she'd said was the most obvious thing in the world. "I went out to go look into it on my own. Me, myself, and I. *Sola*. That's Spanish, by the way." When neither of her grandchildren cracked a smile, she rolled her eyes again. "I left the damn Council room while the other six yahoos took their sweet time to come to a consensus about literally *anything*. They were taking way too long, so I took things into my own hands. Figured an outside opinion might remind them how to get their asses in gear so we could *do* something about it."

The living room fell silent again because it was perfectly clear Greta was on a roll. This time, both Halsey and Brigham understood that when their grandmother started a confusing rant, she was on the precipice of dropping the kind of illuminating info-bomb they were waiting for.

With a heavy sigh, Greta slumped as far back as she could go in her armchair, raised her glass in a stiff motion toward the opposite side of the room, and practically growled, "I was wrong as shit."

CHAPTER EIGHT

Greta downed her lemonade like she was knocking back the last dregs of a stiff liquor drink, then stared into space and said nothing.

Brigham frowned at his glass and took another tentative sniff. Yet it was nothing but pure lemonade.

Halsey stared at her grandmother, waiting for more and hating every second ticking by at a snail's pace.

She's never talked about her past before. She's never talked about any of this, but now we're finally about to hear what actually happened. Why everything's so screwed up with our family. All the secrets they're keeping and the lies they've been telling, and how things got this way.

At the moment, she wanted nothing more than to prod her grandmother into continuing, but the tension in the air balanced too precariously. If she pushed too hard, too fast, there was a decent chance Halsey might push Greta off the proverbial ledge. Then the woman might call this whole thing off, kick her grandchildren out of the house, and leave Halsey and Brigham with nothing to show for the hours they'd devoted to learning what they needed to know.

Did it feel like this was taking forever? Absolutely. Halsey preferred an actual conversation that dragged on but eventually got to the point, rather than coming back to her Meemaw's house over and over again for the truth, one fractured morsel at a time.

She forced herself to breathe calmly and not jump down the woman's throat about it. Clearly, Greta was having a hard time walking down memory lane and not stopping at every landmark along the way.

Finally, Greta sniffed and stood from her armchair enough to reach for the lemonade pitcher on the coffee table and fill yet another glass. Most of the ice had melted at this point, but that didn't seem to matter. As the tiny ice cubes clinked into the glass with slightly watered-down lemonade, she shook her head and sniffed again. "I was *so* wrong. Not that it matters now anyway…"

Once she finished refilling her glass, she pulled the pitcher away as if to set it down again and paused. Then she stood there like a statue, her bright blue eyes glistening and her lips turning down at the corners as she stared at absolutely nothing again. The only proof she *wasn't* a statue showed in the slight tremble of her hand gripping the pitcher's handle and the few strands of silvery-gray hair trembling beside her face as her slow breath fluttered them aside again and again.

Brigham swallowed thickly, and when Halsey turned to look at him, his wide eyes and mouth slightly parted in an O might as well have been words written across his face. *Shit. We broke Meemaw.*

Then Halsey's concern for her grandmother overtook her fear of inadvertently bringing this entire conversation to a premature end, and she asked as gently as she could, "Are you...okay?"

Greta blinked, then looked sharply up at her. "Don't coddle me, girl. I'm not a fan, and you're no good at it anyway." Then she straightened from looming over the lemonade tray on the coffee table, looked down at the pitcher in her hand as if noticing it for the first time, and slowly waved it in front of her. "More lemonade?"

Not wanting to be the target of more hard truths doled out as casual conversation pieces, Halsey shook her head.

"All good here," Brigham replied as he raised his full glass with all the ice nearly melted. He glanced at the drink, realized how unsupportive he looked by not having drank an acceptable amount at this point, and took a long, slow sip. His swallow was loud enough for everyone to hear, but his next smile wasn't nearly as forced when he was reminded of how good his grandmother's refreshing concoction was. "Perfect."

"Nothing's perfect, Brigham," Greta coolly replied as she set down the pitcher, then returned to her chair. With a heavy sigh, she lowered herself back into it and pointed at him. "Anyone who says otherwise doesn't know what they're looking at. Or even what they're looking *for*. So don't go spewing that nonsense all over the place like you're one of those idiots."

He pressed his lips together, his eyes wide, then raised his glass to his mouth again and muttered over the rim, "Yes, ma'am."

That made their grandmother's smile return enough to

make her not nearly as scary as she'd been two seconds ago.

I've seen Meemaw pissed off before. The day she stormed into the Council room, waving around the scroll with all the blood runes on it, she was pissed. This is something else.

Halsey wasn't sure how to categorize her grandmother's current mood because labeling the woman's current emotion on display as either anger, resentment, or sadness didn't quite fit. Now she had a feeling whatever Greta was experiencing right now, part of this conversation would end up spreading that emotion farther than the woman's own personal bubble.

We're not gonna like what she has to say next. I can deal with that. As long as she doesn't try to use it as an excuse to bow out.

"So." Brigham took another sip of lemonade, smacked his lips, then cleared his throat. "You went off on your own to find out what was happening to the monsters back then. Because everyone else was too busy arguing and trying to make up their minds, right?"

"Or arguing *about* trying to make up their minds." Greta scoffed. "Like I ever had a clue what was going through any of those plugged-up heads. Still don't. But they want to blame me for it, that's for damn sure."

"And?" he prompted, nodding slowly.

"And what?"

"And...where did you go looking for answers?"

"Oh." Greta tossed a hand in the air as if her grandchildren should've already known the answer through osmosis. "I went to the Order of Skrár. Obviously."

Brigham wasn't even taking a drink of lemonade, but he choked anyway. "Wait, *what*?"

"Don't act like you have no idea who I'm talking about."

He quickly recovered from his shock, then tried to play it off like he'd been expecting this the whole time. "Yeah, I've heard of them. Even got a name or two in Turkey, but..."

"What?" Greta smirked. "Can't picture your old Meemaw roaming around the globe and talking to important men with their cigars and whiskey and big ol' hats?"

"Huh?" Brigham blinked slowly, taken aback once again by the odd imagery he couldn't quite get rid of as quickly as he would've liked.

Apparently, Greta took his confusion for complete cluelessness once again. She widened her eyes at Halsey and gestured toward her befuddled grandson. "You mean he doesn't know *that*, either?"

Crap. She's gonna blow the lid open on my *secrets, too, if we keep at it like this.*

"Hey, I'm not an idiot," Brigham retorted, quickly shaking his head before trying to get down to the point. He had to pause for a brief moment longer before turning toward Halsey. "What's she talking about?"

"For the love of all..." Greta growled in frustration. "You two are killing me. You know that, right? Or at least giving me indigestion, and that's basically the same thing."

"Maybe it's the lemonade," Brigham muttered.

"Now *you* can't have any more than what's already in your glass." The woman grimaced at him in mock moodiness, then gestured toward Halsey this time. "Because I'm not a *complete* airhead, I'll tell you what I'm talking about. The last time your cousin came over for a nice chat and a cup of What the Hell Is That Glowing Ball, I told her exactly what she needed to do next if she wanted to—"

"*That's* what you meant by 'living records,'" Halsey cut in. Because if she'd let her grandmother keep talking about her last visit, the woman was sure to spit out a few other priceless little nuggets Halsey hadn't gotten around to sharing with her mission partner quite yet. Plus, they'd already had enough distractions today, and Halsey *knew* they were getting close to something big.

Greta gazed back at her with wide eyes as if she could see right into her granddaughter's brain and thoroughly disapproved of the entire strategy.

"You were sending me to the Order of Skrár," Halsey added with a slow nod.

"Well. I *had* hoped you'd be smart enough and dedicated enough to figure it out on your own without me having to spell out every little detail, but apparently, I was wrong."

"Hold on." Brigham wrinkled his nose again, and now he was clenching his fists so tightly in his lap he looked like he might explode. "You came back here *again* without me?"

Halsey fought back a cringe. "Just to see if Meemaw knew anything about the weird not-sand and the ball I turned it into."

"Hal…"

"Hey, it's not like you would've come with me if I told you I wanted to talk to her about that. You hate the thing."

"For a good reason!" Now he didn't try to hide it when he stared pointedly at the copper orb in question. "You're snuggling a fucking *bomb* in your lap right now—"

"I believe," Greta barked, interrupting the argument

before lowering her voice to a normal volume. "We agreed to no more yelling."

Brigham clapped his mouth shut.

Halsey stuffed the copper orb between her thigh and the armrest, then murmured, "I had no idea the *living records* were supposed to be the Order of Skrár."

"Well, that's a rather large oversight on your part, girl, isn't it?" Greta eyed her granddaughter a moment longer, then clicked her tongue. "Should we keep going? Because I'm getting the feeling neither one of you wants this to continue."

"Don't say that." Halsey fixed the woman with a disapproving frown. "You know we do."

"Good. Then act like it."

"Wait." Brigham pinched the bridge of his nose and drew a deep breath. "Twenty years ago, this obviously wasn't a thing, but you know what those people are doing *now*, though, right?"

"Who?" Greta asked innocently.

"The Order, Meemaw."

"Oh. The Order's been around forever, kid. They do a whole slew of things, and unless it has anything to do with me, it's none of my business."

"Okay, but it *does* have something to do with you. With all of us." Brigham's next heavy sigh did more to show how frustrated he was than any amount of shouting previously could have. When he finally met Greta's gaze again, he didn't look remotely happy to have to be breaking the news to her like this. "Because whatever else they're supposed to do, the Order of Skrár added handing out recommendations for world's best monster hunter to their list."

Greta blinked at him, then snorted. "Good one."

"He's not kidding," Halsey added. "That's how we got our last job."

"In *Turkey?*"

"The Order of Skrár gave out contact info for someone on the Ambrosius Council," Brigham added. "Because somebody had a paying job for the best monster hunters out there, and they were willing to make an offer only a complete moron would refuse."

"Right. There are plenty of those out in the world already. Don't assume I'm one of them." When Greta realized they weren't trying to screw with her, she threw her head back and released a honking, bitter laugh. "*Contracted* missions now, huh? Our holier-than-thou Council actually took the bait! Not because any of us actually need the money. Oh, no. They can't handle the fact that their own fragile egos aren't enough to hold this fraying rug together anymore. Who wants to admit something like *that?* Ha!"

Halsey and Brigham exchanged another confused look, but Greta was having the time of her life laughing about the whole thing.

"Hoo-wee!" She slapped her thigh, then chortled again before shaking her head. "You know, I try not to live in the past. It's a hell of a lot easier for me than a few select elementals we all know. I'm not naming any names, but *damn.* Hearing all that makes the years sink in, know what I mean?"

"Not really, no." Halsey shrugged. "Now I'm wondering if we're talking about the same Order of Skrár."

"Of course we are. They cover their tracks well enough to avoid some up-and-coming joker with a giant noggin snatching up a name like that and calling it their own!" Greta had another good laugh at that. "Trying to ride *those* coattails is one helluva stupid business move if you ask me. Now the Order's playing supernatural agency, is that it? Yeesh. Here I was, assuming all along they were still doing what they'd been doing for the last several *thousand* years."

She continued. "Which, judging by the blank looks you're both giving me right now, I'd say neither of you can grasp at the moment. So I'll lay some knowledge on ya. The Order's main purpose, right? Gathering and preserving records to carry them on for posterity."

For a moment, the living room fell silent again. Then Brigham cleared his throat. "Yeah, Meemaw. We…kinda figured that part out already."

"Huh. Then you should've said so before I wasted all that breath back there."

"Why'd you call them *living records*?" Halsey asked. "You could've told me they were a giant library."

"Oh, so you *want* me to lie to you, is that it?" Greta raised her eyebrows, and Halsey immediately clapped her mouth shut. "I didn't think so. I called them what I know them to be, girl. The Order of Skrár is more than a giant library and a hell of a lot more than some two-bit agency handing out elemental Clan contact numbers like candy, apparently."

She sniggered, shook her head, and sipped on her refreshed lemonade. Fortunately, she didn't require any further prompting again to get back into the conversation. "As far as I know, the Order goes as far back as our family tree. They existed before the Ice Age and the great war, like elementals did, and I'd bet my lemonade recipe they'll be hanging around even longer than us. If we're lucky. Not that I think elementals are dying out anytime soon. Then again, our family as a whole certainly doesn't inspire confidence in the survival-of-the-fittest arena."

Brigham narrowed his eyes as his grandmother chuckled at her own harsh joke. "So they're...what? Another magical family?"

"Of course not. They're an *Order*. Blood relation isn't a requirement. Actually, it might even be the *only* way to keep somebody out of the fold if they've passed all the other tests. You don't want a single family responsible for protecting and maintaining all the magical and supernatural histories for all eternity. Someone's bound to pull a nepotistic rewrite somewhere along the way..."

"They have to be magical *somehow*. You can't be responsible for something like that if you aren't actually involved in magic."

"Hmm." Stroking her chin, Greta scanned her grandson, then shrugged. "You might be onto something there. You know, I honestly never bothered to ask. All magical abilities aside, the Order has their own ways of doing things. I'd say they perfected their methods a hell of a lot faster than the rest of us. Especially *our* Clan, if the way things are headed is any indication..."

"They're a Clan?" Halsey asked.

Her grandmother clicked her tongue. "No, girl. What's wrong with you? Pay attention. The Order of Skrár is an *Order*, which... Huh. Anyone else getting déjà vu right now?" When she didn't get another prompt to continue or a laugh or so much as an eye-roll, Greta puffed out a sigh. "Fine. They're an organization. Highly detailed, meticulous, and interested in all the major *and* minor details. Larger by far than any elemental Clan, and they have been since the very beginning when they were created to maintain more *objective* records than any one elemental Clan alone. For reasons previously discussed, among others. I'm assuming I don't have to spell *that* out for you.

"When I say objective records, I do literally mean objective in the broadest, macro-est sense. Most macro? Whatever. They're big. Their only real purpose is to keep tabs on *everything* magical. We're not only talking about the fact that magic exists or pinning up new headlines on a giant Order corkboard, okay? I do mean *everything*.

"The Order's got a wing on monsters. A wing on massive historical events and all their trickle-down, ripple-effect consequences. You better believe they've got a wing or two devoted specifically to those of us on this planet *with* magic."

"Ew." Halsey wrinkled her nose. "As in, they have a file on our whole family?"

"Not just ours, kid. Not only elemental families, either."

"Wait..." Brigham looked lost again until he remembered he'd recently received the answer to his question. Or at least most of it. "Okay, I get it with the whole missing-record thing. A few blood humans must have survived the great war if the Mother of Monsters got called up from the ocean in the tenth century or whatever. Fine. It sounds like you're saying we didn't have to figure that out on our own, though. Like we could've just gone to the Order of Skrár and *asked*."

Greta's smile disappeared. "That's not what I'm saying."

"I seriously hope not," Halsey added. "Otherwise, it'd be kinda hard not to think you've been screwing around with us this whole time."

"Oh, right. Yes, well, hmm…" Greta squinted at her. "That didn't work out too great for you the last time you tried, did it?"

Brigham shot his cousin another questioning look, but she shook her head and forced herself not to keep shaking the other can of worms their grandmother had almost opened. Multiple attempts to meet in person with Halil Aydem was a topic for another day.

"Then what *are* you saying?"

Greta huffed and turned slightly away from her grandchildren to haughtily take another sip of her lemonade. "All I'm saying is the Order of Skrár has something on literally everyone, including blood humans. Since the very beginning of our existence in this world, they've been keeping tabs. Watching. Recording. Organizing. Never stepping in to muddy the waters but aware of absolutely everything. Who those surviving blood humans were. Where each of them went and what happened to them over the ages. What every elemental Clan has done since before the great war was even a speck of thought in our ancestors' minds."

She paused, then added, "They've definitely got something on the two of you."

A shudder skittered across Brigham's shoulders, and he grimaced. "That's just… Come on."

Greta shrugged. "It's true. Go ahead and ask 'em yourself. If you ever get the chance."

"How do they even *do* that?"

"How should *I* know? They've got some kinda magic all their own, probably. Something totally new the rest of us don't have a clue about, but it's not our job to know everything there is to know about magic. It's the Order's."

"Great. We know what the Order does now." Halsey folded her arms. Then she realized how perturbed and impatient she looked, though she was both of those things, and flung a casual arm over the armrest. "Meemaw, we've been talking in circles forever. Can you please tell us what the Order of Skrár told *you* about Cedric's account of the ship? You did take it to them, right?"

"I'm not an idiot, girl. I was prepared when I set my meeting with them."

Whether or not that was a jab at Halsey's inability to get what she wanted from Aydem, including a first sit-down meeting the way she'd planned, Halsey decided to ignore it. She wanted to actually learn something new today.

"After that," her grandmother continued, "they confirmed the validity of Cedric's *little story*. Meaning it was really his, really written down by his hand, and really happened."

"And?" Brigham prompted again.

"And that's it."

"They didn't have anything to say?"

"Nope." Greta stated it like it was the most normal thing in the world. "They work on their own time, believe it or not. Kinda like taking a number and getting in line 'til it's your turn to see the grumpy little man behind the counter who looks at you like he never goes home, never takes breaks, and has somehow figured out how to get rid of the necessity to go to the bathroom... But instead of taking a number, I handed over Cedric's account and called it good."

"You *what?*" Brigham practically shouted.

Greta frowned at him, then leaned forward over her lap and shouted, *"I handed over Cedric's account and called it good!"*

"You can't leave something that valuable with a random organization that probably already knows exactly what happened!"

"Well, I did. So there."

Halsey looked from her incredulous cousin to her attitude-sporting grandmother. "Then what?"

"What do you mean *then what*? I went home. No, I still haven't heard a goddamn thing back from the Order about when, where, how, and why I could use what I found to help my Council and the other Clans prepare for what I guessed was coming somewhere down the line. So there's one more question you can tick off your never-ending list. Then *you* two went out to Ireland, stumbled upon a whole bunch of shiny new crap I couldn't manage to pull together on my own, and proved me right anyway."

CHAPTER NINE

At first, Halsey was certain she'd misheard everything her grandmother had said.

She went to the Order of Skrár and got absolutely nothing from them? No help, no answers, no direction for twenty years, and she thought that would be a great first place to send me for answers about the weird sand and its magic?

She could only sit there and stare numbly at Greta, occasionally blinking to reaffirm she was still alive and still breathing.

If the Order of Skrár was as useless as Greta made them out to be, Halsey had wasted so much time and energy on trying to use both a meeting with Aydem and the contents of Cedric's missing record as proof for the Ambrosius Clan Council. Which, apparently, Greta Ambrosius had never been able to do, either.

"Okay..." Brigham shifted, rolled out his shoulders, and cleared his throat. "Well, that was anticlimactic."

"Oh, so sorry," Greta grumbled. "I wasn't aware a nice long story of *the truth* from your grandmother was supposed to end with a bunch of explosives and pulse-pounding action."

"No, not that." He vigorously scratched his head and tried to find the right words for what he actually wanted to say. "I get there's a lot of history to be learned and discovered, and now we know the truth and the proof of it, even if the Council doesn't wanna hear it. Not like it matters, though. We can't *show* them the one thing that'd get them to change their minds either way…"

"That little scroll I couldn't get them to *read* the first time, kid. It wouldn't do anything for us now, either."

Halsey sucked in a sharp breath before she even fully knew what she was about to say. "Then why bring up the missing record? What was the point?"

Looking confused by the question, Greta gestured toward Brigham. "You needed help getting *him* to see the light. Now he's seen it."

"Meemaw, that's not why we're here."

Greta winked at her granddaughter and chuckled. "You sure about that, kid?"

"*Yes!*" Halsey almost leapt up from the couch but somehow managed to maintain control of her frustration despite it starting to boil and bubble up all over again. "I came here for answers because some random dude from the Order of Skrár told us to go digging through our own family history first. That we weren't ready for the truth we wanted from them until we got the truth we *needed*. From *you*."

"Really? Did he mention my name specifically?"

"No," Brigham replied as his cousin fumed on the opposite end of the couch. "You did make us think you were getting to some giant revelation that was gonna change everything for us from here on out, though."

"I see." Greta looked between them again. "Judging by the insane tension in this room, I'm gonna go ahead and say it hasn't done that."

The woman's complete disregard for what she'd known her grandchildren had been expecting was the last straw on Halsey's figurative camel, and she lost it. "Are you fucking *kidding* me right now?"

"Hal," Brigham warned.

Greta scoffed. "Well, *now*…"

"This whole time," Halsey fumed. "You've been running around your private little garden *this whole time*, alluding to all the secrets and the lies and the fact that you and I know better. That we can *do* better than the rest of the family."

"All right, girl, it's time to cool your—"

"You sent me on a wild history chase for absolutely no fucking reason," Halsey shouted, her voice growing louder and higher in pitch with every other word. "Then you promised me answers. You said you'd tell me everything I've needed to know my entire life but hadn't been *ready* enough to handle until now."

Greta cleared her throat and dipped her head in acknowledgment. "Maybe in not so many words…"

"Now you're telling me these secrets, these lies, all the answers I've always *deserved* but was denied because of our fucked-up family politics…that it's all because you were too impatient to sit around with the Council twenty years ago and wait for them to *agree* with you?"

"Well, that's—" Greta's mouth popped open for the next word that never came. Her mockingly amused expression faded beneath a frown of real confusion. "Wait. What are we talking about again?"

"You're not crazy *or* hiding any life-changing secret. You're too fucking proud to admit you made a mistake, and *that's* what got you kicked off your own Council."

Greta flinched back as if she'd been slapped in the face.

Brigham drew away from his shouting cousin, too, equally surprised by Halsey's conclusion and the daring manner in which she'd chosen to deliver it. "Whoa, dude..."

"No, not *whoa*. She's been playing *us* this whole time like she tried to play everyone else twenty years ago. Greta Ambrosius couldn't get the job done on her own, so instead of admitting the truth, she thought it was better all around to paint it up as one giant family conspiracy. Which is a shitty way to try to build a relationship with your grandkids, by the way."

"Ah. Right." Greta lifted her chin to stare down the bridge of her nose at her granddaughter. "What, exactly, would the immutable truth be that you so suddenly discovered?"

"The real reason you got kicked off the Council and sent out here was that you went to the Order of Skrár with a family record that should've been kept private and didn't tell anyone what you were doing."

"Ha! Trust me, kid. Our family's petty, but even *I* think that's taking it too far."

"Then they kicked you off because you went behind their backs and handed over what might've been the most important pieces of elemental history over to complete strangers."

Greta wrinkled her nose and glanced at Brigham. "She's grasping for straws now, isn't she?"

He could only stare in mute shock at the scene unfolding before him, but Halsey still wasn't finished.

"Of course you won't actually tell us the truth." She leapt to her feet and kept shouting, bearing down on her grandmother without having to take a single step forward. "*You're* the one who's been lying to us this whole time! To *me*!"

"Jesus, Hal." Brigham swallowed and pressed himself against the couch's corner between the back and the armrest. His gaze had left his cousin for the copper orb floating up off the opposite end of the couch and pulsing with golden light.

Though Halsey hadn't seemed to notice the effect her emotional explosion was having on the orb, Greta certainly had. She glanced once behind Halsey's shoulder, then met her granddaughter's gaze steadily and firmly, all trace of her previously amused humor gone.

"All right. After the last hour, I'll admit I can see how you might draw those conclusions. Yes, I've left out more than an acceptable number of details. Lies of omission, some might even say. But I want you to listen to me very carefully right now, Halsey. I have *never* in your life lied to you. Not once—"

"You made me think you actually understood me!" Halsey bellowed as a streaking blur of strobing golden light shot over her shoulder and darted across the room with tiny pop and a violent flurry of air. "That you *knew* who I am!"

"Which is why I could never tell you the truth!" The

second the words left Greta's mouth, her eyes widened, and she pressed herself back into her chair. Because hovering right in front of her, mere inches from the center of her forehead, was the copper orb pulsing with light and letting out a low, shuddering buzz.

"Hal!" Brigham leapt to his feet to head toward his cousin. Now the thought that she might kill Greta with her freakish magical ball was more terrifying than the actual orb itself. "What the fuck?"

"Don't." Halsey jabbed a finger at him without once removing her scathing glare from their grandmother's face. "I shouldn't have brought you into this, Brigham. It has nothing to do with you."

"Holy shit, Hal, do you *hear* yourself right now?"

"No, it's okay," Greta added.

"The hell it is! She ripped apart a whole fucking chimera with that thing, Meemaw. An *invincible* chimera. Like…literally! Now she's using it like a fucking gun with her own—"

"Brigham!"

His grandmother's short, hoarse bark startled him from his incredulity. He found himself in the disorienting position of being pointed at by both women but not remotely included in the ongoing staring contest. He didn't know whether to back away or stay still, which only left turning around and fleeing as the final option.

Before he could make up his spinning mind, the tense and possibly life-threatening conversation between the Ambrosius women picked up again, starting with the breaking tremble in Halsey's growling voice. "If you knew me, Greta, you'd know I'm not falling for that again."

"Of course I know you." Greta's chest rose and fell in a calm, natural rhythm. Yet the visibly pounding vein at her neck and the dry click of her next swallow made it clear she knew how dangerous her granddaughter's copper orb was. Even if she had no idea *what* it was. "I know how badly you want this, Halsey. I know what it means to you. And I know you will do whatever it takes to protect this family and possibly the rest of the world."

Halsey stood perfectly still in the center of the living room, fully aware of what the orb had done in response to her roiling emotions and of how serious her grandmother was finally being. Somewhere in the back of her mind, she was also aware of how disgusted with herself she was for letting things get this far out of control. Part of her wanted to drop the orb at Greta's feet, run to the woman, and beg for her forgiveness despite the fact that she hadn't technically done anything wrong. Not yet, anyway.

The other part of her knew Greta was still keeping something from her. Now, *finally*, she would hear what it was.

She's right. I will *do whatever it takes. But it's not gonna take me doing anything to her 'cause now we're on the same page.*

"Hal," Brigham tried again. "This isn't right."

Greta aimed a hum at him, though she didn't dare break from Halsey's gaze. "I wouldn't necessarily say any one of us in this room right now has an especially pristine definition of right and wrong. We can get to that later if you're still interested. Right now, Brigham, I'd recommend staying out of this."

That kind of warning from his grandmother scared him

more than his best friend acting like she'd been possessed by a demon. Yet he gazed at Halsey a moment longer in case she could feel his pleading stare. Then he rubbed his mouth, sighed, and slowly lowered himself back onto the couch.

If there had been a viable way to stop his cousin from these insanely drastic measures, he would have. If they'd been here for this conversation a few days ago, he definitely would have tried. Yet, in those two days, he'd seen exactly how dangerous Halsey was with that copper orb in her possession. There was nothing even the strongest elemental magic could do in comparison, so there was no point trying.

He did wonder when the incredibly tense, potentially deadly standoff between his cousin and their grandmother would end. Now the two women were merely staring at each other.

Finally, Halsey broke the silence. Her voice was low and hoarse, almost a growl. The copper orb of light stayed exactly where it was, hovering in place two inches from the center of Greta's forehead. "You shouldn't have waited this long to tell me the truth."

"You're absolutely correct," Greta replied firmly, her voice unwavering as she tried to ignore the rather deadly weapon directly in front of her.

"So why did you?" A renewed flare of rage shot through Halsey's entire body, and the copper orb released a warning flash of even brighter light, accompanied by a louder surge of its own humming whine.

"Because I'm a fool. That's always been on the back

burner of personal hurdles for me, which I'm sure you can understand after all the—"

"Stop stalling and tell me why!"

"The truth might make you hate me!" Greta shouted back. The force of her words echoed through the living room, and she drew a deep, halting breath. "As careless and apathetic as I might come across sometimes, Halsey, that's the last thing I want. Our family can toss me off the Council, magically lock me out of the house, and run around telling everyone else I'm a psychotic woman looking for a power grab. That's fine. But if I lose *you*?"

The shimmer of tears in her grandmother's eyes immediately snapped Halsey from her rage. All the boiling frustration, anger, and resentment tightened into another knot. Only this time, it was hard and heavy and sank like a stone into the deepest pit of her stomach.

What the hell am I doing?

A small, strangled cry of awareness and shame escaped her, and the copper orb instantly dropped from right in front of her grandmother's face. The sphere *thunked* onto the rug before rolling slowly beneath Greta's armchair.

Halsey heard the thing topple off the edge of the rug and keep rolling across the hardwood floor until it eventually stopped, but she didn't pay it any more attention than that. The only thing she could think about now was that she'd threatened her own grandmother with who knew *what* kind of magical violence to get what she wanted.

Like an out-of-control toddler.

Like someone who'd forgotten what it meant to be an Ambrosius elemental. What it meant to be family.

Like someone who would rather use pain, fear, and violence than do the right thing.

This isn't me.

"It's all right, girl," Greta soothed, still holding her granddaughter's gaze. She was willing to ignore the copper orb in order to give the girl what she really wanted.

Brigham, on the other hand, struggled not to leap toward them both, shove them aside, and scramble to retrieve the copper orb before chucking it out the window into the river running beside the bungalow. Fortunately for all of them, he stayed put.

Halsey staggered backward, appalled by what she'd done. "I'm so sorry."

Greta slowly stood from the armchair and absently set her glass of lemonade down on the fireplace mantel. "I know."

"I don't know what I was thinking—"

"There's nothing wrong with your thinking, girl. You've been put through the wringer more times than most, and none of us have been helpful in getting you back out again."

When her grandmother stepped toward her and wrapped her in a gentle hug, Halsey wanted to melt right there in Greta's arms and maybe not get back up again. She'd taken this whole thing way too far. Further than she'd ever intended or wanted. The copper orb's magic was foreign, different, and still not completely understood, but it had acted as an extension of her emotions and what she'd really wanted in the moment.

"I didn't want this," she murmured into Greta's shoulder.

"Neither did I, kid. Trust me."

"Whatever you tell me, Meemaw, I could never hate you."

Greta breathed deeply, sighed, and gently patted her granddaughter's back. "I wouldn't jump to any conclusions until you've heard the rest of it."

That made Halsey instantly stiffen.

Feeling the change, Greta released her and stepped back, dipping her head as she studied the reaction on her granddaughter's face. "I went about this all the wrong way, Halsey. I'm sorry too. I can bitch and moan all I want about the injustices within our family, but I didn't have it in me to lay out what started it all."

"It…" Halsey blinked furiously, acutely aware there were no tears in her eyes despite feeling like she'd been crying. "It doesn't have anything to do with the missing record, does it? Not really."

"Well, it's all pretty convoluted, but no. Not really." Greta brushed down the front of her loose linen blouse and nodded toward Brigham, who still sat on the couch like he'd fallen onto it and didn't know how to get back up. "It's not a little thing, girl. If you want privacy for the rest—"

"No." Halsey stepped slowly backward across the room, then gestured toward her cousin. "Brigham and I are in this together. He can handle it."

Greta rubbed the back of her neck and finally broke their gaze. "*He's* not the one I'm worried about."

CHAPTER TEN

She's worried about me and how I'll take the news? After that stupid stunt I pulled, I guess I'd be worried about me, too.

After she walked back to the couch, Halsey didn't think she was capable of sitting back down right now. She leaned against the armrest instead and folded her arms. "Go ahead, then. Tell us what really happened."

Greta tilted her head in consideration, then almost looked like she was rolling her eyes as she slowly lowered herself into the armchair again. "Everything else I've already told you is true. It's what happened afterward that just…spiraled out of control way faster than any of us ever could've expected."

The woman gathered her thoughts before diving into what was supposed to be "the real truth."

Halsey didn't know what that was supposed to mean anymore. The truth, the telling of it, and the admission of so many secrets had twisted what she'd thought she'd known about the history of her family and her part to play in it. Now it was all a jumbled mess.

She better tell me something that makes sense. Or I might end up flying back to Ireland and accepting Cillian Havalon's invitation to stay.

"The Ambrosius Clan Council used to be one of the most powerful, intelligent, critical bodies of gathered elementals," Greta finally continued. "We used to be *united*. We were *still* united when I found Cedric's account proving those bedtime stories and hinting at so many darker things to come. I wasn't truly the only one who saw the importance of asking for a second opinion back then.

"Aidan was right there by my side."

Halsey widened her eyes. "My dad?"

"Unless you know another Aidan Ambrosius." Greta snorted, but the sound lacked her usual humor. "He backed me up in so many of those deliberation meetings we held, one after the other. This was all top-priority stuff, obviously. With Aidan standing next to you, agreeing with everything you say and adding to it in a way everyone else could connect with... Well. You know what that feels like, don't you?"

"You feel unstoppable," Halsey muttered, remembering the day her dad had stood beside her in the Ambrosius Clan Council room while she'd dumped half a dozen severed ogre hands out on the low central table as proof.

He didn't say anything, but he still had my back.

Greta nodded slowly. "He got the Council to let me head off to the Order of Skrár without a fuss. Wanted to come with me, even, but I told him to stay. To look after his wife and little girl and try not to go off hunting too many monsters for fun while I was gone. Even back then, I knew those monsters were changing. Didn't know it would take another twenty years for everyone else to see the same thing, though."

With another massive sigh, Greta shook her head and grimaced at the rug in front of her bare feet. "I should've let him come with me."

The instant foreboding in that one sentence made Halsey swallow thickly. *Something happened here, then. While she was gone. Wait, has she been taking the blame all this time for something* he *did?*

Her grandmother shrugged. "Not that either one of us could've known what would happen, or how to approach it, or exactly which words caused it all and which might have protected her. You never know. We still don't."

"Wait." Halsey's voice came out as another harsh croak. "Protected who?"

Greta slowly looked up from the floor with more sadness and regret in her eyes than either of her grandchildren had ever seen. "Your mother."

"What?" She wasn't quite sure if she'd asked the question in her mind or had actually said it out loud in little more than a breathy whisper. Her folded arms lost all their rigidity, slithering away from each other until the feeling of one of her hands thumping against the couch's armrest brought her slightly back to reality. Then she was able to form words again, though the words that came out weren't exactly the ones she'd wanted to say. "My mom doesn't have anything to do with this."

What she'd really wanted to say was, "Leave my mom out of this," the way Gillian Ambrosius had been left out of their lives for the last twenty years. For good. Still, saying *that* wouldn't have changed the fact that Greta had finally crossed the threshold into the kind of subject matter everyone had been avoiding ever since. Including Halsey.

"I know it's easier to think that way, kid," her grandmother replied gently with another grimace that was probably supposed to be a smile. "Hell, that's what we've all been trying to do for as long as you can remember, and it obviously doesn't work. Now we're peeling back the curtain, aren't we? I can tell you Gillian had everything to do with it back then. Part of me thinks she's still got everything to do with it. Might even be her ghost sitting right beside me, telling me it's time to finally let it all go..."

The woman's voice trembled as she spoke, and Halsey couldn't wrap her mind around how any of this was possible. "She married into the family. She wasn't an elemental."

It sounded ridiculous, but it was the only thing she could think of to say.

Greta nodded, her lips flickering into a weak smile as she finally let herself go back to the part of their past that truly mattered. "That didn't stop her from being one of the best damn Ambrosiuses I've ever known. Hell, one of the best *people*. Gillian was too good to your dad when he deserved it and especially when he didn't. That woman... Ha. That woman poured her heart and soul into being an Ambrosius.

"A lot like your Pappy did, honestly. Granted, she didn't pick up a weapon and charge off into the sunset on missions, but her heart was there. It was *here*. She was proud to be Aidan's wife and *your* mother, and everyone around here saw it plain as day. You couldn't *not* see it. We all... We all loved her, girl. Very much."

Hearing those words from her grandmother's mouth

brought a freshly stinging wave of hot tears to Halsey's eyes. For as long as she could remember, no one in her family had had a good, decent thing to say about Gillian Ambrosius. The woman was mentioned only in relation to Halsey, to the fear that Aidan's only child might manifest the same issues as her mother. Never that they'd *loved* her.

I can't listen to this. But I have to.

"Gillian was your dad's hearthstone before, during, and after every mission, every Council meeting, every surprise, and every boring moment." Greta's smile grew as the memories she hadn't let herself touch in so long flooded back in. "We might as well have put her *on* the Council for all the knowledge she had about our militia and how helpful she was to your dad. Of course, we didn't, for obvious non-magical reasons. I doubt anybody would've objected to the idea if it had ever been brought up, though.

"When I made my decision to take Cedric's story to the Order of Skrár for a second opinion, Aidan *supported* me in it one hundred percent. The Council wasn't quite on board, and they went off into a tizzy about it. Like I said." Greta met her granddaughter's gaze with pleading eyes, but Halsey was too shocked and confused about the fact that they were having a conversation about her *mom* to notice. "Needless to say, your dad went right to Gillian about the whole thing. And I do mean all of it.

"The record I found, what it meant for our family and all other elementals. Our very strong and almost proven theory that there were still blood humans out there in the world, alive and well and most likely biding their time. For what? We had no idea. We all knew *something* was coming, though. The way I heard it, Aidan didn't leave out a single detail. He never did with your mom. Married for five years before they had you and another three at this point. They were... Well, it sounds mushy as hell, but your parents were like one person split into two bodies. If anyone knows what that looks and feels like, I guess it'd be me."

This time when Greta paused to gather up the next round of her thoughts, her eyes shimmered with unshed tears again. The same look of not-quite-sadness Halsey had noticed earlier in this very strange, painfully illuminating conversation had returned again. This time, Halsey recognized it instantly.

That's regret. Remorse. How long has she been carrying that around?

Part of her was concerned about her grandmother and the kind of heavy wound keeping all this inside for so long would have caused. The other part of her, the stronger part, still couldn't trust what was right in front of her, even when she was looking at it with her own two eyes.

Instead of gently prompting the woman to continue, Halsey blurted, "What did you do?"

Brigham sucked in a sharp breath. She felt him once again staring at her in disbelief and shock, but she could only focus on her grandmother's bright blue eyes shimmering with tears that still hadn't spilled.

The look of absolute devastation reflected back to her from Greta's glistening bright blue eyes, however, seemed at odds with the woman's next words. "That's the thing, girl. I didn't do a damn thing. None of us did. None of us even knew anything was wrong, and we sure as hell didn't expect it to crumble apart in such a landslide the way it did.

"Gillian did what she always did. She comforted her husband. Told him to be patient. That everything would work itself out. She even—" She closed her eyes and sucked in a sharp breath. "Ancestors help me, she even told him to trust *me*. That I was head of the Council for a reason. She had faith…"

Suddenly, Greta didn't seem capable of saying anything.

In an odd reversal of what she knew about her grandmother, Halsey faced a woman who apparently couldn't find the words but had absolutely no problem feeling everything all at once. This wasn't the Meemaw she knew. *This* woman looked so old, so tired. So full of regret. She looked guilty too, but nothing she'd said so far pointed at her having been the one to make whatever unforgivable mistake Halsey expected her grandmother to reveal at any second.

"So…what?" she murmured, trying to pull the woman from her pained silence. "The Council decided to go after my mom instead? Teach Greta and Aidan Ambrosius a lesson?"

"What?" Greta's eyes flew open, and she quickly blinked the tears away while somehow managing not to let a single one of them slide out from between her lashes. "No. Have you heard a single thing I've said, or are you so dead-set on making somebody pay that none of it actually matters?"

Halsey pushed herself away from the couch's armrest, wanting to shout and storm toward her grandmother and say…what?

She's right. She doesn't like talking about my mom any more than I do, but this is…

"Sorry," she murmured, then paced behind the couch because she couldn't stand still. "I'm listening."

"Uh-huh." Greta watched her granddaughter pacing slowly behind the couch in her agitation, then raised an eyebrow at Brigham. The young man leaned slightly away from the back of the couch whenever his cousin passed him, but he didn't look at her. He stared at Greta with the same expression she'd gotten from the rest of her family over the last twenty years. Including Aidan and her four other children she'd raised to know better.

That look said only one thing. *How could you?*

She'd been asking herself that for the last twenty years, too. It had been easy to keep punishing herself for everything that had happened, even when the whole thing had been out of her hands. Even when she'd done nothing wrong, and they all knew it.

The next time Halsey spun from the end of the couch where Brigham sat still as a statue to continue in the opposite direction, she met her grandmother's gaze and raised her eyebrows.

Greta took the simple expression and all its implications in stride and dipped her head. "Maybe if we'd seen the signs, we could have figured out what went wrong and how to fix it. There might not even have *been* any signs, and who's to know anyway. Oh, you could ask thirty different people in this family about what actually happened, and you'd probably get thirty different answers. That doesn't help anyone. The only thing I *do* know is the day I left for the Order of Skrár with that damned scroll, the day Gillian told her husband to *trust his mother*, everything changed. *She* changed."

With a tight, thick swallow, Greta glanced at the ceiling again as if it would suddenly absolve her of whatever needed absolving and relieve her of this storytelling burden at the same time. Halsey's steady footsteps across the living room floor only served as a constant reminder that the telling wasn't finished. Not yet. It wouldn't be until Greta got to the part she'd hoped she'd never have to speak about again.

"That was when everything went downhill, Halsey. I was gone, and the Council was a mess trying to figure out how they felt about me taking off and what they should actually do about it. If anything. Your dad was caught up in the middle of it, trying to hold both ends of the rope for everybody all at once. You know Aidan. He'll hold onto whatever he needs to hold onto and won't let go until he knows he'd done his part, no matter what. Except the man only has two hands like everybody else. I'm sure he assumed Gillian would be right there behind him like she always had been.

"The day I came back from my little sit-down with the Order, though..." Greta shook her head. "It couldn't have been more than two weeks. By then, Halsey, your mom was already heading downhill fast."

"Downhill." Halsey stopped pacing behind the couch and whipped her head up to stare at her grandmother again. "What's that even supposed to mean?"

"Her *mind*, kiddo. Everything about her started to fall apart—"

"No." Halsey thumped the heel of her fist against the back of the couch, making Brigham jolt in his seat before she picked up her pacing again. "You don't go from being the perfect wife, mom, and...*normie* everyone loves one day to falling apart the next."

"Gillian did."

"Something happened." Furiously shaking her head, Halsey started pacing again, though it was halting and uncertain now. "It had to."

"That's what we all thought too. Trust me. I spent years trying to find the cause, the missing piece, what exactly went wrong... It all happened so fast. Something inside her snapped, Halsey. When I came back from asking the Order for help, I didn't recognize her. Your *dad* didn't recognize her. She'd completely withdrawn. Isolated. Wouldn't talk to any of us, no matter how gentle we were or how patient we tried to be. When she *did* talk, it all turned into a bunch of nonsense about monsters and magic. Not just *our* magic, either. She was rambling about blood magic—"

"That's not true," Halsey snapped. "She didn't even *have* magic."

"She had all the knowledge and resources of someone who did." Greta frowned, her eyes moving slowly back and forth as they followed her granddaughter's jerky pacing across the room. "She knew as much as any one of us. The knowledge was too much for her."

"And her mind broke." Halsey stopped again with a baffled frown. "That's what happened. *That's* why everyone's been looking at me my entire life like I'm a bomb about to go off at any second?"

"Halsey."

"No, that's bullshit. So my mom couldn't handle being deeply involved in magic and monster hunting and all the extra crap that goes into it. So what? *She was normal.* That's obviously not an issue with *me…*"

"She went too far with it," Greta insisted. "In the end, your mother was *terrified.* Who could blame her? The issue wasn't how she felt anymore but *why.* She kept going on and on about some dark force we had to be ready for. She was convinced someone was coming for her, Halsey. Coming for *you.*"

"That doesn't mean it's *my* fault!"

"No, of course not. If it's anyone's fault, it's mine."

Halsey scoffed and kept pacing. "Because you're not all-knowing. Big failure, Meemaw."

"Because I tried to convince her to stay." Greta practically shouted the words. The regret and horror behind them sent a shudder skittering down the back of Halsey's neck.

She looked up to meet the other woman's gaze anyway. "Stay where?"

"Here. Home. With her *family.* I found her trying to sneak off in the middle of the night with a tiny suitcase in one arm and *you* in the other." Her voice broke at the end, but she pushed on anyway as tears returned to her eyes. "I tried to get her to come back inside with me, but she wouldn't have it. She was so sure someone was coming for both of you, and there was no way to convince her otherwise. She couldn't *see—*"

A strangled choke erupted from Greta's throat, which was as close to crying as either of her grandchildren had seen her get. She closed her eyes and took another slow, deep breath. "I told her if she really wanted to go, she should go, but I wouldn't let her take *you.* You belonged here, with your family. With those who knew how to care for you. Gillian was so far gone at that point we had to watch both of you around the clock. You would never have made it out there in the world on your own, the two of you. Not the way she was."

"You took me away from her," Halsey muttered. "You took her *child*—"

"I thought it would get her to see where *she* belonged too. I thought it would get her to see the safest place for both of you was to stay right here. That if she had to choose between some wild delusion and her own daughter, she'd choose you. Yet when I took you in my arms and offered your mother the choice, she actually looked…"

The pitch of Greta's voice had become so high it bordered on shouting. Then she brushed away her unfinished thought and continued telling this awful story with as much calm and composure as possible. "She left. Just like that. I couldn't go after her on my own. Not with a three-year-old clinging to me and falling asleep.

"I woke your dad first. He did what he does best and rallied everyone else behind him to go after Gillian and bring her back. She didn't get very far. Only a few miles. By the time we found her…"

The living room filled with another heavy, tense silence that made Halsey's ears ring.

That's why no one else in this family actually wants to listen to what I have to say. Because I'm too much like her...

The thought was nearly unbearable, but she had to get to the end. She had to know.

"She was right, wasn't she?" she murmured.

With her eyes still closed, Greta shook her head.

"She was right about being followed. About someone coming for her."

"That's not what happened."

"You all thought she was going crazy. She wasn't an elemental, and she didn't have any magic, so she couldn't possibly have known what would happen. Is that it?"

"You're barking up the wrong tree, girl. That's *our* fault for leading you toward the wrong tree this whole time and hoping you never noticed the other one."

"Cut it out with the riddles, Greta," Halsey snarled as she stormed around the side of the couch again. "Gillian never lost her mind, did she? She knew what was happening. None of you wanted to admit you couldn't see it coming, so you ignored her. You took her *child* from her, and you sent her out there to face what she knew was coming, all on her own—"

"The only thing following Gillian Ambrosius that night was a search party, Halsey. Her family."

"You don't know that."

"The hell I don't!" Greta launched herself so quickly and furiously from her armchair that Halsey jolted and took a stumbling step back. "I was there. I saw it. That woman took her own life out there in the woods, and she would've taken yours if I hadn't stopped her. I wish to high heaven it wasn't, but that's the God's honest truth, girl. Now you know."

CHAPTER ELEVEN

Halsey's entire body trembled with shock, anger, and distrust as she stared her grandmother down.

Mom killed herself? That's...

There weren't any words. After the last twenty years of imagining her mother as some kind of Rapunzel, locked away in the tower of her own broken mind until she'd withered away, hearing something so outrageously different felt like a physical blow to the gut.

To the center of her entire being.

She had no idea what to do with it. At all.

Her knees felt like they would buckle at any second, but she somehow managed to stay on her feet.

"How..." She blinked, cleared her throat, then tried again. "Why would everybody *keep* something like that from me?"

"Because that's when our family fell apart," Greta replied matter-of-factly. She looked like she wanted to hurry toward her granddaughter and wrap her up in another hug, but they both remained perfectly still, with a good four feet between them. "You remember what happened with your dad. Traded his role as a full-time father for a full-time seat on the Council. Stopped hunting. Stopped...living.

"He was the only one who'd stuck with me through our family's little tiff about what Cedric's entry meant. Without Gillian? Well, I guess he didn't feel the need to follow his heart anymore after that. Instead, the whole damn family shut down, and every one of them tried to pretend it wasn't happening."

"Fuck..." Brigham murmured from the couch.

Hearing him say anything after he'd sat there for so long in complete silence somehow brought the next wave of tears to Halsey's eyes when they probably would have otherwise remained dry.

"They swept everything under the rug," Halsey murmured, furiously blinking as her nose burned and her vision blurred with heat.

"Pretty much." Greta gently nodded. "Kicked me off the Council and out of the estate house and sent me here. Sent us *both* here, actually. You and I, we did the best we could together for as long as it took to get *you* ready to move on."

"So everyone just...tried to pretend it didn't happen." The sheer enormity of what her family had been hiding from her nearly her entire life felt like a ton of bricks bearing down on her. Halsey had to take a few slow breaths to try calming herself down, but it wasn't nearly as effective at the moment as she'd hoped. "They kept raising a whole new generation of us on a lie. A *massive* lie. Not even... I mean, yeah, there's my mom—"

The short sob that burst from her took her by surprise.

"Hal?" Brigham gently asked as he rose from the couch.

"They *knew*." Halsey took another staggering step backward as she tried to process the full extent of the last twenty years she'd known nothing about. "This whole time. They *knew* what the silver coffin meant, that monsters would be changing, and the Blood Matriarch was probably already here because *they already knew about Cedric*."

"It's hard enough to change someone's mind when they don't know what they don't know," Greta murmured. "Even harder when someone's fully aware of everything else around them, and they still choose to act like it isn't there. They don't *want* to see it, Halsey."

"But they already *knew*!" Halsey was well aware of the fact that anything she said right now, feeling like she did, couldn't be taken back if she later changed her mind about it. And she didn't care. "This whole time. They knew about the silver coffin and the Mother of Monsters. They knew it was *possible*. I wasn't making any of it up or blowing some tiny thing way out of proportion. They made me think I'd been losing my mind!"

"You and I both know that's not the case."

"And *Brigham*!" Halsey swung an open arm toward her cousin, who still sat on the couch in frozen shock. His eyes widened when she spoke his name, but he didn't move.

"Well, yeah," Greta conceded. "Of course he knows—"

"They kept sending him out on missions *knowing* any of those monsters could've been the seriously screwed-up kind. *Without* me. They sent him and Cadence after those ogres without so much as a warning, and the whole time, they could've been training us how to better face something like that. They almost got him killed!"

Brigham's expression fell like he was immensely disappointed with the conversation going from secrets of the past to partially reliving his near-death experience between a tree trunk and a blood-cursed ogre's fist.

"Hindsight's always twenty-twenty, kid," Greta replied gently, trying not to get her granddaughter riled up any more than she already was. Now that the truth was out, she also wasn't willing to throw the Council under the bus. "We can't blame them entirely for that little mishap."

"Mishap?" A bitter laugh escaped Halsey as she spun in a tight circle and nearly picked up her pacing again. "He came home from that mission on a *stretcher*. The only reason the Council sent my dad and me back out there to finish the job was that they wanted to make sure nobody else got seriously hurt because of them."

"Because they knew you could handle it, Halsey. Plain and simple."

"Why the fuck are you *defending* them?"

For a moment, it seemed like her grandmother wouldn't be able to come up with a reply to that. Then Greta sighed and spread her arms. "We may have magic, girl, but we're all still human. We all make mistakes."

"Yeah, and *your* biggest mistake was not telling me all this the *first* time I came to you for help." Halsey spun tightly around again and, this time, didn't in any way intend to face her grandmother again. "Or at any other point in the last twenty years, but I guess that never occurred to you."

"Halsey, certain things had to—"

"I don't wanna hear it." She stormed across the living room toward the bungalow's front door.

"The first time you asked, none of us knew anywhere near as much as we know now, girl!" Greta called after her, stretching her neck as far as she could without actually going after her granddaughter. "Hell, I try my damnedest, but I can't always see when it's the right time for everything." When the only reply Halsey offered was an abrupt slamming of the bungalow's front door, Greta cupped a hand around her mouth and shouted at the window closest to the front porch. "Fine! At least take this creepy-as-shit magical ball with you and out of my house, 'cause I ain't babysitting the damn thing—"

A violent thump rose from the armchair, and the woman jumped. First in surprise, then to get out of the way as the copper orb lurched out from beneath the chair. Then it zipped dangerously across the room, humming and glowing in readiness, and might have taken Brigham's head off if he hadn't ducked into the couch at the perfect moment.

Then the living room filled with the crack and echoing tinkle of shattered glass a split second after Halsey's orb of foreign magic smashed the window her grandmother had tried to shout at her through.

Then everything was silent again.

Too silent for Greta's liking, she smacked her lips as she stared at the broken windowpane in her living room. "You know, I never liked that window anyway."

Brigham huffed a humorless puff of air and turned on

the couch to eye the damage. Glass all over the floor, window curtains fluttering in the breeze that should have been insanely warm for mid-August in Texas but actually didn't feel like anything. "At least your magical AC didn't break down with it."

"I should go after her."

He spun on the couch again and almost toppled off it. "That's probably not a—"

"I need to tell her I'm sorry. For real." With a determined nod, Greta started across the living room toward the front of the bungalow. "She needs to know none of this was her fault."

"Trust me. She knows *now*." Brigham almost turned to look over his shoulder at the mess of glass all over the floor, but seeing his grandmother walking across the room from the corner of his eye brought him back to the present. "Seriously, though, Meemaw. You should stay here."

"Why? You think she's gonna try to hurt me again? Blast me to smithereens? Drown me in the river?" She released a hooting laugh that didn't sound amused. "I'm the one who *raised* her, boy."

He leapt off the couch in a mad-dash scramble to stop his grandmother from leaving before it was too late. "*I'm* her partner. You gotta believe me when I say you don't wanna—"

A coarse scream rose from outside, muffled by the bungalow's closed front door and insulated walls and only slightly louder than it would have been because of the broken window. Despite the scream sounding like it went on forever, the sound only made Greta slow down on her way to the door. Then she doubled her efforts to get out before a new sound joined the furious scream.

Splintering trees.

One after another, she counted at least five deafening pops outside as the willows and dogwoods lining the river outside snapped in quick succession, followed by the roar of stones and rocky chunks of earth being ripped from the ground. After that came a shower of pebbles spraying against the side of the house, massive splashes in the riverbed before the sound of waves crashing violently against a rocky cliff face even though no rocky cliff faces were in sight.

A tremor buckled the earth beneath the bungalow's foundations, making the entire house shudder and a few of the floorboards crack against each other before everything settled back into place.

When the chaos outside settled, Greta stood two feet from the front door with her hand outstretched toward the doorknob. With a sharp breath, she lowered her hand and turned to face her grandson. "On second thought, maybe she could use more time to process."

"Yeah." He nodded at her with wide eyes. "Good idea."

"Thank you." She shot him an obviously fake grin as she sauntered back across the bungalow toward the kitchen this time. Then she stopped again. "How long does she usually need after…something like this?"

Brigham almost choked on his surprise and managed to turn it into something resembling a laugh. Once he realized laughing made no sense right now, he stopped abruptly and sighed. "Hal's usual *anything* doesn't apply right now, Meemaw."

"Why not?"

"'Cause there's never *been* something like this." He glanced quickly between his grandmother, frozen halfway into the kitchen, and the front door. It was suspiciously quiet outside again. With Hal, that usually meant more was coming. "She needs time, okay? Don't ask how much, 'cause I don't know. When she's ready to…get back to it, I guess, she'll let us—"

The sound of the ATV's revving engine outside wasn't particularly loud or startling, but after the recent silence, it was easy to notice. Brigham knew what it meant.

"*And* that's Hal letting me know." He hurried across the house toward the front door and paused to give Greta a quick peck on the cheek. Then he remembered what had gone down in the woman's living room, and he quickly added, "She'll come around. Probably. I hope."

Greta shot him a humorless smirk. "No promises, though, huh?"

"Not ones I can keep." He wanted to stay longer so he could come up with something else that didn't sound so ridiculously hopeless, but the ATV's engine made an altogether different sound. If he didn't hurry up, he'd miss his ride.

Like he'd almost missed his ride on the way out to Greta's bungalow earlier today.

Brigham darted toward the front door, jerked it open, and hopped from the top porch step to the gravel in front of the house in one scrambling leap. "Hal. Don't even think about—hey!"

Halsey had already kicked the vehicle into gear and

lurched away from the house with a spray of gravel. Before her cousin could get too upset about it, though, she pulled an incredibly tight U-turn for such a clunky vehicle and skidded to a stop right in front of him, this time with the ATV pointing in the direction of the estate house.

She didn't say anything, and she didn't look at her cousin, but she didn't need to. Brigham knew the drill at this point and was happy enough to climb aboard behind her, this time without having to chase her down first in order to do so.

As soon as he was on, Halsey sped away over the rolling hills making up their family property. Brigham tried to ignore the stand of trees missing several branches and large chunks of their bark right beside the river, which seemed to have been halfway drained onto Greta's side yard, newly landscaped with uprooted boulders in addition to being halfway drowned.

Inside the bungalow, Greta listened to the ATV's engine grow fainter and farther away. When she finally couldn't hear it anymore, she walked casually back into her living room, where she collected all three glasses of lemonade, the pitcher, and the serving tray to take back with her into the kitchen.

Without saying a word, she refilled her glass yet again, then reached into the smallest, narrowest bottom cabinet on the floor beside the fridge. In addition to the clinking of fresh ice cubes in her lemonade glass, the kitchen was also filled with the sound of several ounces of bourbon trickling down on top of it all.

Greta Ambrosius wasn't all that certain if anyone else in

the family at this point would have cared one way or the other about her newly formed drinking habit. She did know if Percival McAllister, her late husband and the love of her life, had been here, he would have approved.

And he would have joined her.

CHAPTER TWELVE

Halsey and Brigham didn't say another word to each other as she drove them back to the estate house like a crazy person.

Maybe that's taking it overboard a little, Brigham thought when he noticed the way he'd been thinking about his best friend and her eccentric habits for pretty much their entire lives. *Hal's not crazy. Meemaw's not crazy. Still, this whole thing is one giant shitshow, isn't it?*

The ATV came to such a sudden stop behind the estate house that the front of his head almost cracked right into the back of hers. Whether or not Halsey noticed, she didn't show any sign of it. Instead, she angrily jerked on the keys to cut the engine, then hopped off the vehicle and stormed right up to one of the rear access doors.

"Okay, hold on…" After clumsily tugging several times on the leg of his jeans to get it unstuck from whatever had caught it, Brigham freed himself with a loud rip, then tore after his cousin next. "Hal! Can you *wait* a minute?"

"I've already wasted so much time on bullshit,

Brigham," she practically growled as she jerked open the door. "I'm not interested in wasting any more."

"Well, can't you at least... Oh, come on." With a grunt of frustration, he caught the door before it swung shut again. Then he slipped inside and felt like an idiot looking both ways down the hall like a kid before crossing the street.

Halsey's steady gait down the hallway stretching to his left was hard to miss, her sneakers clomping down the worn carpeting of the halls mostly used only by the estate house staff and her fists clenched tightly at her sides.

"Just for a second." Brigham raced after her and easily caught up, though he would've preferred not to feel like he was in a speed-walking race while simultaneously trying to have an important heart-to-heart with his cousin. "'Cause *I'm* not a waste of your time. Right?"

That knocked her from her one-track mind for the briefest moment. She blinked, slowed a bit, then turned to scrutinize her best friend. "No. You're not."

"Well...thanks." He only realized she'd picked up the pace again once she'd gotten six feet in front of him down the hall. "I honestly didn't expect that answer, but I appreciate it. So can you tell me where we're going now?"

"We're late for our debriefing from the Turkey mission." She didn't look at him again, and her voice was so flat and toneless it almost sounded robotic.

Brigham knew better, though.

Halsey had stormed into their grandmother's bungalow earlier today, shouting and pacing and making semi-threats with a weird glowing orb she'd made from someone else's magic, sure. Yet that had been out of fear.

Fear of what might actually be uncovered now that

she'd reached the end of her patience for accepting Greta's doled-out factoids one little bit at a time. Fear of what it would mean for her and her cousin and any of their future missions after the deadly horror their last one had become. Maybe even a fear that Halsey was the one who'd done something wrong, that she'd somehow missed an obvious sign for some integral piece of information.

Now, though, she stalked through the back halls of the estate house with a different but not dissimilar emotion swelling through her. Halsey wasn't afraid anymore.

She was livid.

Brigham knew this by the way she walked, the blank look on her face, and the fact that she seemed to have checked out.

In some small, hidden part of herself, Halsey knew this too. The rest of her was operating on furious autopilot until she figured out a better way to deal with what she'd discovered today. What they'd both discovered.

He couldn't let her keep going like this without at least trying to get through to her.

"Okay, well, first of all, I totally support checking in for official militia business, even late. Still, don't you think we should slow down for a second and maybe talk about all—"

"Nope."

There it was again. That flatness in her voice, like they hadn't gone through the last few hours of mind-numbing revelations with their grandmother.

Mind-numbing for her, *dude. You're only the guy who got caught up in this mess. Not that I'd ever change anything about my mission partner or anything we've been through together, but you gotta remember this isn't about* you. *It's all Hal.*

Brigham had to push himself again to catch up with her even though she'd been traipsing along at normal human speeds the whole time. It was difficult for him to think and move simultaneously. As far as he knew, Halsey never had that problem.

"Hal, come on," he tried again as he settled beside her. "You got some serious bombs dropped on you back there. Don't you think it's, like, a *little* important to try to work through at least some of it before you go—"

"I'm fine, Brigham." She turned the next corner down yet another hallway that would eventually lead them to the even wider corridor serving as the first line of defense for the Ambrosius Clan Council room.

"You're pissed," he muttered.

"You're right. At least now I know everything I need to know. Doesn't mean I like it, but the monster's finally out of the bag. The big, hairy, slobbering fucking monster that's been getting a free ride on my back for my whole life. Now I see it."

They turned another corner and immediately came to the wide hallway leading up to the enormous Council room doors. She paused for a moment on the side of the hall as if she wasn't sure she could cross it without bursting into flame or melting into a quivering puddle. After glancing furtively at the intricately carved doors to the Council room at the end of the hall, Halsey drew a deep breath, walked across the hallway, and didn't look back. "Eventually, I'll drop that fucker, keep walking, and move on."

"Eventually, yeah." Brigham shot a furtive glance at the double doors, but it was more to make sure there was nothing there they needed to see instead of through some unspoken disdain for the room on the other side. Knowing his cousin as well as he did, that was likely the only reason she'd bothered to look.

Then his mission partner was already on the other side of the hallway, and he jumped after her to catch up, silently berating himself for falling behind again. "Hey, I get it, cuz. I mean, I don't *get*-get it. This is *your* story, you know? I don't have anything to do with it other than—"

He abruptly stopped because Halsey had done the same. Now she turned to look at him for the first time since she'd stormed from Greta's bungalow to let off a little steam *outside* instead of *inside*. "Don't say that."

"What? That this is your story?"

"That you don't have anything to do with it."

There might have been a shimmer in her eye hinting at some other emotion beyond cold, flat rage, but he couldn't be sure.

"You're the only person who's never lied to me, Brigham."

Not quite sure how to handle her unexpected responses, he huffed out a laugh and shrugged. "That's just being a decent person."

Halsey's eyebrows flickered toward each other, and she fixed him with a pseudo-grimace before wiping it off her face. "Yeah, well, it looks like you're the only decent person I know. I…can't thank you enough for that."

"Uh…you're welcome?" He glanced down the hall in the direction they were headed. Directly for the debriefing room where Cavanaugh was, of course, waiting for them to arrive. "Look. Forget about the mission, the debriefing, and the reports, okay? I only wanna make sure you're okay. Like, for real."

"Excluding the fact that I've been lied to my whole life and everything I've been driving myself insane over for the last two months was totally unnecessary, yeah. Sure. I'm okay for real."

"Hey." His hand wrapped around her wrist even before he realized what he was doing, but he pulled her back toward him anyway, so they had time to finish this talk before Cavanaugh expected their complete focus for his damn reports. "You don't have to do that. Not with me."

Halsey stared at his hand around her wrist, but then she let it go before he even had a chance to release her. "I know. I'm sorry, and thank you, and I'll be okay. Eventually. Right now, I'd like to get through this stupid meeting so I can stop thinking about anything for the next few days, at least. Fair?"

"Totally." Brigham released his cousin's wrist to clap his hand down on her shoulder instead and nodded. "Totally fair. I got your back. If you want me to handle most of the talking for this one, I'm down."

"Thanks." She turned away and walked out from under his hand to head for the debriefing room like this conversation had never happened.

For a moment, the only thing her cousin could do was stand there and watch her walk off with a heavy knot tightening in the pit of his stomach.

Sure. She'll be okay eventually. *No way in hell is that gonna be today.*

CHAPTER THIRTEEN

Their second cousin Cavanaugh, Blanche's son who looked old enough to be her brother instead, scowled at the team of young elementals when they finally stepped into his office.

"Just felt like screwing around today, huh?" he intoned, folding his arms as Halsey went for a chair at the table, and Brigham silently paused to pull the door shut behind them. "I thought your flight got in this morning."

"It did." Brigham shot his cousin a sidelong glance, but Halsey only stared across the room at a spot somewhere behind Cavanaugh's head. Slowly, he headed toward the chair beside her and chose his words as carefully as possible. "We just…hit a few bumps in the road on the way here."

"So I need to give *Connor* a reassessment. Is that it?"

"No, Connor's great," Brigham replied quickly. "No issues there."

"A *personal* reassessment might go a hell of a long way,

though," Halsey replied flatly without meeting Cavanaugh's gaze.

The man's frown deepened, but trying to stare someone down who wouldn't so much as look at him was a useless endeavor, so he soon gave up.

Trying hard not to grimace, Brigham shot their blood-relation debriefing commander a quick nod. "Personal road bumps, Cavanaugh. That's it."

"So you had to take a whole three hours out of everybody's day for a little personal time." Their cousin scoffed and shook his head. "Sounds like somebody left their brains behind."

Halsey cut him a sharp glance. "If you'd been on this Turkey mission, or *any* mission, instead of planting your ass behind a table and insulting the actual monster hunters all day, you'd leave your brain somewhere too."

Cavanaugh raised his eyebrows in mute shock, and when he looked at Brigham for some kind of explanation regarding his mission partner's terrible mood, Brigham could only press his lips together and look at Halsey.

"Or *maybe* once we get to the actual debriefing," she continued stoically, "you'll give us a fucking break."

"Hal," Brigham whispered. "Do we need, like, another five minutes or—"

"Nah, that sounds like a fun challenge." Cavanaugh nodded curtly, but the tight smile on his lips made him look like a wild predator mere seconds from devouring its prey. "So let's get started."

Debriefings were Brigham's thing anyway, so he had no problem diving in to relay their account of what had happened with the chimera in Turkey. He might have dived in faster and more enthusiastically than usual, but he didn't want to give his cousin an opportunity to say anything else that could get them in even deeper shit than they already were. So far, they'd managed to stay on the Council's good side, relatively speaking. At least after Halsey was preemptively relieved of her thirty-day suspension to go after the corpse-eating ogres.

After he began, it was easy enough to drop back into storytelling mode like he did every time they returned from a mission.

As usual, Brigham hit all the important mission points. Meeting with Burakgazi at the Grand Bazaar, their brief stint in a palatial hotel suite while they formulated their plan, and exactly what the plan entailed. Things got bumpier when he started talking about their actual trip out to Burakgazi's enormous property with tons of commercial steel beams at their disposal.

The only time Cavanaugh looked surprised was when Brigham relayed the information he and Halsey had received from their mission "client" during that first meeting in the secret tent set up behind the cushion vendor. "The chimera was immune to *all* those methods?"

"Every single one." Brigham nodded and paused in case Halsey wanted to add anything. Then he had to keep going on his own because she was obviously intent on sitting through the entire debriefing with nothing to add. "We didn't believe it either, at first. When we made it to the target location and actually found the thing... Well, I guess we could say all the impossible stuff Burakgazi told us didn't seem impossible anymore."

"Such as?"

"It grew wings," Halsey interjected, though her voice was still flat and emotionless as she glared at their second cousin. "Apparently overnight."

"That's..." Cavanaugh cocked his head in confusion, then looked down at the paperwork he'd laid out in front of him next to his smartphone set to record the audio of this entire conversation. After clearing his throat and eyeing his phone briefly, he looked back up at the monster-hunter team sitting across the table from him. "Sounds like you had some kind of miscommunication when you sat down with the client—"

"Nope." Halsey blinked at him. "Burakgazi had no idea about the wings before he sent us in like a couple of canaries in a mine. Yet the chimera sure as shit was flying around like a pro when we got there."

Brigham tried to subtly nudge his shoe against his cousin's ankle under the table because she still hadn't given up on pushing the envelope during this little meeting.

She felt his attempt to get her to straighten out, but Halsey was done playing the Council's game. At this point, her personal issues had grown beyond the Council. She was done with the Ambrosius Clan militia. She was done with their entire family.

Yet she was still a monster hunter. This was still her job, and she still had a responsibility to do what she did best in the interest of keeping everyone safe and preparing for the worst.

That didn't mean she had to be a good little operative sitting down for a polite, formal, efficiently succinct debriefing.

Then she went in the complete opposite direction

Brigham had intended by trying to bring her attention to the way she was handling herself.

Halsey leaned slightly forward in her chair and pointed at Cavanaugh's phone. "You might wanna pay special attention to that part, so I'll say it again. Over the course of the three to seven days between the client's last sighting and the day Brigham and I walked onsite, the *chimera* grew fucking *wings*." Then she slumped back in her chair and fixed Cavanaugh with a tight smile. "It's a good story, right? You know, for posterity's sake."

Brigham actually kicked her leg under the table this time, and she kicked him right back without ever taking her eyes off the ranking Ambrosius militia commander while it was only the three of them in this room.

Cavanaugh had been handling mission briefings and debriefings for nearly every team of Ambrosius Clan militia operatives for the last eleven years. Only recently, during a new and unexpected upsurge in small-monster missions, had he commandeered another senior family member as his backup to handle the overflow. Either he had specifically wanted to save the Turkey debriefing for himself, or there weren't many other teams of hunters coming in from their own missions at the moment.

Halsey had a feeling it was the former, but she wasn't about to ask.

For the first time in the team's five years of hunting, Cavanaugh actually showed some form of emotion during a debriefing. Today, that emotion happened to be a tense, heavy, and entirely uncertain concern.

It was his job to move these conversations forward in the necessary direction so he could gain all the necessary information for his report. Which meant the next thing out of his mouth would have been ridiculous in any other situation but was perfectly suited for this one. "Obviously, the chimera wasn't entirely invincible. What did you do that the client hadn't already thought to try?"

"We thought steel alchemized into a massive spear would do the trick," Brigham replied.

Cavanaugh fixed them with a humorless smirk. "Trying to duplicate legendary victories, huh?"

"That was the idea. We figured the first spear would work, but—"

"We'd miscalculated the chimera's weaknesses," Halsey cut in flatly. "Had to go in for a second round with the thing before we finally figured out how to take it down."

Cavanaugh looked between them before feeling the need to prompt further. "Which was?"

"Well." Brigham looked dumbstruck for a moment, clearly unsure how to broach the subject of Halsey's deadly golden ball made from someone else's leftover magic. Swallowing thickly, he turned to look at his cousin and feebly tried again. "We, uh…"

"Strategic placement of alchemized metal with an emphasis on the most likely points for an intersection of three different beasts' bodies," Halsey fluidly continued as if she'd been practicing this explanation the entire time. "That's pretty much what it came down to."

"Three different…" Cavanaugh stared at her, blinked once, then looked at Brigham again for clarification. "I don't even know what that means."

"It means we started with a chimera and ended with a lion, a goat, and a snake," Halsey snapped. "All of them dead. Plus a pair of wings, but those were obviously an add-on."

"I see." It didn't look like their second cousin was seeing anything clearly at the moment. Yet he was smart enough, and maybe not interested enough, to pry any further. "Meaning you did successfully neutralize your target and complete this mission."

"Really?" Halsey gestured toward Brigham with a flippant wave of her hand. "Have you *ever* seen us come back for an *unsuccessful* debrief? Other than the time the Council sent Brigham and Cadence out to take on a whole damn pack of ogres without giving them the right intel first, of course. I guess everyone's entitled to a free pass once in a while, right?"

"Yeah," Brigham added with a slow nod, trying to keep his cool. "We completed our mission."

"Also, you obviously don't have access to the militia bank accounts," she added glibly. "Otherwise, you'd already know we did what Burakgazi wanted."

Apparently, there was nothing to say to that grim-sounding remark. For all his experience in picking apart and reassembling a play-by-play of each mission for his reports handed directly to the Council after each debriefing, Cavanaugh clearly didn't want to spend any more time here with these particular two hunters than absolutely necessary. He did ask them a few more questions about the details of their mission. The exact location of Burakgazi's private property, any other contacts they might have made while in Turkey, and if either of the cousins had sustained any injuries while abroad that might have to be documented and treated.

For the most part, however, he kept the questions brief. Halsey and Brigham kept their answers even briefer. Neither of the young elementals said a word about the *real* reason they'd been able to kill the chimera or Burakgazi handing them the contact information for Halil Aydem of the Order of Skrár. They skipped the part about the Ambrosius Clan militia's newest and hopefully first client having effectively captured and maintained a mutant chimera and her *egg* until the beast had gotten smart and wanted out.

That didn't have anything to do with their actual mission, and though they hadn't exactly discussed it between then and now, Halsey and her cousin had come to an unspoken understanding that some things weren't ready to be revealed to the Council. Plus, a conversation about contracted missions, random normie civilians capturing monsters on purpose, and glowing golden balls that literally broke monsters apart with a member of the Ambrosius Clan who wasn't involved in active field missions or Council business would have been even more of a waste of time.

Cavanaugh clearly couldn't handle that kind of mind-blowing information, anyway. He'd been assigned the organization and overseeing of all mission briefs and debriefs.

When he'd run out of questions, their second cousin didn't look satisfied with the answers or the information he'd received. Yet his job was finished. He turned off the recording on his phone and signed off at the bottom of whatever paper he'd currently been filling out. Then he regarded Halsey and Brigham with a pinched expression as if he'd bitten into a hunk of prematurely moldy cheese. "All right. That's…everything I need."

"And then some, I bet," Halsey muttered under her breath.

Brigham dipped his head to stare at her sidelong, but Cavanaugh was clearly more concerned about getting these two the hell out of the debriefing room so he could be alone with his reports.

So he ignored her blatantly useless comments and shuffled his papers around to look more official. "We're done here. I'll let you know if—"

Halsey slammed her hands on the table and lurched to her feet, kicking the chair noisily out behind her in the process.

Brigham sighed and stood in a much more respectful way, though he still wanted to move as quickly as possible to make sure she didn't get away from him before they could have a nice little chat of their own about what the hell she'd been thinking. "See ya later, Cavanaugh."

The sound of Halsey throwing the door open with a bang and storming into the hall made it perfectly clear any other conversation would be a bad idea—or too little, too late.

"Uh-huh." Cavanaugh nodded toward the open door, then looked back down at his paperwork and muttered, "Good luck."

"Yup."

Brigham spun and raced after his cousin.

CHAPTER FOURTEEN

The moment he stepped out of the briefing room, what he really wanted to do was shout at her to quit being such a pain in the ass. Maybe even pull a lighter from his pocket and toss a fireball her way to get her attention. Let her know he wasn't screwing around nearly as much as she was all of a sudden.

Instead, he half-walked, half-jogged down the hall and waited until they were far enough away that hopefully, nobody could hear them. "Hal!"

"There's nothing else on our plate now, Brigham," she called without slowing down or even casting him a glance over her shoulder. "I'm going home."

"Yeah, great. You can do whatever you want after we…" With a growl, he watched his cousin turning the corner down yet another hall among the maze that made up the rear of the enormous estate house. He pushed himself to move faster, to catch up with her, and he almost ran into her from behind as he turned the corner. "Wha… Shit!"

Halsey spun to face him and spread her arms. "What, dude?"

He looked behind him around the corner, then searched their current corridor. So far, he and his cousin still seemed alone. He cleared his throat, brushed past Halsey, and tugged on her arm to get her walking with him again. "Listen, Hal. I know you're pissed—"

A bitter laugh escaped her. "That's like saying a dying animal is 'momentarily out of energy.'"

Brigham wrinkled his nose, blinked as he tried to put that one together, then shook his head. "Fine. You're furious."

"I don't need you to tell me how I feel, Brigham. I'm the one feeling it."

They turned another corner, but this time, Brigham knew which route his cousin was taking toward one of the estate house's rear entrances, so he was able to anticipate the rest of the way without having to backtrack or catch up with her. Yet he couldn't shake the feeling he'd have to work harder to anticipate what his cousin would do next. Because now she seemed…unpredictable.

"I get that, okay? Look. I'm not trying to get all up in your face about any of this, but you're not exactly—"

"I'm not exactly what? Huh?" Halsey stopped abruptly in the center of the corridor, once again forcing her cousin to quickly become aware of her disappearing from his side before he slowly turned to face her. "You're not sure I can handle this? You don't think I should keep going? Maybe taking, oh, I don't know…a thirty-day leave would help me calm down and screw my head back on straight before continuing with my *life*? Is that it?"

"I mean..."

"Listen, I'm not gonna tell you I'm fine. 'Cause I'm not." She folded her arms and gazed down the hallway, not quite able to center her gaze on her cousin's face but not willing to act like she couldn't see him. "Sure, maybe I need time to process things, but I wasn't gonna charge off into the sunset for some *me-time* without at least taking care of my responsibilities. Like a debrief. All right? So if you're freaking out about me going off the deep end 'cause I'm starting to act like whoever the hell—"

"You're acting like the pissed-off, hotheaded version of yourself that doesn't always see the full picture of what's happening," Brigham snapped. "So I'm gonna say what I've been trying to say, and you're gonna shut up and listen."

Now that he'd reached the end of his patience with her, his tone caught a lot more of his cousin's attention than it had a few seconds before. Halsey's gaze cut toward him, but she didn't try to say anything else.

Brigham had her full attention now, and not necessarily in the way he preferred. He cleared his throat and looked up and down the still-empty hallway. "The first thing I *was* gonna ask is, what were you thinking in there?"

She stared back at him with a perfectly blank expression. "What?"

"Come on, Hal. I get the attitude. Throw in a few little barbs for the Council to get all butt-hurt about later when Cavanaugh sends over his report. Fine. But *lying* about our mission?"

"I didn't lie about anything."

"You basically told him we killed the chimera by hitting it with a spear *at strategic juncture points.*" Brigham clicked his tongue and spread his arms. "You think that's a good idea right now? Especially after everything we heard from Meemaw?"

For a moment, it seemed like he might have gotten through to her. Or at least Halsey looked like she was contemplating his question, though her eyes still held the glazed, far-off emptiness he'd only ever seen when she was about to fire or throw a weapon at target practice. Which meant she was probably more focused on coming up with some other kind of off-the-cuff strategy for something Brigham wasn't sure he wanted to be a part of yet.

Then her hazel eyes flickered back toward her cousin's face, and she snorted. "Obviously, I thought it was a good idea. 'Cause that's what I did."

"Hal." He stood exactly where he'd stopped and slowly turned to stare after her as she brushed past him with a renewed dedication to get the hell out of the estate house. She didn't stop, so he sighed heavily and eventually gave in to catching up with her again. "Will you listen to what I'm actually saying and take this seriously? I'm not questioning *you—*"

"Sure sounds like it."

"No, I'm questioning your choices. Like storming into a debriefing without giving your mission partner anything remotely resembling a heads-up or a wink or *some* kind of sign to let me know about your plan going into it."

"We handled it."

"With enough subtlety to kill a horse. Hey." Brigham grabbed her wrist to stop her before she could reach the door at the end of the hall that led out into the late-afternoon heat, where it would be a lot easier for her to get away from him.

Halsey hissed in irritation at being held back. She jerked her wrist from his grasp but still turned the way he'd wanted her to. "You're worried about *subtlety*? Brigham, what's the point?"

"The point is, Cavanaugh knows *something's* wrong. The Council's gonna know it, too. You won't actually talk to me, so I have no idea if stirring up a whole lot more suspicion and making the Council more nervous was actually your plan or if you've decided blatantly lying in our debrief is one of those militia rules you don't care about anymore."

"You know what?" Halsey laughed as she turned toward the door again. "The Council's been lying to us our whole lives. Was it part of some elaborate plan I cooked up on the ATV ride over here? No. Do I give a shit at this point? Also no. You shouldn't, either."

Her hand slammed against the metal release bar, and the door swung open into bright sunlight and yet another wave of cloying August heat blasting against their faces as they stepped outside.

Brigham forced himself to keep up with her because he wasn't quite sure they'd had much of a productive conversation, and he also wasn't sure he'd be able to find her again today if she sped off on her own. He wasn't trying to hop onto the back of a moving ATV again, either.

He called after her. "Well, now that I know you're throwing caution to the wind with all this, can we at least make sure we're on the same page about everything? *Before* we have to show a united front to…whoever we're blatantly lying to in the future?"

"Sure. I'll call a meeting next time I'm about to say a word to anyone who isn't you."

"Dude." He stopped a few yards away from the ATV, which Halsey once more intended to ride off across the immense Ambrosius Clan property because it was too hot to walk all the way out to her little cottage in the woods. "You're obviously having a hard time seeing it right now, but I'm on your side, Hal. Always. I'm not trying to start a fight or anything, but, like…"

"Like what?" Halsey swung a leg over the ATV's seat, then grabbed the keys she'd left in the ignition and paused to watch her cousin with as much sarcasm as raised eyebrows and complete silence could get across.

Brigham sighed and spread his arms before hopelessly dropping them back to his sides. "I'm trying to make sure you're okay. I know you're not *okay* right now, and I know there's not a whole lot I can do. I just… I don't know. Maybe you want somebody with you right now? Feels like forever since beer and pizza, and I'm totally down to cover all of it."

"Ha. Right. With the insanely massive independent contractor check we *didn't* get from the Council." When her cousin didn't laugh, snort, or so much as crack the tiniest smile through his concerned stare, she finally dropped the pissed-off-killing-machine routine to have a real conversation with him again. Or at least to finish this one. "Look, I know I'm being kind of an asshole right now."

"Totally justified, if you ask me." He shrugged. "I know *I* didn't do anything."

"No, you didn't. But I'm sorry anyway." She started to release the keys in the ignition, then paused and slightly tightened her grip on them instead. "Right now... I'm pretty sure *I'm* gonna end up starting fights with literally anyone and everyone. Which isn't what I'm trying to do, either. I think it's better for everyone if I'm alone. For now. Maybe a day or two. You know?"

"For sure." Biting on his bottom lip, Brigham nodded slowly and looked the ATV over from front bumper to rear. "If you change your mind..."

"I'll tell you." It wasn't worth it to try smiling right now. Halsey already knew it would turn out to be a complete disaster anyway, and at this point, she was beyond trying to pretend she felt or thought one way when it was the complete opposite.

More than that, she was done trying to do everything she could to make sure the Ambrosius Clan, her *family*, would finally accept her for who she was. Not because she'd so far managed to avoid becoming like her mom.

A twinge of remorse, disgust, and fear flared up in her gut, and she sighed.

Gillian took her own life. Which would've been great to know sometime before I was a grown adult going against her family and trying to figure out how to save the whole fucking world from the Mother of Monsters, but hey. At least I know taking the easy way out isn't an option for me. Not like it was for her...

After that, she didn't have anything else to say. She *really* needed to get back to her house, her things, and her space. To figure out how to work through this before she actually exploded and either said or did something she'd immediately regret.

Brigham seemed to pick up on exactly what was going on, as he usually did no matter what they were going through, and folded his arms while Halsey wordlessly started the ATV's engine.

She couldn't bring herself to look at him again before taking off across the rolling hills and open meadows of the property immediately behind the estate house. She found it a lot easier to glance at the warped, cloudy glass of the rearview mirror to see him still standing there, exactly as she'd left him. Watching her until neither one of them could see the other anymore.

Once the next stand of trees had wiped Brigham from view, she let herself go with the gas and raced even faster across the open land toward her cottage.

At least they'd gotten on the same page *before* she'd taken off, or as much on the same page as was possible for the current circumstances. Yes, Halsey still had a few major confessions to make to her best friend and mission partner, and in retrospect, she was actually glad she hadn't opened those particular cans of worms right there in Greta's living room before Halsey's whole world was systematically turned upside-down by the kind of revelations she couldn't in a million years have anticipated. The things she had yet to share with Brigham were between her and Brigham, though.

Like the knowledge of the copper orb hidden back in the pocket of her light canvas jacket and how it had gotten there in the first place. The fact that they'd tried to reach out to the Order of Skrár together. Or that they'd spent three hours with their grandmother today hashing out the details of the past that the family didn't want them to know. Neither one of them would take any of that information outside their long-standing partnership until they'd agreed it was the right time.

Halsey knew Brigham had her back. He'd had it when they were kids running around along the river beside Greta's bungalow and when they'd first discovered the full extent of their magic while going through their militia training together. He'd had her back since the moment they both stepped foot off the Ambrosius Clan estate property for their very first monster hunt together.

She knew he'd be waiting for her to reach out when she felt like coming out of her cottage, talking, or being around other people again.

Right now, the only thing she wanted was to be totally alone. Nothing else to think, worry, or care about but herself and however she wanted to spend her time at any given moment.

Halsey and Brigham were a team, had always been a team, and would always be a team. Yet now, more than ever, she realized some things in life simply couldn't be shared.

CHAPTER FIFTEEN

In the last two months, Halsey had spent more time shut up in her little cottage in the woods than she had in the last year, starting with her mandatory thirty-day leave that had been cut a whole week short by the Council's inability to effectively deal with changing monsters and the *real* threat they posed to the entire clan. Funnily enough, this was the first time she truly appreciated the time alone. Though it was still a far cry from the vacation she'd been saying she needed back in June when all this craziness started.

However, it was plenty of time alone without being assigned new missions left and right or any impending meetings looming over her head. She could sit, think, and be with herself.

More importantly, it gave her the extra time she'd wanted to go through all the clues. To keep piecing together the greater story and the greater threat the Ambrosius cousins had been drawn into.

She was more convinced than ever they were on the right track.

The only difference was that Brigham completely believed both her and their grandmother after more or less seeing the evidence for himself. No, since Halil Aydem's refusal to meet with them in Turkey, it seemed impossible they'd get any second chances with the Order of Skrár. Which made taking a look at their ancestor's handwritten story of finding the ship that had borne the first monsters on Earth since before the Ice Age equally impossible.

Halsey didn't need to look at the record to know in her bones they'd figured it out, though.

Almost two thousand years ago, someone aboard a Viking longship had summoned the Mother of Monsters from the bottom of the ocean. The Blood Matriarch had clearly created more of her own terrifying monsters, the way she'd been known to do way back when. Suddenly, she'd been buried again for another two thousand years until the same necessary conditions were met.

A full moon. A Summer Solstice. And…what?

Halsey spent the next few days in her cottage, racking her brain over exactly what the missing piece of the puzzle might have been. The only other common denominator she could come up with was the silverback alpha had been present during both occasions. She also couldn't give the alpha all the credit for either of those occasions.

Rolfr Magnusson, the two-thousand-year-old werewolf alpha who'd died happily and willingly under the blade of Halsey's axe, had been aboard the longship way back when. That could only mean the Mother of Monsters had turned him. She couldn't think of any other explanation for the combined variables that actually made sense.

Even after they'd apparently hashed it out at Greta's

house, something still niggled in the back of her mind. Halsey realized she hadn't had the time to even consider looking up one last little piece of the puzzle. A seemingly small detail that anyone else might've overlooked or written off as unimportant. Both Seamus Havalon and Halsey's own grandmother had written it off, but the young elemental couldn't let it go.

Especially since now she finally had the time to sit down and take a look without Brigham constantly asking what she was doing or the Council calling her in for more mission meetings before shipping her off to wherever they thought best.

By her third day of R&R, after the slightly upsetting news she'd received at her grandmother's and the frustration of essentially working for a monster militia of lies and deceit, Halsey was finally feeling in good enough spirits to attempt some research.

This time, going to the Ambrosius Clan library was out of the question. Not only because Greta's brother Charlemagne had banned her for life, or so he'd said, but because Halsey already knew she wouldn't find what she wanted there. The whole reason she hadn't immediately known what she'd heard that night behind the Havalon estate was the Ambrosius Clan library had nothing on effectively dead languages the Clan hunters would never need to use.

Except for now, of course, but she couldn't blame generations of her own family for not having foreseen this little bump in the future timeline.

Plus, sometimes, an even greater resource than a massive family library full of magical tomes and texts was as simple as getting on the internet.

Holding a freshly poured pint glass of Monster Bash blonde ale, her and Brigham's favorite local beer, Halsey sat down at the outdoor patio furniture in the back room she and her cousins had dubbed "the greenhouse." She opened her laptop and had absolutely no idea where to start.

"Okay..." Narrowing her eyes at the screen she hadn't had the time or the need to look at in the last two years, she opened the internet browser and instantly realized she'd have to work off her cell phone's hotspot all the way out here. The lack of internet or cable TV was one of the many perks of this little hidden cottage that made her want to claim the abandoned building for herself.

After five years of living here alone, with the greenhouse in a constant state of magical improvement and all the quiet and privacy she could ever want, this might have been the first time she wished getting internet in the middle of Nowhere, Texas, was an option.

When she finally got it sorted out with a decent Wi-Fi hotspot signal from her phone, she was able to play around on the internet long enough to remember how much she didn't know about the internet.

Jeez. I'm twenty-three, I've been all over the world, I hunt monsters the human population still doesn't know exist, and I have no idea where to start looking for stuff about dead Nordic languages. This must be how the normies of Meemaw's generation feel about technology in general.

That thought made her snort before she took another long sip of her beer and started typing things into her internet browser's search engine.

Halsey could handle the newest phones and tablets like

everyone else her age or younger. Whenever she went over to Brigham's place near downtown Lufton rather than him coming here to hang out, she knew her way around an Xbox. Yet when her entire personal life revolved around her family, the Ambrosius Clan militia, and hunting monsters, there hadn't been a lot of impetus for learning to navigate the internet beyond email, paying her bills, and online banking.

Social media was a bust because she didn't *know* anyone. She didn't *want* to know anyone. Her schooling between the ages of eight and eighteen had all been right here, on Ambrosius Clan property, with the rest of her cousins and extended cousins and whatever other Ambrosius elementals were the same age and ready to go through their training together.

"Yeah, I probably wouldn't have been popular in a normal elementary school with all the other normie kids. 'Oh, look. There's Halsey with her throwing axe, turning all the soda cans into gold nuggets for her friends.'"

For some reason, laughing at herself in a way she hadn't laughed for what seemed like a long time felt natural. Normal. Hell, it felt good, which only made it clearer how much of her time and energy she'd spent on "finding proof" for the Council and worrying over when the Mother of Monsters would show up.

Now, though, she knew the truth.

The truth about her mom, Gillian's death, the Council's duplicity, the reason Greta had gotten kicked off the Council and exiled onto the property and branded an Ambrosius lunatic. The truth about why Aidan had all but abandoned his three-year-old daughter for his mother to raise instead while simultaneously turning against her and swearing off monster hunting altogether, at least for the next twenty years.

The truth was probably the same reason the Ambrosius Clan had denied the Havalon Clan's request for help with Ireland's burgeoning werewolf problem years ago. Secrets didn't stay secret for very long when they were shared. Especially with other families.

The truth had suddenly made all the other questions Halsey had been asking seem like the kind that never needed to be asked in the first place.

Except this one.

"All right. Here we go. What did Rolfr Magnusson actually say with his dying breath?"

Thinking about it now, she found it amazing that the man within the alpha werewolf had managed to speak to her in perfectly clear English, albeit heavily accented, right before he'd passed from the land of the living into the realm of the dead. Only a single sentence had been in a different language, which probably meant those foreign words had marked the seconds before Rolfr would never draw another breath again.

A small shudder racked Halsey, and it wasn't from the mix of water and air magic she'd perfected with the fountain in the center of the greenhouse for climate control, even in one of Texas' hottest months. She shook the thought of a dying red-haired Viking out of her mind and focused instead on what she did know for sure.

It wasn't much. Seamus Havalon and Greta had both seemed confident in their assessment of that foreign language being some form of a Nordic language, either

Icelandic or Old Norse. The latter generally didn't exist anymore. Knowing what she knew now about the silverback alpha having been spotted by her ancestor Cedric on a Viking longship way back in 953 AD, Old Norse seemed far more likely.

The one other thing Halsey knew was that she had something of a photographic memory, but only with things that caught her interest enough to cement them in her mind. She could remember all her favorite passages from books she hadn't read in over five years. She could recognize any of her family members from a mile away while blindfolded by the individual feel of their unique brand of elemental magic.

She could recall every moment of a monster hunt down to the smallest detail. Which was also part of what had made her and Brigham's last debrief from the Turkey mission so out-of-the-norm for all parties involved.

She could also pull from the deepest parts of her mind anything she'd heard once already, no matter how far in the past it had been. Verbatim.

Today, that meant she had no problem drawing up the last words of Rolfr Magnussen as he lay dying beneath the full weight of one confused elemental with her axe in his chest and his fractured wolf claw embedded in her thigh.

"Munkurinn hafdi rétt fyrstur."

They were so easy to say, rolling off the tongue as if she'd been repeating the phrase her entire life. This particular skill no doubt added to the ease with which Halsey had studied, learned to read and write, and eventually learned to speak a whole slew of languages during her militia training. Yet if she hadn't seen the words before and didn't know anything about the mechanics of a nearly dead language, figuring out how to type them correctly into internet translation sites was more difficult.

The first issue she discovered was how easy it was to find a translation website for an almost-dead language that excelled at getting the translations entirely wrong. Over the next hour, she typed the same series of words into dozens of different translation sites and got startlingly different results from all of them. Worse still, none of those translations into English made any sense. When she rearranged those English languages to then translate them back into Old Norse, the end result sounded absolutely nothing like what Rolfr Magnusson had actually said.

Yeah, the internet's great and all, but it sure as hell doesn't account for two thousand years of linguistic evolution. Even for a language nobody speaks anymore.

It took her another twenty minutes to find the best the internet had to offer in terms of translators. What little knowledge she had about what was out there meant the winner turned out to have been right there with the original search engine all along. That search engine didn't happen to have an option for translating Old Norse into English.

Of course it doesn't.

Halsey gulped a massive chug of her second poured-at-home pint, then figured she'd see what other languages the search engine's translation capabilities *did* cover. Norwegian was one of them, but whatever she typed into that box didn't come back with a single word in English. She went through a few Slavic and Germanic language options, but that didn't give her different results. Finally, because she couldn't think of anything else, she selected the Icelandic language option and tried again. And again.

"This is ridiculous. How many different ways do I have to spell something to get the words right?"

Using her previous translate-and-retranslate method, she got a few different renditions that seemed a lot more likely in their English versions. "The man on a mission," "the wise man," "the man was first." Still, it sounded wrong when she tapped the little speaker icon to hear how the words were pronounced.

"Right. A dying man isn't gonna use his last breath to talk about some other guy *being first*."

The closest thing she got to an actual translation was achieved by pure coincidence.

As she started over from scratch, typing in the phrase she remembered so well yet again, Halsey raised her pint glass to her lips with one hand and typed with the index finger of her other hand. Then her phone buzzed on the table beside her laptop with an incoming text.

She chugged more beer, then set the glass down to pick up her phone, all while still staring at the obnoxiously inaccurate online translator. The combination of condensation from her beer and not paying enough attention came together for a perfect storm. It didn't seem like anything beyond an annoyance at first when her phone slipped from her hand and toppled onto her laptop's keyboard with a clatter.

"Oh, come on…"

She snatched her phone off the keyboard, wiped her palm on her jeans, and tried again.

It was a text from Brigham.

So the last time I gave you three days to chill in your own house, you almost took my head off with an axe. Figured I'd send you a message first this time, just in case. I actually kinda like my head. How you doing?

Halsey snorted and started to text him back. She felt worlds better than she had three days ago despite not having found any intelligible translations for Rolfr Magnusson's final words.

If he wants to pop over for a bit, I won't throw anything at his head this time. Probably.

In the middle of her typing a reply to ask if his previous offer of pizza and beer still stood, she looked up at her laptop screen and almost dropped her phone all over again.

"You've gotta be shitting me…"

As was often the case when inanimate objects abused keyboards, her phone had pressed a few extra buttons. Namely, a space bar in the center of the last word of her indecipherable sentence. Because the translation site pulled up an automatic version of the words in English, she saw what she'd been trying to find.

The Icelandic word she'd pegged as "first" had become two nonsense Icelandic words, but looking at it this way, she realized she'd been picking out the wrong sounds. She'd spelled it incorrectly the whole time.

Not *"fyrstur"* but *"fyrir sér."*

It changed everything because now Halsey had a feel for how those words were *actually* spelled. She only had to change a few consonants from harsher sounds to softer ones and try a wild guess by typing a U instead of an O.

"The man was first" suddenly became "the monk was right."

"Holy shit…" Halsey stared at the screen, then hastily switched the translation to change "the monk was right" from English to Icelandic. When she read it out loud again, the words were exactly what she remembered the redheaded Viking telling her a few weeks ago. "*Munkurinn hafdi rétt fyrir sér*… Damn, he really *was* on that ship. With the monk they found dead with a hole in his gut."

She was well aware of talking to herself now, but it felt right. In the scheme of things, talking to herself in her own house was last on her list of things to be concerned about.

Okay, now I know. What does that even mean? The monk was right about what? Right about warning the Vikings not to read from the blood-magic ritual scroll? That would mean at least one of the first monsters let back into the world was a blood human. No one else would have been able to read the runes. Or maybe it was the monk…

Her phone buzzed again, startling her from her hypothetical conjectures. Halsey had to tear her eyes away from her laptop screen before looking down at her phone and another incoming text from Brigham.

Can't blame me for trying. But if you take longer than a day to get back to me, I'm coming over anyway. It's not like you're so busy you forgot about your phone, right? Or your best friend who may or may not have already picked up a steaming pizza and a six-pack…

He'd ended the text with a nervously smiling emoji at

the end, which was his way of saying he was joking but not really.

Halsey glanced back up at the words on her computer, "the monk was right," and barked out a laugh.

Definitely something to break my radio silence over. Brigham's gonna freak when he figures out it's the same monk.

With her previously furious mood now having morphed into an excited elation over the last three days, especially now, she typed up a reply to her cousin but didn't get halfway through it before she remembered one tiny little problem with sharing the news.

"Crap. I still haven't told him."

Revealing yet another secret she'd kept from him, even something as insane as the silverback alpha having *spoken* to her in both his forms, wasn't best done over a text. The fact that she hadn't talked to Brigham in three days would only make it worse.

Halsey deleted everything she wrote and typed up a completely different response.

All good here. Almost like the vacation I always wanted. You already know I never turn down pizza. But I might still throw an axe at your head, so come prepared.

At the end of her text, she added a deviously smirking devil-face emoji and paused. She wanted to say a lot more to Brigham, but neither of them was the phone-call type. There was no smooth, kind, gentle way to break any sort of news to him if she added it to a few lines of text and a ridiculous purple image. Giving her cousin the old "we need to talk" spiel over text probably wasn't the best way to go about it.

While she mulled over possible ways to subtly prepare her cousin for yet another important chat about certain things she'd kept secret for weeks, Halsey lost the opportunity to actually send the text she'd intended as a semi-immediate reply. Three slow, muffled knocks on the front door of her cottage interrupted everything else.

CHAPTER SIXTEEN

Halsey forgot all about getting back to her cousin and stood from the table, frowning at the sliding wooden door that led from the living room of her cottage and into the magically created backroom greenhouse. After absently setting her phone on the patio table's metal mesh surface, she cocked her head and waited.

Nobody ever stops by for fun. Except for Brigham, and he opens the door and walks right in.

When the firm, steady knock came again, she snorted and finally walked across the greenhouse toward the sliding door into the cottage proper. Reaching out to the thick, ropey vines she and her cousins had erected all over the greenhouse to create the cozy-yet-natural feeling of an enclosed space was as easy and inherent as breathing.

Halsey's magic called out. The life force within the vines replied instantly, and three of them peeled away from the greenhouse walls to wrap around the tarnished brass handle of the sliding wooden door. The soft rumble of the door sliding open mixed with the constant calming burble of the enchanted fountain in the center of the greenhouse, and as soon as she stepped through the open door into the living room, she made sure to send the vines one final command.

The door slid smoothly shut behind her again, and now she stared at the front door of her cottage.

I hope I'm not imagining this. Or maybe Brigham's playing up the "don't chop my head off" theme today.

That thought made her smirk until whoever it was on the other side of her front door knocked yet again.

"Jeez. *Someone's* in a hurry all of a sudden," she murmured as she crossed the living room toward the front of the cottage. Then she stopped again because she was apparently close enough to pick up on a different magical signature. Within this space, where the only other energy belonged to her and to the plants in the greenhouse, the feeling of a familiar but completely different magical source felt intrusive and violating. As if the owner of the magic had simply busted down her front door instead of remaining respectfully outside and continuing to knock.

For better or worse, the person this magic belonged to hadn't once set foot on this tiny, innocuous plot within the borders of the Ambrosius Clan property during the five years Halsey had lived here.

So why now? It's not like we suddenly have anything to talk about.

Another round of three hard knocks pounded away on the front door, and she rolled her eyes.

Points for persistence, I guess.

Then, because she didn't want to hear any more of the firm knocking that was bound to quickly become obnoxious, she hurried across her living room, past the dining room turned monster-hunter workshop and armory, and finally past the exterior kitchen counter on her right that extended to the front wall of the cottage.

The feeling of foreign, uninvited, not-necessarily-welcome magic within the elemental on the other side of that door was nearly overpowering. Usually, a feeling like that meant another elemental was on the verge of calling up a seriously powerful attack. In zero cases was attacking Halsey Ambrosius on her own doorstep remotely warranted.

Yet it wasn't exactly an attack. *This* was somebody desperately using their own magic to call on the elemental life forces around them as a remedy. To eradicate fear, anger, or nervousness, or maybe to hide any and all emotions.

Halsey inhaled, reached for the doorknob, and paused. She forced herself to twist it with a quick jerk before opening the door as if she had no idea who she'd find on the other side of it.

The charade played off better than she'd expected. Although Halsey was grown and stood at an average adult height of five-foot-five, she'd forgotten how enormous Aidan Ambrosius really was. She had to compensate for the oversight by flicking her gaze up from the center of the man's huge, barrel-shaped chest to the mess of coarse, wild, bushy black hair covering the bottom half of his face.

Then she stopped, her hand still clamped around the doorknob as she held the door open and blinked. "Dad."

Aidan's one-eyed gaze flickered across her face, his other eye gone to some crazed beast in his prime days of monster hunting. Where that eye had once been, the socket was now perpetually covered by a large, soft brown leather eyepatch so frequently oiled that it had taken on a dark, chocolaty sheen.

Even if he hadn't worn the eyepatch every day since sustaining the injury years before Halsey was even born, Aidan would have made a terrifying sight at six-foot-five with shoulders almost wider than the doorframe and a gut that some might have mistaken for soft until they discovered it was solid muscle. Anyone else probably *would* have been scared to see the man standing there on their doorstep, unannounced, scowling slightly the way he scowled down at his daughter.

Or, at least, Halsey imagined that was the expression currently gracing her dad's face. More often than not, with almost all of it covered by either the unruly black beard tinged with gray or the bushy black eyebrows or the glistening brown eyepatch, it was extremely hard to tell. It wasn't like she'd spent enough time with her dad over the last twenty years to know what his micro-expressions meant. If he even had any.

For a moment, they merely stood there staring at each other without a word. Halsey silently dared her dad to start harping on her about something else she'd done that the Council disapproved of.

Instead, Aidan's remaining green eye flickered toward the top of the doorframe as if he were noticing the existence of doorframes for the first time. "I haven't been here in…years."

The man's voice was a rolling growl, which only added to the effect of Aidan Ambrosius being the human equivalent of a massive, grizzled, solitary bear past the height of his prime but still a far cry from lying down and giving up.

Halsey blinked at him and couldn't think of anything to say.

"It looks a lot less...abandoned now," he added before his good eye narrowed and his muscle twitched.

She imagined that was what it looked like when her dad grimaced at the awkward way he'd chosen to greet his own daughter. Not by saying anything to or about *her* but by commenting on the state of her front doorframe.

Then, because he looked so miserable standing there without much of anything else to say, Halsey blurted, "Well, that's what happens when you put time and energy into taking care of something."

The words came out much harsher and with more venom than she'd intended, but it wasn't surprising.

If he thinks I'm still his ignorant adult kid who gobbled up all the lies about my entire life and why we are the way we are with each other, he's not gonna get the docile welcome he was expecting.

When her dad looked down at her again, the lines of his face softened. His good eye widened a little, smoothing out the worn age creases at its corners. Then he raised his eyebrows and dipped his head in one of the most passive gestures Halsey didn't know he was capable of making. "Can I come in?"

"Uh...yeah. I guess." She didn't know why she hadn't launched some other smartass remark at him instead. Maybe it was the pleading look in her dad's eye or the fact that he was clearly so uncomfortable with being here for the first time, specifically to see his daughter. She might have felt sorry for him. Then again, she simply might have been curious enough to let this strange encounter draw out before she called it off.

Stepping aside, Halsey opened the door even wider and gestured toward the cottage's living room.

Aidan nodded with a grunt that was probably supposed to represent gratitude, then dipped his head farther and hunched his shoulders to step inside. The man had to practically squeeze through the doorframe that clearly hadn't been built for anyone remotely his size, and Halsey released the doorknob to take a few steps back and give him the room he needed.

With a little shuffling and slight turning at the right angle, her dad managed to make it inside without any damage. Though the damage was more likely to have been done to the doorframe than to him. After he was through, he turned immediately around to swing the door shut behind him with a soft click. For a man so enormous and seemingly intimidating, he handled Halsey's front door with an unexpected gentleness that almost made her feel bad for being irritated with him.

Almost.

After that, with nothing else on which to center his focus, Aidan gazed around the front entryway and looked lost. "Wow. This is…"

"A lot different than the last time you came all the way out here. Yeah." Halsey folded her arms and studied her dad's face, pressing her lips tightly together and hoping it was enough to get her point across. He'd spent the last twenty years being remarkably uninterested in her life beyond her performance as a militia operative. Now seemed like the absolute worst time to start taking an interest, especially when the man was apparently trying to sweep the entirety of those twenty years under the rug without even acknowledging what he was doing.

Whatever he's here for, I'm pretty sure he couldn't make it any weirder.

Aidan sucked a deep breath through his nose, then walked slowly past the kitchen and toward the living room. He only turned his head slightly to glance down the narrow, darkened hallway opposite the kitchen that led to the cottage's single bedroom and bathroom, but there clearly wasn't enough there to catch his interest.

Once he made it past the relatively low ceiling at the front of the house, the man straightened to his full height again, now that the living room provided him the space to do so. Halsey watched him from where she stood, waiting for whatever kind of berating or verbal discipline her dad had been sent here to deliver. The more she watched him, the more she had to admit Aidan didn't look like a man on a mission. At least, not one he particularly wanted to accept.

He looked lost. Small. Uncertain.

He looks like a kid dropped off at a new school and told to figure it out on his own.

"Dad," she called gently but couldn't bring herself to follow him yet. "I'm not sure what—"

Aidan stopped again when he caught sight of the long dining room table that had been converted into Halsey's workspace. The weapons she kept in store for any and all monster-hunting occasions covered the surface. Pistols, two crossbows, a slew of arrows with custom-made tips for different types of monsters, a hatchet, two daggers, her Pappy's old but still beautifully functioning bolt-action rifle, boxes of ammunition, and her trio of throwing axes.

The man released something between a hum and a snort, then gestured toward the table with one enormous hand as he turned slightly back toward his daughter. "Getting ready for some secret mission I don't know about?"

Halsey chortled. "Subtle."

"How's that?"

"Dad, if I was getting ready for a secret mission the Council didn't know about, do you really think I'd fess up and tell you all about it the second you asked?"

Aidan's eyebrows flickered together, then he cocked his head and turned back toward the weapons table. "I guess not. So what *is* all this, then? Cleaning day?"

"That was yesterday." The sarcasm in her voice was clearly lost on her dad, so she sighed before adding, "It's where I keep everything, okay? Weapons at the ready, you know? Building a secret walk-in closet in this place wasn't an option."

"It's a dining room table, Halsey."

She could have taken the statement as more condescension toward the way she lived her own life as an adult, way out here on the property. Except her dad sounded so confused that she couldn't help but take everything he said with a grain of salt. "No. It's an armory."

"It's a table in a dining room. That's what it's for. You leave all your weapons and munitions out here for anyone to see…"

"It's not like I'm throwing elaborate parties or letting small children run around in here. I don't have a lot of guests. And it's *my* house." Halsey finally had to give up standing in the entryway for this very strange conversation because her dad had picked up one of her cases of very special, very explosive arrow tips and was now rummaging through the case with his thick fingers. The click of the arrowheads' casings bumping dangerously up against each other filled the cottage until she all but jogged toward her weapons table and swiftly took the case from her dad's hand. "Maybe I should have a rule about giant men with beards not having free rein in here either, huh?"

Aidan stared blankly at the ammo case as Halsey returned it to the table, unmoved by her attempt at a joke even when she offered an uncertain chuckle to lighten the mood. Then he scanned the weapons on the table again and frowned. "So, where do you eat?"

Seriously? The first in-person visit he'd ever bothered to make, and he wants to know where I eat? Come on. If he asks where I go to the bathroom next, I'm calling this thing.

With a snort, she tried to play it off like some kind of joke, but her dad looked at her with nothing but earnest curiosity. He was serious.

"Um..." Halsey turned to gesture toward the couch and loveseat in her living room. "Sometimes on the couch. Sometimes back in the greenhouse, I guess."

Aidan's bushy black eyebrows lifted again, and he searched the cottage for evidence of whatever this greenhouse might be. "You added on a *greenhouse*," he mused, "but you couldn't be bothered to take your weapons off the dining room table."

"That's where they go. It's not a *greenhouse*-greenhouse the way you're thinking." She would've felt ridiculous trying to explain to him what the greenhouse really was while they were standing there in her workshop, mere yards away from the door that separated the back of the cottage from the addition in question. With a sigh, Halsey pointed at the sliding wooden door on its wheeled tracks and headed past her dad. "Here, come on. It's easier if I show you."

He released a muffled hum of consideration, amusement, or something else entirely, but she didn't bother trying to figure out what that noise meant. She didn't look back, either.

Part of her was excited to show her dad around the formerly abandoned cottage she'd put a lot of work into making her own. That part was getting something Halsey had wanted for a very long time. For her dad to put any kind of effort into getting to know his only daughter and her life. Not as Halsey Ambrosius the monster hunter but as Hal, right here in her element.

The other part of her couldn't believe she was leading her dad, a man from the previous generation and a member of the Ambrosius Clan Council, toward the single best-kept secret among *her* generation. The greenhouse had been here behind this cottage for a decade before she'd graduated from militia training and snatched up this little plot for herself. No one else had wanted it, but it was still a secret place for the younger Ambrosius elementals. Away from the estate house, far from the prying eyes of the Council and anyone else in their family who'd made it a habit to continuously tell them what they were doing wrong.

She paused at the sliding wooden door, drew a deep

breath, and gave herself a moment to make sure she really wanted this.

Who knows? Maybe he'll wait another twenty years before bothering to check in on me again. He's trying, I guess. The least I can do is let him in and see what he does with it.

Halsey grabbed the brass handle and slid the door aside.

CHAPTER SEVENTEEN

The perpetual burble of the enchanted fountain at the entrance of the greenhouse sounded incredibly loud now. It was the only sound in the still silence of Halsey's home, even when Aidan slowly lumbered across the living room to join her.

She sensed her dad coming up behind her and didn't quite want to give him the opportunity to turn this into some kind of overly mushy, heartfelt moment. So she quickly walked through the doorway and stepped aside to give her dad a full view of the room that had been nurtured, grown, and added onto by the next generation of Ambrosius elementals, hiding out from the grownups and putting together their own little clubhouse.

"And…greenhouse," she murmured, failing to sound remotely excited about the big reveal.

Aidan took his sweet time assessing the scene in front of him.

The massive dead oak tree on the left served as part of the left-hand wall but had clearly also doubled as a focus point for target practice. The remaining walls were made of vines, leaves, and the branches of two willow trees enchanted to perpetually bend toward each other to serve as the center of the roof, all of it punctuated with enough space between them to let through slivers of bright sunlight. The enchanted fountain burbled away in the center, surrounded by half a dozen tree stumps and hammocks woven from still-living vines.

Somewhere from within the branches of one of the willow trees, a cardinal twittered at the disruption.

Halsey looked up with wide eyes but couldn't find a sign of the bird or its nest. "That part's new."

Her dad grunted again, then snorted. His low, rumbling chuckle made her turn to eye him warily. The only changes in the man's perpetually concealed expression were the laugh lines crinkling at the corner of his eye and a slight twitch in the place where his beard and mustache met. It was rare to see Aidan Ambrosius' lips in any situation beneath the wiry mess of black hair covering his face, but today, Halsey was graced with a flash of white teeth as her dad laughed again and let his gaze roam in every direction around the greenhouse.

The sound of his laughter was more poignant and more powerful than Halsey ever could have anticipated. It made her feel small again, hopeful again, taking her back to a time when her dad laughed every day, and his smile alone promised her the world was safe with the two of them in it.

That he would always be there for her, no matter what.

And then he wasn't.

A lump formed in her throat, and she quickly forced it back down again because this wasn't the right time to let herself feel everything all at once. That was then, and this was now. Three-year-old Halsey might have thought the world of her dad, but twenty-three-year-old Halsey knew better.

"You did all this?" he asked, whipping her from her angry attempt to get ahold of herself.

Halsey cleared her throat and shook her head. "Yeah. I mean, not *all* of it. Not by myself, anyway."

Tilting his head back to look up at the high ceiling of interwoven tree branches and ropelike vines, Aidan folded his arms and chuckled again. "Meaning you and Brigham."

"Along with a few other cousins, yeah." Half of her wanted to leap forward and start diving into all the stories of how each part of the greenhouse had become what it was, and the other half of her was screaming in the back of her mind that this was a mistake and she should never have brought him here. "It was a work in progress for a while."

"I'll say."

"The fountain was all me, though."

"Well, it doesn't feel like a jungle in here. You made the right call." Aidan nodded slowly, his long beard fluffing against his chest. "So this is where you all ran off to after a day of training, then. Makes sense. I'm not one to generally get jealous about much of anything, but…" He released a sigh that bordered on a laugh and finally looked at his daughter. "I would've loved to have a place like this back in my own school days. Hell, even a chance to hone our magic by *building* a place like this."

Halsey couldn't help but fix him with an uncertain smile. "What, you guys hadn't figured out how to build clubhouses out of trees back then?"

"Wouldn't have taken us years to do it, either. If we'd had nearly as much downtime as the next generation in line."

"Ha. Kids these days, right?" For a moment, they only stared at each other. Then Halsey suddenly remembered the reason she and so many of her cousins had had so much downtime was that their parents had been too busy holding seats on the Council.

Also trying not to spill the beans about how Meemaw was never actually crazy, and everyone wanted to pretend we wouldn't have to face the Mother of Monster again someday...

As soon as she had the thought, the entire mood changed again. Halsey slid her hands into the pockets of her cutoff jeans and shrugged. "Why are you really here, Dad?"

His smile faded until his lips disappeared beneath his thick, bushy mustache again. Then he inhaled deeply. "I can't check in on my kid for no reason?"

"For the first time since I moved in here five years ago? That's not suspicious at all. Come on. You send Jasper or Brigham out here after me when you wanna get my attention. It's great that you finally made it, but I can't help thinking it's 'cause you want something."

"That's one way to put it." Raising a massive hand to his face, Aidan rubbed his mouth, then swiped his hand down over his entire mustache and beard until finally tugging on the end of the wild mass of unruly black hair. His beard fell back against his chest again, and he nodded toward the patio table and matching chairs in front of the fountain. "Can we sit?"

"Uh…sure." Halsey headed for the table, trying not to

act like they both didn't already know that was a bad idea. She casually closed her laptop to avoid any questioning about her little linguistic investigation, then pulled her chair out again and sat. Her gaze fell onto her cell phone, still on the table, and she fought back a grimace.

Crap. Whatever this is about, he'd better make it fast. Or Brigham actually will end up at my front door, and won't that be super-fun to see them both here gawking at each other?

"Where'd you find *this*?" Aidan asked as he approached one of the other empty chairs, studying the metal mesh of the patio furniture like it was some kind of fragile antique. Which, for a man of his size and weight, it might as well have been.

"I don't know. Some garage sale in town a few years ago." Halsey shook her head and eyed the chair her dad had selected to be his latest victim. None of these chairs were suited for holding up such a bear of a man, but she didn't dare say a thing about it. Sometimes, there were things even *she* was too smart and too scared to bring up around her dad.

He's not really gonna sit in that, is he?

"I like it." Aidan grabbed the back of the chair and gave it a sturdy little shake as he gazed around the greenhouse again. "Might as well be a back porch anyway. Lot cooler than most of 'em, too."

She was on the verge of hopping from her chair and suggesting they go sit inside instead. Her couch wasn't necessarily the strongest piece of furniture, but it stood a much higher chance of surviving fifteen minutes with Aidan Ambrosius than anything else. Before she could figure out the best way to make such a suggestion, the air around them was filled with the sharp tingle of her dad's elemental magic working even more than it had on the other side of her front door.

The metal beneath Aidan's hand rippled and morphed, the thin iron hardening and thickening, taking on a more burnished look as it alchemized before her eyes. He made it look so easy, so casual. As if he were fluffing a pillow before sitting down instead of literally changing the chemical makeup of the metal in front of him.

Alchemy was an Ambrosius Clan specialty for a reason.

In seconds, the man had transformed a slightly lopsided, cheap metal patio chair into what could only have been considered a sturdy steel throne by comparison.

Of course he did. So this is a power play, huh? From my own dad.

"Yeah," Halsey muttered as she leaned back in her chair and folded her arms, pretending not to notice the magical twinge in the air or the fact that her dad had given a whole new meaning to rearranging the furniture. "One of the perks of being the only one who liked it here enough to move right on in. Followed closely by the fact that nobody else is around to touch my stuff. Usually."

Whether or not Aidan picked up on her renewed sarcasm, he didn't show any sign of being affected by it as he pulled his newly alchemized chair across the bits of lush grass and a few pebbles that had made their way into the greenhouse on the bottoms of other people's shoes over the years. He lowered himself into the steel chair, exhaled a heavy sigh, and clearly didn't have any clue what to say next.

Great. Now, all we need is to break out the rocking chairs and a few glasses of lemonade while we're at it. Yeah, no way am I playing Southern Front Porch right now. Especially not with him.

The bird that had apparently decided to build its nest in the enchanted willow branches twittered again, this time rustling its feathers or flapping its wings enough to make the bottom-facing branches quiver a little. A handful of leaves broke from their stems and fluttered lazily down to the floor of the greenhouse, and Halsey could've sworn she heard each one of them settling onto the grass.

"Dad."

Aidan slowly turned his head to finally look her straight in the eyes, which was when she realized he hadn't done that once since she'd opened her front door. "Halsey."

She spread her arms slightly and shrugged. "Why are you here?"

Her dad tried to smile at her again, but all the sense of joy and childlike wonder that had filled Aidan at the sight of the greenhouse had now disappeared under the weight of his true motivation for knocking on her door in person. "You haven't seemed like yourself since you got back from Turkey. Plus, I read the chimera report. Which was…unexpected."

"Ha. No shit." She folded her arms again and shook her head in disbelief, fixing him with a humorless smile. "That whole mission was *unexpected*."

"Clearly." His eyebrows drew together, and a curious darkness spread across his features, surprisingly unencumbered by the large amount of his face hidden behind the brown leather eyepatch. "That's not usually the way you handle debriefings, though."

"A lot's changed in the last few months, Dad. You know that. I know that. Hell, the Council knows that, though you couldn't *pay* anyone else in those other six seats to admit it."

Aidan rubbed his mouth with an enormous hand again, his emerald-green eye glinting in the sunlight streaming through the vines and branches overhead. "I can only speak for what I know personally, Halsey. Which I'm guessing isn't anywhere close to what you've been digging up on your—"

"No. It's not."

"I can't help but feel like you're keeping something from the Council."

Halsey's violently explosive laugh lacked all humor. She pounded a fist on the patio table's metal mesh surface, rattling her laptop, her cell phone, and her half-empty third pint of ale she'd forgotten about in lieu of answering the door. "Well, you know what, Dad? The Council's been keeping a whole bunch of shit from me for *years*. Most of my life, really. So if I'm *keeping* something from the *Council*, the *Council* can fucking deal. Trust me, that's not asking for a whole lot, all things considered."

Her dad fixed her with his good eye again and slowly leaned back against the nearly solid back of the steel throne he'd alchemized just for fun. The way he stared at her, though, she guessed he hadn't been expecting her to throw this level of defiance right back in his face. So she stared blankly at him and steeled herself for the short, succinct reprimand that was no doubt on its way.

Coming from Aidan Ambrosius, anything more than two or three sentences at a time was a damn lecture and would have been more than Halsey's dad had said to her in years. Including their fun little night of fisticuffs with an abnormal pack of ogres, a mass of desecrated graves, and a whole lot of severed hands in a Texas cemetery.

But the lecture she was waiting for never came.

Instead, Aidan reached toward the patio table and gingerly picked up one of the fallen leaves by its stem. Despite the size of his fingers and the awful strength Halsey knew they possessed, her dad was amazingly gentle with the greenery as he spun the stem between his thumb and forefinger.

"I can't argue with that, Halsey. But I misspoke." His bright green eye flickered up away from the leaf of almost exactly the same shade before his gaze settled on his daughter's face once again. "I can't help but feel like you're keeping something from *me*."

Her first thought was how good it would feel to laugh in his face. Maybe she should have because, at this point, she would have felt justified. Instead, as Aidan twirled the leaf and stared at her, urgently awaiting a response, Halsey merely wrinkled her nose before replying, "Come on, Dad. There are plenty of things I haven't told you. Probably most things, actually."

"No. We never got around to that whole father-daughter…bond thing, did we?"

"What, you mean like me calling you every day to talk about boys or writing 'Dear Daddy' instead of 'Dear Diary'? No. Didn't really happen." She snorted, then instantly wiped the smile off her face once her next thought flashed through her mind. "Jesus, Dad. Don't tell me you're trying to start something like that *now*."

A grumbling chuckle rose from what sounded like somewhere deep in her dad's chest. Maybe it was only her imagination, but her imagination wasn't making it easier *not* to think of her dad as some kind of giant, lumbering, unpredictable, deadly wild animal. There were teddy bears, and there were grizzly bears, and there wasn't a whole lot of middle ground between them.

"Not even close," Aidan replied, shaking his head with another chuckle that sounded a lot more human this time. Then he looked quickly at her again and raised an eyebrow. "Unless it was something *you*…"

"Nope." Halsey briskly shook her head and chopped a hand through the air to emphasize her complete lack of interest in buddy-buddy time with her dear ol' dad. "Never even entered my mind until literally just now."

"All right." Her dad scrutinized her, his expression masked yet again by his unruly black beard, then cleared his throat. "Good." Another awkward moment passed between them, but fortunately, Aidan was aware of it enough to try breaking through without further prompting. "I'm not…good at this."

"If being super vague and confusing without actually saying anything is what you were going for, I'd say you're nailing it." When he cut her a sharp look, Halsey couldn't help but huff out another wry laugh and spread her arms again. "What do you want me to say?"

"I thought…maybe if I was *here*, you know, ah…" Aidan's grimace was absolutely recognizable now, even beneath his beard. It scrunched his entire face and threatened to shove the brown leather eyepatch onto his forehead and beyond. "You might feel like you actually had an opportunity to talk about some things. With me. If there's anything you wanna say to me..."

Oh, jeez. He's flailing here.

She pressed her lips together and eyed him in case something else came stumbling out of her dad's mouth. It didn't. "I don't know, Dad. Is there anything you wanna say to *me*?"

Aidan's eyebrows did a strange little dance, moving together and apart, up and down, as if he couldn't figure out how to interpret his daughter's words or what any of those interpretations might mean when applied to real-life scenarios with his own offspring. Then he grunted and scanned the wall of vines *behind* the aforementioned offspring instead of continuing to look her in the eye. "Not at the moment."

He really is here just for moral support, huh?

No way could Halsey and Aidan sit here in her greenhouse for as long as it would take her to open up about everything she'd been "keeping" from him. To start, the Council didn't know about her and Brigham's private little side-trip back to Ireland. Consequently, they also knew absolutely nothing about the leftover magical sand she'd found in an overly secure storage unit from which someone had still managed to steal the silver coffin, not to mention she'd managed to alchemize those leftovers into something she didn't understand but had brought home with her anyway.

They didn't know about the silverback alpha, either. Or about Halsey and her cousin meeting and teaming up with the entire Havalon Clan, who couldn't have possibly been any different than the Ambrosius elementals. Or about

Halsey's attempts to find out more about both the legends surrounding the Mother of Monsters and her own connection to her alchemized copper orb, specifically by trying and failing to set up an in-person meeting with the Order of Skrár.

The Council had no idea what had actually taken down the invincible chimera in Turkey. They wouldn't until Halsey decided to tell them. If she ever did.

Apparently, her dad was still as clueless about Greta's grand revelation in her living room three days ago as Halsey had been about the full truth of what had happened to her mother and why the Ambrosius Clan was as screwed up as it was today.

Yet he has a feeling I'm keeping something from him?

He couldn't show up at her door, unannounced and probably without actually knowing *why*, and expect her to lay everything out on the table for him. That might have been possible once, maybe, and he could have tried any number of times in the past.

The devastating news from her grandmother years and years ago, who had insisted Halsey move out of the bungalow and back into the estate house to prepare for the official start of her militia training. Or when she'd gotten her ass kicked by her cousin Nick in mock-combat because she'd been too worried about actually hurting him and had never held back since. The day she'd graduated at eighteen, or come back from her first monster hunt, or even the emergency meeting after that first mission in Ireland.

All those would have been perfect opportunities for Aidan to get closer to his daughter and exchange truths and secrets that needed to be aired. To ensure Halsey didn't spend the rest of her life not realizing she was choking on all the lies her family had been feeding her and wondering why she couldn't catch a break. Hell, if he'd come to talk to her after they'd both stood in front of that low round table in the Council room to offer a dozen severed ogre hands with crimson blood runes staining the palms, it would have been better than this.

Sorry, Dad. It's too little, too late.

Aidan Ambrosius had run out of chances to get ahead of the lies. He simply didn't know it yet.

Or maybe not...

Frowning, Halsey studied her dad's profile and waited for him to say something else, even though she already knew he wouldn't. That wasn't how he worked, and it wasn't like she'd deluded herself into thinking he might change anytime soon.

For the last three days, she'd holed herself up here in her forgotten little cottage nestled in the woods, mulling over everything she'd learned and how she actually felt about it. Discovering the truth about her mother's death and the entire Ambrosius family's part to play in keeping Gillian's daughter in the dark over the last twenty years had hurt, yes. Especially knowing her Meemaw, the woman who'd taken on the closest motherly role possible at the time, had been as implicit in keeping up the lie as everyone else.

Aidan had been hurting over the truth *and* the lie for the last twenty years.

This wasn't about how badly the Clan had screwed up or the myriad ways Halsey could concoct to get back at them for how they'd refused to be responsible for their past mistakes. It would've been entirely too easy to get back at them, too. That was a given.

This wasn't about waiting for the Council to step into their grownup pants and clean up the mess they'd made, either. At this point, Halsey was all too aware of the high possibility it was too late for her dad and the other Ambrosius elementals of his generation to change. They'd been doing things their way for far too long, and it obviously wasn't working.

This *was*, however, about the power Halsey had to change the tides, break the cycle, and find a better way. She didn't have to keep handling dark secrets and heavy feelings like the rest of her family. She also didn't have to keep denying the fact that monsters all over the world were changing, alphas were coming out of the woodwork again, and the Mother of Monsters was out there somewhere. Waiting for her moment to strike back against the few remaining descendants of the elementals who'd locked her away.

If there was ever a time to start changing things around here, it was now.

CHAPTER EIGHTEEN

"Dad, I know."

That was the first thing Halsey could think of to say, and while it wasn't exactly a show-stopper, it did catch her dad's attention again.

Aidan's bushy black eyebrows did their weird little dance as he wavered between gazing intently at his daughter and trying to act more interested in the enchanted fountain behind her. "Know what?"

"Everything."

He cocked his head, his jaw working beneath his giant beard, which swished across the collar of his button-down shirt with the rhythm. He didn't say anything, though.

At least he's not trying to tell me he has no idea what I'm talking about.

"About Mom," she added gently, and it was easy now to give her dad the courtesy of holding his gaze as she spoke. Or at least gazing only at his good eye so when he *did* look at her, he'd find his daughter thoroughly engaged in the conversation neither one had wanted to start. "About what really happened. She didn't go crazy and wither away. I know she tried to…take me with her. I know why it all started."

It briefly occurred to her she might have broken the bear of a man sitting at her patio table. Aidan stared directly ahead, his green eye open as wide as it would go as he traced across the back of the greenhouse from one of the willow trunks to the opposite wall of vines. His thick black mustache twitched once, twice, three times. Halsey hadn't even realized the man had legitimately stopped breathing until he drew in a long, deep, heavy breath through his nose.

She waited for him to say something. Anything. She didn't even consider the possibility of what came out of his mouth next.

"Right." Aidan cleared his throat, then dipped his head and leaned toward the table as if he intended to get up and run through the wall of vines and over the next hill beyond. "Then I guess there's nothing to talk about—"

"Sit down." The firm command in Halsey's voice surprised them both, though it didn't lack in kindness or compassion. She wasn't finished with this little moment. Not after she'd finally taken the leap of faith to dive right into it head-first.

Her dad was so surprised he dropped into his newly transformed steel chair, making it shudder slightly beneath his weight. He stared at her as if she'd been beamed down from space into the other chair.

"We've been pretending there's nothing to talk about for way too long," she added carefully. "I don't know about you, but I think it's time to change that."

Aidan's lips parted with a puff of air, ruffling the underside of his mustache as his eye narrowed and he scrutinized his daughter. It was unnerving to see that look on him now, aimed at *her*. The same expression he'd worn at the cemetery in Woden when Halsey and her dad had taken up their hiding spots behind a few thick tree trunks to assess the "nine blood-cursed ogres gorging themselves on human corpses" situation.

Either that's his thinking face, or he's looking at me like I'm the monster here. Thanks, Dad.

Fortunately for her, the man quickly got over the indecision hump, and all pretenses were suddenly dropped. Aidan released an enormous, half-growling sigh and rubbed his mouth again before smoothing his beard out. "How long?"

Of all the questions he could have asked, that one seemed like the least important.

Give him a minute to warm up, Halsey. No way is this what he thought he was getting into.

"Since right before the Turkey debrief," she replied glibly.

"Turkey?" It seemed he'd forgotten about the fun little report he'd already admitted to reading. Or maybe he was thoroughly stunned by the fact that his daughter had only known the truth for the last three days and was already handling it better than he could manage after twenty years. "Three days."

"Unless Cavanaugh's been writing all the wrong dates on his reports." Halsey shrugged, but the joke wasn't exactly her dad's style at the moment. "Yeah. Three days."

"How did you…" His eye widened again, then he lifted

his chin and stared at the table like it was the young child he hadn't spent very much time disciplining or admonishing. "*That's* why she called me."

"Who?"

"Greta." Apparently, saying his own mother's name was as difficult as sitting down for a real, genuine conversation with his daughter. The single word came out in a low growl, and he slowly shook his head. "Maybe I should block her number."

"And miss out on a day like this?" At least he snorted at her comment, which was a lot more than Halsey could say for her other attempts to lighten the mood with humor thus far. Now, though, she was starting to feel like the butt of another joke she didn't quite understand yet. "What did she say, exactly?"

Aidan grunted. "Something about family needing each other now more than ever, and when did I talk to you last." The next time he looked at his daughter, he tried to do it without her noticing, but Halsey hadn't stopped staring at him since she'd commanded him to sit down, and he'd obeyed. "Guess I fell for that one, huh?"

"Dad, if there's any trap here, it's the one you set for yourself. Honestly, I'm surprised it took twenty years for the damn thing to finally go off."

"And here I am, checking the line. Thought I'd find a… quivering little bunny and ended up with snarling wolf instead."

"Just making sure." Halsey pointed at him. "I'm supposed to be the wolf, right?"

Bemused by their hunting analogy and clearly loosening up with his own cleverness, her dad snorted again before his attention fell to what little beer remained in the pint glass Halsey hadn't touched for at least an hour now. He pointed at it. "That yours?"

"No, my imaginary friend was drinking that, actually."

Aidan was already reaching for the glass when she said it, but her reply was weird enough to make him pause before he realized this was more of his daughter's wry humor. Which he hadn't spent a whole lot of time getting to know, either, but it looked like things might be heading in a different direction. His beard twitched around a crooked smile as his hand hovered beside the pint glass. "Mind if I—"

"Ew. Jesus, Dad. Yes, I mind." She stood abruptly and snatched the pint glass off the table before tossing its contents over her shoulder and onto the greenhouse's earthen floor. "If you want a beer, just say so." He didn't say anything, and she fought back a laugh. "So *do* you, or what?"

"Got anything stronger?"

"This isn't a pub." Without waiting for him to say anything else, Halsey walked briskly around the patio table and headed for the sliding wooden door with the empty pint glass in hand. Two more vines responded to her magical call and unlaced themselves from the wall of vegetation to open the door for her, even though she could've done it on her own.

Somehow, knowing her dad was watching her and any little trick she wanted to pull with her elemental magic made it feel like she was making a statement.

This was *her* house. Whatever ended up happening here, Halsey was the only one calling the shots.

When she returned to the greenhouse with a full and sloshing pint of Monster Bash ale in each hand, the five minutes it had taken to pour those pints had also given her five minutes away from her dad. Apparently, it was plenty of time to rethink her strategy and realize how grateful she actually was for having a place like the greenhouse to hold this kind of conversation. Anywhere else in her cottage would have felt intrusive. Doing this back at the estate house was out of the question, no matter how allegedly private some of the unused rooms were purported to be.

It did, however, take her longer than she'd thought to get her dad warmed up enough to look her in the eye *while* talking to her instead of before or after. Around the third pint, though, he finally got the picture.

Just because beer was involved didn't mean this was any less a delicate conversation. Which was exactly how Halsey handled it. She didn't yell, point the finger, or act appalled and devastated like she hadn't had the last three days to figure out how she felt about their family's history. Instead, she stuck to the facts.

The missing record of Cedric's story, the Order of Skrár, the brand-new monsters of the tenth century, Greta's attempts to find a more objective interpretation, and all the events leading up to Gillian Ambrosius' attempted "escape" and eventual death. The Ambrosius Council's decisions to both exile their former Council head and to shove what they knew about the Mother of Monsters so far down they managed to convince *themselves* it wasn't real was the cherry on top of the pile-of-lies sundae.

Yet for Halsey, it was the cherry that had hurt the most.

"You had to know what that would do to me," she calmly finished as Aidan downed the first third of his fourth pint in one gulp. "Even if nobody else understood, you *had* to know."

"Yep." He smacked his lips, set the pint glass down on the table, and ignored the thin layer of beer foam still coating the ends of his mustache. "I knew."

"Dad..." The pained lines on his face when he grimaced made her pull back on the disappointment in her voice. "Hey, I get it. From your perspective. Really. You'd been playing the game for so long. Stepping out of it now, with your daughter shoving blood-magic proof in everyone's faces, felt way too big to handle. Too big to keep in once the whole thing started unraveling, right? So you kept playing along because that's what you've always been doing. It makes sense."

"Huh." It didn't look like Aidan would say anything else to move their already tense conversation forward as he stared at the patio table and tapped the pint glass resting in his massive hand. Then he turned his head to face her so she could see both sides of his face. One made alive and bright and aware by his one good eye glinting at her, the other dampened and darkened by grizzled scars punctuating that side of his beard beneath the eyepatch.

Another grunting laugh made it sound like he was giving up. "You never think about it before starting your own family. Sometimes, girl, I feel like you're the one who should've been parenting *me* in this life."

That admission took Halsey by surprise, and her uncertain laugh was startlingly similar to her dad's. "I said it makes sense, Dad. That doesn't mean I agree with the way everyone's been handling things. Yeah, including you."

"I know." With his next long glug of ale, the man looked a lot more refreshed and a lot less stiff, which apparently only took three and a half pints. "I can't speak for everyone else on the Council or for everyone else in our family. Only for myself. If I could go back and change the way the whole thing played out…" Aidan clenched his eye shut and dipped his head. "First of all, I would've paid more attention to your mom. I would've looked for ways to—"

"Dad, it wasn't your fault." Instinctively, she reached toward her dad's hand, but her fingers only ended up brushing slightly against his enormous wrist. Anything more than that felt like taking their little heart-to-heart too far, and it wasn't like they'd spent much time holding hands in general, even when she was a kid.

The gesture got the point across the way it was supposed to. Halsey retracted her arm and tapped the tabletop for emphasis instead. "There was nothing you could've done for Mom. Nothing anyone could've done. Sometimes, people just…can't be brought back."

Her dad had been staring at the place on his wrist where she'd attempted a reassuring touch, and his beard and mustache bristled again as his lips moved somewhere beneath them, unseen. "I loved her so much."

The pain and self-loathing in that one little confession almost made her fall apart. It didn't help that she thought she saw tears glistening in her dad's green eye. Which only made it harder to hold back her own tears, unshed for so long over all this.

Halsey Ambrosius didn't cry. Apparently, it was a common family trait.

"I know," she murmured. "Me too."

"I never really..." Aidan choked on his words, finished his fourth pint with a final long chug, then gently set the glass down on the table and met his daughter's gaze again. "I never did right by you, Halsey. Sure, we got over the hump in the beginning, but it wasn't because I was there with you."

She shrugged. "You did the best you could."

"Uh-huh. And someone else's best turned out to be even better for you."

"Meemaw."

Her dad's nose twitched like he wanted to wrinkle it before realizing he actually didn't believe the lie the whole family had been maintaining about his mother. That Greta Ambrosius was a crazy old woman who'd endangered the entire Clan one too many times and was better kept out of sight and out of the way. "She saved both of us in her own way. Your Meemaw. I can't... Shit."

Halsey chuckled when her dad realized he was all out of ale. She set her mostly full glass in front of him and nodded. "This one hasn't been sitting out for a few hours."

Aidan grunted, pulled her pint glass toward himself, and paused. "We carry a hell of a heavy burden, being what we are. Elementals. Monster hunters. Family. Yet it's the *shame* that gets you. Heaviest damn burden I've ever lugged around, and I put it on my own damn shoulders. It... I can't help..." Apparently unable to finish his thought, the man knocked back another enormous gulp of ale to sturdy himself before continuing.

Damn. No wonder we haven't actually sat down and talked. Ever. About anything. Dad's a big softy wrapped up in a giant hunting machine's body.

Halsey waited patiently for the man to compose himself again, warring between being incredibly grateful for this opportunity and incredibly uncomfortable. Yet everything else about her life, her family, and what she knew of the truth was already changing. She might as well get used to the possibility this might be another part of it.

Finally, Aidan looked up at his daughter and nodded. "You're on the right track, Halsey. Always have been. I should've stood up for you the day you came back from Ireland. Should've said more when you tossed a bunch of bloody stumps onto the table in front of everyone…"

"You weren't the only speechless person in the Council room that night."

He snorted. "One night isn't shit in the scheme of things, is it? All I'm trying to say is, well… You've got your own path to walk, like the rest of us. After everything, I'm telling you right now. I won't be the one to stand in your way."

"Thanks." They stared at each other for a moment longer, and she couldn't quite figure out if he was waiting for her to say something else or if she was supposed to end this conversation now. At this point, it was fairly likely they'd both reached heartfelt-moment overload.

Then her dad cleared his throat. "That's bullshit."

"Wait, what?"

"I'm done taking the easy way out, Halsey. Fuck stepping out of the way and standing there while my own kid handles something that's way bigger than any one of us. Fuck being silent."

I like where this is headed. Not sure how I feel about hearing my Dad curse like Brigham and me almost getting killed by an invincible chimera, but okay.

She couldn't help a small smile as she watched her dad transform from the broken, uncertain, embarrassed, deeply ashamed man who had squeezed silently through her front door and tried to avoid anything and everything related to emotions and connecting with his own kid.

Aidan glugged down what was now his fifth pint of Monster Bash ale, then pounded a fist on the patio table. All of Halsey's electronics jumped and rattled against the metal mesh surface, along with the two empty pint glasses. Fortunately, nothing broke or toppled over, but she was sure she'd find a dent in the tabletop later.

"I'm done watching from the sidelines," her dad added with gruff certainty. "I won't stand in your way, and I won't let anyone else do it, either. Not anymore. Whatever it takes, girl, I'm with you on this. I have no idea where it's going. Hell, I couldn't tell you the first thing about getting the Clan ready for this…war that's obviously coming. The Council thinks we have more time—"

"We don't." Halsey sat up straighter in her chair and shook her head. "That's what I've been trying to tell everyone."

"Yep." Her dad's mustache and beard bristled again as he sniffed. "Might be too late for Greta and me. Who knows? But I hope it's different for us. You and me."

Oh, jeez. Here it comes.

"I don't think it's too late, Dad. I just…need more help."

A muffled choking noise rose from Aidan's throat, then he looked away from her and studied the walls of the greenhouse again, his eyebrows doing their little dance. "I stood back and did nothing once already because it was easier. Because I thought it wouldn't hurt as much. Hell, if I'd known back then that betraying my own family, which I *knew* was right, would only make it so much worse…"

"It's okay." Halsey nodded, wanting to reassure her dad and also wary of what the man was doing with his enormous hands in case he felt like taking out even more of his frustration on her patio furniture. "It's not too late to change any of this. That's the whole point. That's what I'm trying to do."

"Ha. Well, you're doing a damn fine job of pulling everything apart to lay it all out in the open. That's for fucking sure."

"You know me. Dismantling the system and shit."

That brought another genuine smile to her dad's lips, and his eye lit up with the same level of life and vitality Halsey had seen more in her memories than in real life. The same spark of life had shown up again the night she and Aidan had formed their father-daughter team to go after the blood-marked ogres, but now it wasn't only about hunting and fighting and killing.

This gleam in his eye was about living in the here and now. Finally.

As long as he can hold onto that, maybe we do have a chance of coming out of this on the other side. The Mother of Monsters can't stand against the elementals a second time. Not if we're all in it together.

CHAPTER NINETEEN

There was no real ending to their conversation, at least the way endings normally go. Aidan stood from his alchemized chair, picked up the pint glasses, and headed back into the main part of the cottage without a word. Halsey was left to assume they were finished with this particular chat.

After confirming the new dent in the patio table, she stood with a snort, slipped her cell phone into her back pocket, and followed her dad inside.

Almost topping the charts of the most surprising thing her dad had done today was the sight of him standing at her kitchen sink and washing out the pint glasses with dish soap and a sponge. With a crooked, tentative smile, she watched him silently as she slid the wooden door closed again. He didn't seem to notice anything else around him until the glasses were thoroughly rinsed, dried, and set out on a dish rag on the counter beside the sink.

"Thanks," she finally replied as she crossed the living room.

Aidan turned with what might have been a sheepish

smile, but it was hard to tell under so much beard. "Least I could do. Thanks for the beer."

"It's not like I could've gone through the whole case by myself anyway."

Wiping his hands on his pants legs, he walked slowly from the kitchen, gazing intently at everything around the cottage again. Now that they'd gotten their much-needed conversation out of the way, and it was apparently time for him to go, he'd returned to being silent, tense, and awkward.

I'm gonna have to literally push him out the door, aren't I?

Halsey almost laughed, but her dad immediately moved her attention to something else when he pointed at the dining room wall behind her weapons table.

"Didn't see *that* when I walked in."

She wanted to kick herself when she realized he was pointing at the handmade necklace the Havalon Clan had given to her as a parting thank-you gift for helping with their little werewolf problem. She'd strung it up onto the wall as one of the very few decorative pieces she owned or had even bothered to put up around the cottage. The leather strings braided into Celtic knots looked especially intimidating, hanging over her entire array of monster-hunting weapons.

The long tip of broken alpha claw that Fiona Havalon had surgically removed from Halsey's thigh, which now dangled at the end of the necklace, didn't hurt the general ambiance.

"Oh, *that*." She huffed out a laugh and tried to casually wave off the topic. "Something fun I picked up in…Turkey. Thought it looked badass."

Of course, she couldn't tell him where the thing had really come from or why. As far as the Ambrosius Clan Council knew, Halsey and Brigham had never returned to the source of all this chaos. There was no telling how deep the feud between the Ambrosius and Havalon Clans ran, at least on this side of things.

"Turkey, huh?" Aidan cocked his head and leaned slightly forward for a better view of the necklace. "Yep. Badass."

"Thanks." The cottage fell silent again, but it seemed like Aidan was finally ready to call this a done deal.

"Well. I'll get outta your hair, then."

"Yeah, okay. Thanks for...stopping by."

He paused on his way to the front door and snorted, his crooked smile barely visible beneath his black mustache. "Not sure you actually mean that."

"I probably didn't in the beginning, but now I do. I think."

"Uh-huh." With a grunt, he continued toward the door.

Then one more question popped into Halsey's mind like they usually did when she felt she was running out of time. She headed after him and called, "Hey, Dad?"

Aidan turned to look at her with raised eyebrows.

"*You've* seen the chimera report. Has the rest of the Council read it yet?"

His thick eyebrows drew together. "I don't know."

"When they do, though, they're gonna come around to seeing this as all the proof they ever needed, right? They have to."

"Things are still...fragile with the Council, Halsey. You

know I didn't come here on official Council business, right?"

"Yeah, I kinda got that impression."

Her dad nodded again, but his frown remained as he mulled over her question and how he wanted to answer. "I'm on your side of things. Know that. Still, if we push too hard, too fast, there's nothing to stop the Council from kicking *me* off next."

"Oh, good. Then we can build a compound of exile out by the river together. You, me, and Meemaw."

Aidan was thoroughly unamused by the prospect. "We bide our time, girl. Handle things as cautiously and consistently as we can with what we can control on our own. They'll come around eventually."

"Eventually." She shook her head. "I'm not sure we have much time to bide, Dad."

"Uh-huh." Aidan grabbed the doorknob and twisted it gently before pulling the front door open. "A little optimism never hurt anyone, by the way."

Halsey snorted. "Right. Sorry, I guess I forgot that part."

With a low, growling chuckle, he pulled the door open and squeezed himself back through the doorframe that was still far too small for a man his size. Halsey headed to the front door and stood there to watch her dad climb up into the SUV.

When he'd settled behind the wheel, Aidan gave his daughter a casual two-finger salute, then pulled the SUV into reverse before taking off again with a spray of dirt and dry grass behind the rear tires.

Still unsure exactly how she felt about their conversation and the way things between her and her dad might have been headed, Halsey stood there in the open doorway for a moment longer. She watched the breeze rippling across the treetops and over the blades of grass coating the rolling hills of the property.

That was weird. And good. Change is good, I think. Hey, but at least now I have a direct line into the Council again. Maybe I can get Dad to do some undercover work.

The thought made her snort. Then she jumped as her cell phone broadcasted another humming buzz from her back pocket.

"Crap." Halsey knew the text had come from Brigham, and she realized she'd never gotten back to him.

Last call. Just in case you were napping all day or whatever. Pizza's hot, beer's cold, but they're about to switch temperatures.

Shaking her head, she deleted everything else she'd previously typed up and sent back a much simpler text.

Sorry, I got sidetracked. Aidan was here. It was weird. He drank all my beer. So get over here.

After she sent it and effectively let her worrying cousin know that everything was okay, it felt like a massive weight was lifting off her shoulders. Not entirely, and not all at once, but the pressure of being the only one who knew what she did was lifting. The only one who felt, believed, and sensed everything that was coming for the elementals in the foreseeable future despite not yet having *all* the proof. She was actually looking forward to hanging out with Brigham again after the strange visit from her dad.

Maybe she'd even keep the heart-to-heart train running and tell her cousin everything she *hadn't* told him yet about the silverback alpha, Rolfr Magnusson, and "the monk was right."

Before she could head back into her house, her phone repeatedly buzzed with an incoming phone call.

"Jeez, Brigham. If you're gonna blow up my phone, just call the first—"

It wasn't Brigham. The number saved in her phone came up with the name she'd assigned to it, which happened to be a cheeky "Master of Reports."

It was Cavanaugh.

"Great." Grimacing, Halsey accepted the call and pressed the phone to her ear. "Hello?"

"I need you to come in, Halsey," her second cousin muttered on the other end of the line. "Right now."

"I'm doing great, Cavanaugh. Thanks for asking." She rolled her eyes, turned around, and started to pull her front door shut behind her. "Listen, I get people might want clarification on Turkey, but there's nothing else to—"

"Forget Turkey," he snapped. "This is something totally different."

"Like…what?"

"Like a goddamn mission, Halsey. Why else would I be calling you in the middle of the day? Get your gear together for an international trip and get your ass down to the briefing room in an hour."

Then the line went dead with a loud click, and Halsey

pulled the phone away from her ear to stare at the brightly lit home screen. "Seriously?"

A notification for another incoming text popped up, and she quickly opened yet another text from Brigham.

So I guess Cavanaugh gets the pizza and beer?

Wrinkling her nose, Halsey firmly shut her front door and typed up a quick reply.

Maybe if he wasn't such an asshole. See you in an hour.

She hurried down the narrow hall at the side of the cottage toward her bedroom to start packing for another oh-so-critical mission. Everything else would have to wait.

CHAPTER TWENTY

She ended up packing way more than she normally did for monster missions, solely due to the fact that Cavanaugh hadn't said a word about what Halsey and Brigham were going after this time or how to battle the damn thing. So naturally, her duffel bag was insanely heavy and bulging over her shoulder as she power-walked through the halls of the estate house toward the briefing room. Still, it was better to be over-prepared than not nearly prepared enough. The Ambrosius cousins had learned that the hard way.

When she entered the briefing room, Brigham was already there, slumped back in his seat and staring blankly at Cavanaugh, who did not look happy to be heading this unscheduled emergency meeting. The man nodded at the other empty chair beside Brigham and grumbled, "Shut the door and sit."

With a sigh, Halsey did as she was told. The door shut with a click, her duffel bag thumped heavily onto the floor, and she dropped into the empty chair to get this show on the road. Only then did Brigham turn his head to finally look at her with wide eyes and a quick wiggle of his eyebrows.

Both cousins tried to hide their smiles as Cavanaugh fired up to tell them what they needed to know and get them on their way.

"Barghests up in Coningsby in east England," he grumbled. Instead of looking at either of the Clan militia's best monster hunters, the man was apparently far more concerned with shuffling around the scattered stack of papers in front of him.

"Barghest," Brigham repeated with a snort. "Not exactly an emergency monster."

"It is when they're tearing up a whole village in the middle of nowhere and apparently don't give a shit about being seen by almost every villager over the last four days."

"That's it?" Halsey folded her arms and cocked her head. "Four days isn't very long. You don't think we can take this easy instead of running around like a bunch of—"

"You. Shut up." Cavanaugh pointed at her, then stabbed his finger down onto the stack of paperwork in front of him. "This isn't the regular monster-rumor upheaval with a few operatives popping in and out to get rid of the evidence before it hurts anyone. We only got wind of this thing two hours ago, and we need the two of *you* to drop by for a quick and easy cleanup. 'Cause the way it sounds, these people are losing their minds."

"Well *yeah*," Brigham replied with a chuckle. "Barghests are, like...*the* death omen. Of course these people are freaking out."

Cavanaugh looked sharply up from his paperwork to scowl at him, and Brigham shut his mouth. He didn't bother to wipe off the smirk, though.

They're sending us off on another mission three days after we got back from Turkey? This has to be way more of a problem if the Council doesn't think they have another team who can actually handle a few giant black dogs running around to herald someone else's death.

"So what's the catch?" Halsey asked blandly.

"Catch?" Cavanaugh looked clueless as he shook his head. "It's a couple of fucking monsters being seen by a whole village. This thing doesn't need a catch. Lucky for you, Coningsby happens to be way out in the countryside in the middle of nowhere."

"Oh, goodie." Brigham grinned.

Cavanaugh glanced at the ceiling to steady his nerves and drew a deep breath. "Meaning there isn't a whole lot of foot traffic in and around the place, so you don't have to worry about civilian crowds making it even worse than it already is. Because apparently, it only took four days for the people of Coningsby to fall into complete and utter chaos. So this is your objective. You go in, you take out the barghests, then you clean up the area and put a wrap on any crazy idea those normie villagers happened to come up with over the last four days for what they've been seeing. Got it?"

Before either of the cousins had a chance to reply one way or the other, their briefing commander leaned sideways in his chair to rifle through a bag beside him on the floor. Then he sat upright again and slid a small canvas sack slightly larger than a fanny pack across the table toward his two operatives. "Take this with you. You'll need it."

Halsey reached for the odd purse or satchel or whatever the Council wanted to call the thing. When she wrapped her hand around it, the soft clinking of glass against glass rose from inside. Opening the top flap confirmed the purse contained a significant amount of glass. Half a dozen vials of transparent, luminescent green liquid.

Frowning, she handed the purse over to Brigham so he could take a good look and asked, "Care to elaborate."

"Healing potion." Cavanaugh shrugged, then when he found both elementals staring blankly at him, he heaved a sigh like this was the most inconvenient task of his life. "For the barghest bites? Antidotes to the damn thing's magic that leaves an unhealing wound? Not ringing a bell? Shit, how did *either* of you manage to graduate?"

"Well, *you're* not being very nice," Brigham muttered as he shot the man a sidelong frown. Cavanaugh tried to glower him into submission again, but Brigham busied himself instead by leaning down toward his duffel bag and carefully tucking the potion purse in among his things.

Halsey also decided to ignore their second cousin's otherwise insulting remarks. Something about this mission still didn't sit right with her. Not that any of them had, lately, but she had a lot more information to go on now.

"You know, it's weird that we'd already have a bunch of barghest-bite potions ready to go."

Cavanaugh scoffed. "Why?"

"We got the call for this mission a few hours ago, right?"

"Yeah. So what? Florence's always tossing together

random shit from her garden to help with hunts that need extra firepower." When Halsey cocked her head and kept frowning at him, he continued with an explanation he hoped would get her to back off about it. "Listen, maybe you handle things differently at home. I don't care about your personal life right now. In this *militia*, it's always a good idea to have the pantry stocked with a little of everything. Okay? So keep those with you. Use the potion if any of the villagers ended up getting too close to the barghests while their neighbors were running around screaming like a bunch of chickens with their heads cut off."

Brigham choked on a laugh and failed to hide his amusement. "Now *that* I'd like to hear."

Halsey shot him a quick sidelong look that was supposed to be a 'quit screwing around' warning, but she couldn't keep a tiny smirk off her lips.

Cavanaugh clearly didn't like having a team of militia operatives sitting there with their own silent and private inside joke. "Or hey, if you two wanna keep *not* taking this seriously, use the damn potions on yourselves. Just because this mission's all the way across the ocean doesn't mean it's not happening. Right now.

"So. Connor's waiting out front with the car to get you to the airport. Any questions before I get rid of you? Feel free to keep the stupid one to yourselves."

"Nope." Brigham grabbed the strap of his duffel bag, stood, and slung the whole thing over his shoulder. "We'll take it from here, Cav."

"Don't call me that."

Halsey stood as well but paused before picking up her

bag stuffed full of everything she could think of to bring. Now, most of it was probably useless, but she didn't have time to unpack again. She did, however, have time for clarification. "One question, actually."

Cavanaugh had already gone back to scribbling all over his paperwork, and he didn't look up at her. "Make it quick."

"Is this another contracted job? You know, like with extra payment to the Ambrosius Clan with whatever fee the Council decided was worth our *services*?"

That made her second cousin pause to look up at her with another deep frown. "How the hell does that apply to you?"

"It's nice to know what we're actually getting into ahead of time, that's all. It's a lot easier to focus on the mission without all the extra surprises. You know?"

Cavanaugh sighed and shook his head. "No. It's not a contracted job."

"Who, exactly, are our sources for this little tip about barghests running wild in Coningsby?"

Cavanaugh licked his lips in agitation and set down his pen before looking up to fix her with a blank, expressionless stare. "We're elementals, Halsey. It's our job to know when and where there's a monster problem that needs a monster hunter. That's it. Now get out of here. I have way more paperwork than I wanted on a Wednesday, and your flight leaves in two hours."

"Awesome. Thanks." With a nod Cavanaugh didn't see because he'd already gone back to his paperwork, Halsey bent over to retrieve her duffel bag and slung that over her shoulder too.

"I'm guessing it's still too much to ask for first-class tickets this time?" Brigham inquired with a cocky grin.

Neither one of the cousins actually expected an answer. So they weren't all that disappointed when they didn't get one.

CHAPTER TWENTY-ONE

Though the assignment of this new barghests-in-England mission had come quickly and chaotically, not to mention the hasty packing and piling into the car so the Clan's driver Connor could take Halsey and Brigham to the Dallas-Fort Worth Airport on time, the urgent pace abruptly settled the second they boarded their flight.

Because a twelve-plus-hour flight from Texas to London's Heathrow International was incredibly long and incredibly uneventful, and there was nothing Halsey or her cousin could do about it.

At one point, Brigham tried to break up the monotony with what had previously been their team's standard MO before each and every hunt. "Anything else other than death and horror come to mind when I say 'barghest?'"

Halsey paused the movie she'd been watching on her phone, the first of many on a long flight like this, and looked at him. "I'm not sure a refresher course in barghest-neutralizing is gonna help us much with this one, cuz."

"What?" He scrunched his face, glanced at the sports

magazine he'd bought in the terminal along with a snack, then looked up again. "Why not?"

"Because everything we've ever known about every monster in our catalog is pretty much useless now. Using Greek legends to take down the chimera didn't work. It took the entire Havalon Clan militia plus *us* to get rid of the werewolves turning *outside* a full moon. Plus, my dad and I killed a bunch of ogres in the same spot by chopping off their hands until they puked themselves to death. Ever read anything about *those* creature habits in our prep books?"

"Shit." He slumped back into his seat, wobbling it violently and eliciting an irritated huff from the passenger directly behind him. "Yeah, you're right. No more battle strategy and attack plans, huh?"

"Probably not. Sorry." When her cousin didn't have anything else to say, Halsey pressed play on her phone again to keep watching her movie. Two seconds later, Brigham swatted at her arm, and she had to pause the movie again. "What?"

"What about the potions?" He raised his eyebrows and spread his arms as much as the small space in coach class provided. "You think those'll actually work if we need 'em? Or should we just, like, assume we're screwed from the very beginning?"

She chuckled and leaned back in her seat a lot more gently than he did. "Yeah, we do kinda seem to have that going for us, huh?"

"You know me, Hal. I like to be prepared. And if I have to be prepared for *not* being prepared, that counts. I think."

Nodding, she had to take a moment to think about how

they were most likely going to handle this mission that seemed particularly straightforward at a glance. The villagers of Coningsby, way out in middle-of-nowhere England, needed help with the terrible monsters ravaging their streets and driving their friends and neighbors insane with images of their own deaths. Probably.

Yet it was made so much more complicated by the fact that monsters hadn't been playing by the rules for months now. On top of that, Halsey had a persistent hunch there was a lot more to this mission than met the eye. Cavanaugh had no idea *where* the Ambrosius Clan militia had gotten the tip about the barghests. Even if "tips" rolled in like that, they didn't get escalated to full-on mission status four days after whatever monster showed up and started causing problems.

Missions weren't generally assigned in a few hours, either. Especially not before shipping off the best and most capable team of Ambrosius hunters on what felt like nothing but a whim.

Halsey and Brigham were not and never had been "the cleanup crew."

Yet she didn't have any proof of that. Right now, working on a mission that might be easy despite not knowing *how* the barghests had changed from their MO for the last thousand years seemed the best way to focus her energy.

"I think we shouldn't assume anything about anything." She cast Brigham a sidelong glance. "We've gotten good at winging it, anyway."

"Ha. When shit hits the fan, send out Brigham and Hal. Except these days, we're the ones *throwing* the shit."

"Thank you for such an inspiring image, cuz."

"Hey, no problem. I gotcha."

Halfway through their flight, bored out of her mind and unable to sleep and waiting for the next in-flight meal to come around, Halsey considered having the ever-looming conversation with her cousin. Part of her brimmed with excitement to tell Brigham what she'd discovered by Rolfr Magnusson's dying words and the fact that "the monk" in question was most likely the dead monk Cedric and his other elemental friends had found on the Viking ship.

The other part of her decided this wasn't the right place or the right time. Still.

She considered how she'd reacted to hearing the final truth about her mom and the entire Council's reactions to Gillian's death. Not to mention twenty years of sustained lies and secrets the older half of the family had been keeping from the younger half. Revealing her secrets to Brigham could potentially go the same way. If their situations were reversed, the last place Halsey would want to hear even more secrets was stuck in a cramped airline seat for twelve-plus hours with the person who was finally spilling the beans.

So she kept her mouth shut and told herself she'd find the time. Maybe after this barghest mission, she and Brigham could add an extra day or two onto their stay in England and finally have the conversations they needed to have.

It had to happen before they got another mission or ran into any other monsters. Because now, with the Blood Matriarch out of her coffin and walking around on dry land with the progeny of her creature creations, the

Ambrosius cousins were bound to run into another alpha sooner or later. It was better for Brigham to know all the possibilities of what those alpha monsters were capable of before seeing it for himself firsthand.

It was harder to admit the real reason she wanted to tell him about everything when the time was right. Keeping secrets from her best friend and mission partner had worn her down so much more than she'd expected. She'd kept that information from him in Ireland because she didn't want him to think she was as insane as the Ambrosius Council had wrongly predicted.

Now, Brigham was on the same page. He believed in the legends, he understood what was at stake, and he was behind her one hundred percent.

No, it wasn't quite the same as keeping devastating secrets from him for the last *twenty years*. Yet she understood what Aidan had meant when he'd said shame was the heavier burden to shoulder by far.

As long as we don't let that get between us on a hunt, we'll be all right. I'll make sure of it.

The feeling of being in uneventful limbo right before they were supposed to charge into the allegedly chaotic village of Coningsby continued even after the cousins landed at Heathrow. Fighting off jetlag and hauling their duffel bags along with them, they found the rental car agency with which the Council had booked them a ride.

"Classic English ride." Brigham twirled the keyring around his finger as they walked out onto the lot where their car waited for them. "Has to be."

"Did they tell you what it was?"

"No, but come on, Hal. I have a feeling about these

things." He clicked the key fob and listened for the telltale beep from the classic English ride.

Both cousins spun to face the sound, and Halsey laughed. "Oh, yeah. A *Camry*. That's where it's at, cuz. This thing looks older than both of us."

"Shut up." Grimacing, Brigham opened the rear door, slung his bag inside, and all but slammed the door shut again before heading toward the driver-side door.

Halsey found it incredibly disorienting to sit on the left side of the car in the front passenger seat, but it was easier to ignore while smirking at her cousin and giving him hell for being so excited about a Toyota Camry that looked like it had been sitting under the scant English sunshine in the wind, the rain, and the chill for a few years. "Very posh."

At least the engine turned over, which was honestly more than she'd expected. Brigham didn't say anything else about the car. However, after fifteen minutes of following Halsey's co-pilot GPS directions, his mischievous smirk had returned.

Then there was the long, monotonous, *flat* drive out to Coningsby. It took them a total of four hours, punctuated by two different stops. One to refuel the gas tank and the other to refuel their stomachs. Mostly, that came in the form of as many energy drinks as they could safely imbibe on the way to their target site.

Two hours into the drive, Brigham fiddled with the dashboard's radio buttons and got nothing but static. For the first time since being hauled from their normal lives in Texas to be assigned this mission, he let his frustration show by pounding on the dashboard, then pounding on the horn in the middle of the steering wheel.

Halsey shot him a dubious look and muttered, "There are easier ways to stay awake, dude. Do we need to stop again for more caffeine?"

With a hiss, he shook his head and gripped the steering wheel harshly with both hands again. "It's like they want us to be miserable."

"If I wanted luxury, I wouldn't exactly leave it all up to a rental agency we've never used before—"

"The *Council*, Hal," he snapped. "I'm talking about the Council."

"Right."

That pretty much put a stop to the conversation. Halsey couldn't have agreed more with her cousin, but saying it out loud wouldn't do much of anything to improve his mood at the moment.

At least he's finally starting to see how much they've been failing us lately. I wouldn't necessarily go so far as to say they want us to be miserable, but they aren't pulling out any of the usual stops to give their top monster-hunting team the best experience.

Brigham wasn't finished fuming and surprised her by actually talking about it out loud. "It's not just me, right? I mean, we're *good*, Hal. Maybe even the best."

"No need to be humble…"

"Sure. But *this* mission? Shit, I feel like an underpaid janitor working the night shift. Tell me it's not just me."

Halsey stared at the long stretch of road racing ahead of them across the English countryside. "It's not just you."

"You've been feeling like this for way longer than I have. Haven't you?" Brigham looked at her for as long as he possibly could before the necessity of driving safely made him turn back toward the road. "Of course you have. And I kept laughing it off like everyone else. Damn it, Hal. I wish I'd known."

Halsey shrugged, acutely aware once again that there were *still* things he didn't know. Yet they were stuck in a car together in the middle of nowhere, headed out toward even more nowhere. It still wasn't the right time to lay it all out there. So instead, she simply replied, "You know now."

"Uh-huh. And it sucks." They shared a wry laugh at that, and Brigham's tight grip on the steering wheel finally loosened a little. "Think we'd get anywhere with, like, a petition or something? You know, asking for better treatment of Ambrosius workers."

"You mean monster hunters?"

"Same thing. Seriously, though, these working conditions are starting to go downhill."

Halsey snorted. "Makes Turkey feel like a luxury spa retreat, huh?"

"Shit. I'd take Turkey again over this any day."

"You'd rather have an indestructible chimera with wings that required non-elemental magic to kill?"

For a moment, it seemed like Brigham wouldn't respond. Then he sighed and clicked his tongue. "No. You're right. Turkey sucked, too."

"Now we're on quick and easy cleanup duty." She shot her cousin a blatantly fake grin and nodded. "Go us."

"Moving up." He raised his hand for a sideways high-five. "A-Team for the win!"

Though Halsey had never enjoyed his super-unoriginal name for their two-man super-team, she snorted and met his awkward sideways high-five with a satisfying smack.

CHAPTER TWENTY-TWO

By the time they were within minutes of approaching Coningsby's outer limits, the Ambrosius cousins' mood had greatly improved. A good deal of it had to do with the unseemly amounts of caffeine they'd consumed along the way. The rest of it could easily be attributed to the fact that they'd officially been *on* this mission for almost seventeen hours at this point. Other than the Camry not being up to Brigham's needlessly high expectations, they hadn't run into any problems or gotten into any arguments.

Nothing felt like it was looming over their heads.

In fact, it seemed like everything was working out for them. The last time Halsey felt like this was when she and Brigham were making their way along western Ireland looking for those pesky werewolves. Then they were attacked by a pack three to four times larger than any pack had a right to be. Their first sign something wasn't quite right.

"Here we go." Halsey pointed up ahead at a small sign

along a narrow paved road, almost hidden from view. "Take a right here."

"With the 'Welcome to Coningsby' sign? Pretty self-explanatory, cuz."

"Okay, well, I'm making sure you're paying attention."

"I'm driving. I can't *not* pay attention."

"All right. Jeez." Laughing, Halsey dropped her phone into her lap because they obviously didn't need GPS anymore.

"So here we are. Coningsby." Brigham slowed down to take the turn, then leaned forward over the steering wheel to peer up at the buildings on either side of the village's main road and the trees rising tall beside them. "Nice little place, actually. Bet we'll find a wooden bridge out here and everything. Maybe snag some trolls while we're at it."

"Totally. Extra side hustle to help out a few locals, right?"

"Hey, you never know. So… Any idea who we're supposed to meet with here? I'm guessing a place like this has some kind of major. Or, like, whatever you call the head honcho around here."

Halsey pressed her lips together to fight back a laugh. "Probably."

"You think Coningsby has a tavern too? Like an inn or whatever. We'll roll right up, ask for a room, and sit down in the pub underneath to listen for all the gossip about monsters. Sounds like some kinda fantasy videogame, right?"

"Ha. Sounds like our last trip to Ireland."

"That too. Oh hey. What's that big building up there on the right?"

She leaned forward with him and squinted, trying to make out the sign over the door. "I don't know. Looks like a—"

The incredible force striking the right side of their rental car wiped all thoughts from both cousins' heads. The sound of crunching steel and squealing tires and splintering glass overwhelmed everything else as the vehicle lurched and spun sideways across the road. Fortunately, Brigham knew enough about handling cars to correct and keep them from toppling sideways to roll down the short, shallow embankment on the left side of the main road.

The first thing Halsey felt was the car's right-side tires lifting precariously off the pavement before settling back down with a jolt that rocked the Ambrosius cousins in their seats.

Then everything was still and quiet.

Eerily quiet.

The only sound was the rhythmic tick of the car's engine failing and the hiss of steam coming from the hood.

Halsey blinked heavily, gathered her wits again, and finally managed to croak out, "What the hell?"

"Ah, shit…" Brigham rubbed the back of his neck, then looked up to stretch it out from side to side. "Fucking whiplash, man. And I'm a *good* driver."

"Brigham." Halsey stared past her cousin and through the splintered driver-side window, which now faced the other side of the street because they'd been hit and spun in a quick and disorienting one-eighty.

"Yeah, I'm good. But seriously, you'd think at least *one* of us would be able to see something coming at us out of the blue like that. Damn." He turned in his seat, craning his neck to look out the rear windows and scan the road. "Was there even a side street there? Talk about T-boning."

"Brigham." Her first attempt to grab his arm fell short because she couldn't bring herself to look away from the enormous beast hunched over on the side of the road.

Staring back at her with glowing red eyes.

"Not to mention a good first impression with the locals," he continued, oblivious. "*That's* shot to hell."

"It's not the locals!" She managed to grab his wrist on the second attempt, and whether it was the shouting or his cousin's death grip on his arm, Brigham finally got the picture and started paying attention.

"Ow. What?" He half-heartedly slapped her wrist.

Still trapped in the gaze of a creature that shouldn't have been allowed to grow nearly as big as it was, she slowly retracted her hand and nodded out the splintered window. "Target in sight, dude."

"What? Come on." Brigham swiveled in his seat, looking everywhere but at the actual barghest crouched on the side of the road. "I don't see shit, Hal."

"You don't see the giant fucking black dog with demon eyes staring at us?" Halsey finally had to look away from the beast to grab the collar of her cousin's shirt and force him to look in the right direction. "It's standing right *there*."

Except when they both looked at the previously indicated spot on the side of the road, the barghest was gone.

"Shit." Gritting her teeth, Halsey released her cousin's shirt, unintentionally shoving him away from her in the process, and urgently unfastened her seatbelt.

"Not a funny joke, cuz," Brigham mused. "I don't see—"

"Yeah, it was there, and now it's not." She shoved her door open, climbed stiffly from the seat, and opened the rear door to grab gear. "Which means we're gonna have to skip the introduction with the locals and go right for the throat."

"Dude." Brigham watched her from the driver's seat without making a move to get out. "You hit your head on the dashboard or something? This car definitely sucks. No airbags. Maybe we should take a look at—"

"Get out of the fucking car, Brigham." Halsey lugged her duffel bag strap over her shoulder, which was already sore from some definite whiplash and from hitting her seatbelt as hard as she had. They didn't have a whole lot of time to screw around with sore shoulders and possible head injuries, though. One of the barghests had clearly found them first. The Ambrosius elementals had to work fast to take the first one down before the others showed up and formed an attack pack.

Brigham hadn't seen a hint of the black death-omen dog his cousin was so sure had been standing right there at the side of the road, but he knew Halsey. He'd promised he wouldn't pause again when she asked him for a leap of faith. Except he didn't expect to have to keep that promise so soon after making it. "Yeah, okay."

He turned the keys in the ignition automatically despite the rental car's engine having already sputtered out on them after the crash. Then he whipped off his seatbelt and climbed from the car, groaning and stretching out his back. Halsey rifled through her stuffed duffel bag on the ground, throwing shirts, pants, and toiletries into the back of the car to lighten the load. As she did, Brigham studied the incredible damage done to their rental car.

The entire right-hand side had been bashed in, buckling like they'd been T-boned by another car instead of what was apparently a glancing blow from a barghest.

"Damn. That asshole had some serious speed to hit us like this."

"Serious speed, yeah. Serious claws. Serious teeth. Serious tendency to rip people apart limb from limb. Especially when it's got all its little buddies around to help it out—Brigham!"

"Yep." Trying to blink away lingering dizziness, he opened the other rear door and pulled out his duffel bag. "Are we going with best-guess weapon, or…"

"Just take everything."

"Right." He smirked at her as she finally zipped her much lighter bag and slung it over her shoulder. "So this *is* kinda like Turkey. Everything and the kitchen sink, huh?"

Halsey paused to stare at him. "What is it with you and old-people phrases?"

"*Old*-people phrases. Please. I don't even know what that means."

"Yeah, okay." With a wry laugh, Halsey turned in the middle of the main road to orient herself toward the center of Coningsby. "Guess we're making it the rest of the way on foot."

"Nothing we haven't done before." Brigham cast the rental car a final glance over his shoulder and grimaced. "I swear to God, Hal. If they didn't at least spring for insurance on that thing, I am *so* starting a petition."

"I'll sign it. Come on."

With the wrecked car behind them and the barghest once again nowhere in sight, the Ambrosius cousins trekked down the main road of Coningsby in pursuit of their monsters.

CHAPTER TWENTY-THREE

It didn't take them very long to realize something was very wrong about this quiet little village, other than the apparent barghest infestation.

First of all, the place was *too* quiet. No birds singing in the trees, no rush of water from a river or fountains. No fluttering branches, buzzing bees, or flitting hummingbirds in the quaint little gardens in front of nearly every building. No rumble of other vehicle engines or crackle of tires crunching slowly across gravel. No murmur of voices.

In fact, there was no sign of a single living thing here in the village of Coningsby. Which was a serious problem.

"Hal," Brigham murmured as he scanned his side of the main street, and Halsey scanned the other. "This is creepy as hell, right?"

"It's not just you, man." Moving slowly, Halsey unzipped her duffel bag as quietly as she could and reached around inside for the weapon she wanted. All her weapons stood out to her by feel, and she quickly found her fingers wrapping around the solid, oiled handle of one of her throwing axes before she pulled that out of the bag.

Brigham shot her a glance before returning his attention to the buildings and the tiny alleys between them. "Oh yeah. Sure. That's gonna get the people on our side. Let's walk down the center of the main road with a damn *axe*, right out in the open."

"There aren't any people to *see* it, Brigham." She tightened her grip on the handle. "I wanna be ready."

"Right there with you. How many of 'em you think we're gonna find here?"

"As many as we can get rid of, I guess."

"Great."

The eerie silence continued until the echoing bark of a dog made its way toward them. It sounded like a regular dog, but even that became strange when other dogs joined in. Howling, barking, yipping, snarling. In seconds, it sounded like a thousand dogs on the other side of the village waiting for the two elementals to barge in and break up the party.

"No way those are all barghests," Brigham muttered.

"Probably not. No way to tell until we get eyes on another—"

"Hal! Watch out!" Brigham dived toward her, grabbed her by the arm, and hauled her down to the paved road as an enormous black shadow hurtled toward them both with a terrifying snarl.

Both cousins hit the ground hard, and Halsey almost lost her grip on her throwing axe as she skidded painfully across the pavement.

The barghest's claws cracked and grated on the same road as it landed without having caught its target. Sparks flew from where those enormous, razor-tipped claws struck the road, and a cloud of shadow whipped out behind the terrifying creature like an ethereal cloak.

"Shit, shit, shit..." Brigham rolled away from Halsey and tried to scramble after his weapons bag, which had flown off his shoulder and was now halfway across the road, out of reach.

"Brigham, wait!" Halsey gave up on trying to get him to listen to her. Instead, she reached out with her magic for the life force of the earth beneath the road and found two enormous mounds of solid stone beneath. The road trembled and buckled, then exploded in a shower of stones and pavement and dirt before the giant boulders she really wanted surged up from underground.

She tossed the giant new projectiles right over Brigham's head as her cousin half-crouched, half-ran toward his weapons bag.

The barghest was faster than both of them. It lunged at Brigham with a glinting paw, striking him in the hip and knocking him off his feet. A second later, Halsey's boulders whizzed right for the black beast's head, but the barghest snarled and leapt directly up and out of the way.

Halsey saw the thing's rear legs come down onto one of those boulders in mid-air, which it then used to launch itself again.

Directly toward *her*.

She didn't have the time to wonder how that was even possible before the creature landed right in front of her with a snarl and another spray of sparks as its claws scraped across the pavement.

Gritting her teeth, Halsey scrambled to her feet and stepped back. She tightened her grip on her axe again and stared at the beast that clearly knew a lot more about what it was doing than either of the elementals sent after it. Yet she didn't look away from those glowing, hellish red eyes. She had a strong feeling doing so would be the last thing she ever did.

This is what a barghest does, Halsey. You're not gonna die. Deal with this thing.

"Come on, then," she snarled, mimicking the enormous black dog's crouch and baring her teeth in the same way. "You wanna do this? Come on!"

With a low, warning growl, the barghest hunched its back, and its entire body rippled from the base of its spine up to the back of its head. Then in one swift, unforeseen motion, the creature stood fully on its hind legs, glaring at Halsey and growling and looking a hell of a lot more like a werewolf than a dog.

No way. Now I have a death-dealing man-dog on my hands?

She backed up a few more paces, trying to draw the thing toward her again and closer to the side of the road where two particularly strong-looking trees grew up between the little buildings. If she could get close enough to those, she could call on the roots and the branches for backup.

Where the hell is Brigham?

The barghest threw its head back and howled, which sounded a lot like a werewolf. The madly barking dogs in the distance went even crazier at the sound, and Halsey risked looking across the road to find her cousin.

Unfortunately, Brigham's weapons bag had been tossed under a car parked at the curb, and he hadn't quite managed to pull it free.

"A little help over here would be great," she called.

"I'm *trying*!"

"Brigham!"

The barghest advanced, holding its front paws out at either side like it *was* a werewolf, though there were some real differences. The barghest's bite *and* its claws were the deadliest obstacles. Unlike a werewolf bite that only made another werewolf, a barghest wound would remain forever and never heal. Then its victim dropped dead on the spot.

Jesus, did it kill the whole village?

Then she had no more time for thinking because the creature lunged toward her again on its hind legs and swiped a massive paw toward her.

Halsey called on the power of the tree roots she was finally close enough to command, but they only made it halfway toward her target. Because the barghest was so much faster than anything else she'd fought before.

The next thing she knew, it was on her. Driving her down, slamming her back against the pavement.

Halsey cried out against the jarring pain in her hips and back and the effort of holding a snarling, slavering, demon-eyed beast far enough away to keep its jaws from snapping down on her face. It took her another split second to realize she was literally holding the barghest at bay with her throwing axe. The handle was long enough to fit into both her hands and served as a relatively effective chokehold as she pressed the handle up into the monster's throat.

Apparently, that was the only thing keeping the barghest from tearing her apart.

It wouldn't last much longer, though.

She kicked out with both feet as the barghest strained against her, her sneakers thumping against the pavement amidst the grating shriek of monster claws on pavement and showers of sparks. If she wanted to get out of this, she had to get at least one leg up between her and the creature to somehow pry it off her. With a knee, or a thigh, or even a swift kick to the barghest's more vulnerable parts. Whatever those happened to be.

Strings of steaming-hot, viscous saliva dripped from the monster's snapping jaws as it growled and snarled and fought desperately to get closer to its prey. Even, it would seem, at the expense of crushing its own throat against the handle of Halsey's axe.

Then Brigham shouted, "Don't move!" and she almost laughed out loud at the ridiculous command.

There was no time.

A wave of intense heat overwhelmed her as a red-hot glow nearly drowned out everything else. Halsey instantly recognized the powerful magical energy of fire all around her, realized that Brigham had abandoned his weapons bag for the lighter in his pocket, and while he blasted fire at the crazed barghest seconds away from ripping apart his cousin, he somehow also managed to shield her from the flames at the same time.

Good thinking, but fire won't do shit. All the monsters are changing—

Her brief moment of doubt was cut short when the barghest launched a furious, pained, howling cry. The full extent of its body weight on top of hers faltered, joined by the gut-churning scent of singed hair and bad breath.

Halsey seized the moment, finally got a leg up between herself and the black-dog beast bearing down on her, and managed to kick the thing away from her and buy herself some more time.

The barghest tried to bear down on her again, though now it had been caught off guard by the sheer agony of being set aflame by a second elemental and the surprise of its latest potential victim fighting back with an impressive level of success. As Halsey kicked the monstrous beast up and away, roaring with the effort, the barghest snapped at her in a final effort to bite her face off.

Instead, those powerful jaws clamped down on the handle of her throwing axe right between both of Halsey's hands. She felt the coarse fur of the black dog's snout brushing against the sides of her knuckles before the monster's jaws clamped down even tighter with the crunch of splintering wood.

The axe head flew, spinning end over end until it landed somewhere down the embankment where Halsey could never get to it. The rest of the polished wooden handle would've fallen apart in her hands if she hadn't followed her instincts and let go.

Then the monster was off her, torn away by a combination of her fierce kick and shove and the enormous column of precisely targeted flames Brigham had sent right into the creature's side.

The barghest was gone in the direction of the

embankment off the side of the road, and Halsey rolled the other way toward the middle of the street, gasping for breath.

"That's right!" Brigham shouted as he flicked his lighter again and pulled up another raging wave of flames. "Fucking stings, don't it?"

Halsey only had a moment to watch her cousin valiantly fighting off the monstrous barghest with nothing more than his elemental magic and a cheap gas station lighter.

The creature howled and snarled, stumbling around beneath the onslaught of flames that were clearly hurting it.

Just like fire was known to do when facing down the black dog demon-omen of death.

Why is that actually working?

The stench of burning hair was overwhelming. Halsey pushed herself to her feet at the same instant Brigham shouted, "Yeah? You want some more?"

Instead of producing another flame he could manipulate with his personal magic specialty, the lighter only released a grating click.

No hiss of butane escaping the lighter. No spark of flame. No roar of a churning inferno he could send at their target.

"Shit." Brigham furiously shook the lighter, then tried to ignite it again to no avail. "Shit, shit, shit…"

He tried several more times, but that was because he'd started to panic now and had run out of last-minute ideas.

Which gave the impossibly intelligent barghest time to slap the flames from what was left of its fur before it turned its hellishly glowing red eyes onto the young Ambrosius elemental who'd tried to burn it down.

Brigham knew he was screwed the instant those red eyes locked onto him. Then he froze. He'd been counting on a working lighter to help him defeat a monster using the tried-and-true methods that had neutralized the world's barghests for the last thousand years. Without fire, he had absolutely nothing else he could do.

His hazel eyes widened.

The barghest snarled, coiling into a crouch on its hind legs before springing off the mowed grass lining the top of the embankment. The monster launched itself directly at Brigham, claws outstretched and strings of saliva streaming out behind it from its open, snarling jaws.

A blistering crack filled the main street of Coningsby, echoing over and over against the street and all the little houses lined up neatly in a row but somehow eerily empty and silent now.

Brigham flinched, thinking he was about to go down beneath the weight of the only monster he hadn't been able to defeat.

The barghest, however, went down first.

An unseen force knocked the creature from its forward trajectory, and instead of landing on Brigham's chest to tear the young elemental apart, it dropped right there onto the road in a crumpled heap of black fur and snaking streams of smoke from all that singed hair.

"What the..." Brigham jerked in surprise and preemptively ducked as he spun to face the source of the deafening crack.

He found Halsey standing there in the middle of the

road beside her open weapons bag, both hands clamped down around the stock of the deadliest-looking bolt-action rifle Brigham had ever seen.

She stood stock-still in the center of the road with the firearm in her hands, glowering at the pile of crumpled, singed, unmoving barghest.

Her cousin's jaw dropped. "That actually worked."

"Yeah, you can thank Pappy for that one." Halsey didn't move, still watching the barghest with her full attention because she wasn't convinced they were out of the woods yet.

"You packed Pappy's *rifle*?"

"I packed everything, dude. Apparently, fire and a solid shot to the chest are still everything we need to bring this asshole down."

With his mouth still hanging open, Brigham turned back toward the barghest and cocked his head. "Is it…dead?"

"I don't know. Are you volunteering to go check?"

"Not really—whoa."

As if the barghest were reacting to their actual conversation, the crumpled form in the road disintegrated, blown into a thousand fluttering pieces like ash in the wind. The breeze carried those fragments up and away as the bulk of the beast's once-living body crumbled. The last of it morphed into thick black smoke, churning and roiling across the road and down the embankment before dissipating.

Then there was no more barghest.

Brigham smacked his lips and pointed at the spot where

the creature had been lying. "I'm gonna go ahead and say it's dead as shit now."

"Yep."

"That wasn't supposed to work, was it?"

"Nope." Finally, she lowered the rifle and met her cousin's gaze. "I mean, yeah, back when monsters were following the rules, that was supposed to work. But now? It shouldn't have been so easy."

After taking a quick moment to consider this surprising revelation, Brigham snorted. "Maybe we're finally getting the lucky break we needed."

"Right. That's totally it." Rolling her eyes, Halsey squatted beside her weapons bag and carefully set her grandfather's rifle down on the pavement beside it. She couldn't bring herself to look away from the place where the barghest had vanished. "Fire actually hurt the damn thing, and all it took was a single shot from a normal round. That doesn't make sense."

"Hal," Brigham uttered. "I think we might have another little problem."

"Yeah, I know. There's something seriously not right about any of this. What happened to all the people who live here? Where did they go? We need to find them. See if anyone's been hurt. Damn it, if the whole village got attacked, Cavanaugh only gave us six vials of antidote."

"Five, probably. I hope."

"What?" Frowning, Halsey finally tore her gaze away from where the barghest's corpse had been and looked up at her cousin. "Why would we only have—"

Brigham grimaced, grunted in pain, and stumbled

forward. His legs gave out, but he caught himself on one knee with a short groan.

His face had gone completely white.

"Whoa." She leapt to her feet and headed toward him. "What's wrong? What's going on?"

Her cousin sucked in a sharp breath through his teeth, then slowly lifted the bottom of his shirt to expose the top of his right hip and lower abdomen. "Guess I wasn't as quick on my toes as usual, huh?"

For a moment, the sight of her cousin's wound made her freeze up.

A three-inch gash had been opened in Brigham's side, clearly made by the barghest's claws when the creature bashed him aside to get to Halsey. Yet where any other painful slice would have been red, angry, and bleeding profusely, this wound already looked like it had been festering for days.

There was hardly any blood. Only a black gash where there should have been glistening layers of fat and flesh. Snaking black lines grew quickly across Brigham's skin like an infection. The wound was clearly draining him of his energy.

"Oh shit," Halsey whispered.

"Yeah, no shit." Her cousin laughed bitterly and grimaced at the pain even that small movement brought.

"Okay, we got this." She set a gentle hand on his shoulder and turned slightly to scour the empty street. "Where's your bag? The vials are still in there, right?"

"Yep." Grunting again, Brigham pulled his shirt back down over the nasty wound. "It's under the car…"

"The *rental*?"

"No. That one. It's under…"

"Right. Got it." She took off toward the plain-brown sedan, having caught a glimpse of the duffel bag's strap beneath the carriage.

Losing more and more of his strength by the second, Brigham wobbled on his knee and half-sat, half-collapsed onto the pavement. Then he gave up trying to tell her anything and pointed weakly in the direction of the only other car parked on this street.

Halsey sprinted toward the car, dropped to the ground on her stomach, and reached as far as her arm could go to get to the strap of her cousin's weapons bag. When her fingers finally locked onto it, she pulled it roughly toward her, scraping her elbow and the underside of her forearm in the process. She barely felt it.

Her hands fumbled with the zipper, which got stuck several times in her haste. She rifled urgently through the extra gear Brigham had packed for this particular mission.

"Jesus, it was a regular barghest," she muttered, shaking as she shoved aside various weapons and ammo cases to find the purse Cavanaugh had handed over. "Why the hell did we pack so much *stuff*?"

"Hal," Brigham croaked.

"I'm coming, I'm coming. Hold on. I just—got it!" The glass vials clinked violently together when she practically ripped the canvas purse from the duffel bag. Grimacing, Halsey fumbled with the purse's latch, then finally managed to pull out one of the fortunately intact vials before pushing herself to her feet. "Got it. Right here."

"Great." He swallowed thickly, then drew in a rattling breath. "Way to be prepared, right?"

Halsey ran toward him with the precious vial of barghest-poison antidote, the glowing green liquid sloshing around inside as she clamped her fist around the whole thing and hoped to hell she wouldn't crack the glass in her grasp.

By the time she reached him, Brigham was already laid out on the pavement, breathing shallowly and paler than ever.

"Here. It's right here. I'm here." She dropped to her knees and slid toward him, heedless of the painful thud and scrape of her own legs. Taking the stopper out of the vial took far longer than she wanted, and she released a desperate, frustrated growl before finally digging her fingers in and pulling it out. "Okay, sit up and drink this."

She had to slide a hand under her cousin to help him up enough so he could drink, but her shaking hand almost made it impossible to get the top of the vial to his lips.

Brigham chuckled weakly and reached up to touch her wrist. "Take a deep breath or something, huh? Won't work if you spill it all over me, and I'm pretty sure potion stains won't come out of this shirt easily…"

"Shut up." The fact that he was still joking in spite of his current terrible state made her laugh a little, though there was no humor in it. Still, Halsey managed to follow his suggestion. She drew a bracing breath, steadying her hand enough to keep it from violently trembling all over the place, and finally got the vial of glowing green potion to her cousin's lips.

Brigham had no problem drinking it down in seconds, and though a few luminescent drops fell from the corners of his mouth, most of their Aunt Florence's healing potion went where it was supposed to go. He coughed once, then sighed and gently let his head fall back onto the pavement. "Thanks for that."

"Ha. Yeah, no problem. Part of the job and everything." With a sigh of relief, Halsey sat back on her heels and watched her cousin closely for signs of improvement. "How do you feel?"

"Like…roadkill, honestly."

Fighting not to roll her eyes, she reached for the bottom of his shirt and gingerly pulled it up to reveal the wound. The hole in Brigham's flesh was bigger now, and the black streaks had spread up his ribcage and disappeared under the rest of his shirt. "No…"

"Hey, gimme a break, Hal. I was out of the gym for almost a month after those ogres put me out, but the washboard abs will come back super-fast. You'll see." The crooked smile on his face belied the proof in front of them. His face had lost all its color, and his closed eyes looked gaunt and weak. Like they were being sucked back into his skull.

"It's not working," Halsey muttered.

"Maybe it needs a few more seconds."

Absently tossing the empty vial onto the pavement, Halsey leaned closer to study her cousin and found the tip of one of those black streaks now creeping up from beneath the top of his shirt collar. "Fuck. I don't think it has anything to do with timing, Brigham. The potion didn't work."

Despite the news that should've made him as scared as she was, the lazy, almost dreamy smile on Brigham's face remained. "If you say so. I guess that's...that. What do we do now?"

"I don't know. I gotta think."

"Sure. Just don't take too long, Hal." Opening his eyes again, Brigham slowly lifted his right hand to see the black streaks were now making their way up his forearm and grimaced. "That might be all I've got left."

"Don't say shit like that."

"Like what? The truth?"

"Just stop talking. You'll wear yourself out even faster. I'll...I'll fix this."

Another thick swallow clicked in the back of his throat, followed by another ragged breath that sounded like he had a five-hundred-pound weight resting on his chest. "I trust you."

Hearing those words brought an instant sting of hot tears to her eyes, which Halsey had to close to keep her cousin from seeing them in case he happened to be looking up at her.

He trusts me, and I led him right into a barghest fight that's gonna be the last thing he ever does if I don't fix this. I have to fix it!

While she tried to calm her breathing and search through all the facts in her mind about poisoned wounds and barghests and healing, a warm, tingling buzz of energy caught her awareness.

She recognized it instantly, and her eyes flew open again as she spun on the pavement to face her weapons bag. As she knew it would, the pulsing golden glow rose from within the open top of her duffel.

The copper orb had responded to her magic since the

very beginning. It had formed itself into this shape, moved at her slightest wish, and melted an unkillable chimera into three dead parts. Now it was responding to her emotions and her needs once more when all else had failed.

Since finding the pile of leftover magical sand, Halsey had used the alchemized orb both to create and to destroy. Now she would use it to save Brigham's life.

Knowing in her bones what the orb was capable of didn't seem like enough to go on, but it was the only option she had.

Halsey only had to reach out toward her open duffel bag for the orb to respond to her silent command. It lurched up from the bag and darted toward her open hand, settling there with a solid thump of metal on flesh. The thing's magic lit up inside her, buzzing into her hands, up her arms, and into her core with a force more powerful than she'd felt any other time she'd used the thing. Intentionally or otherwise.

Taking another deep breath, she pulled up the hem of Brigham's shirt and turned her focus onto the wound.

Blinking quickly at the movement, he looked down along his body to see his cousin kneeling there beside him again with that damn glowing ball in her hand. "What the... Aw, *hell* no, Hal. You brought that thing with you *again?*"

"It's a good thing I did, too. Hold still."

"What the fuck are you gonna do with it?"

"I said I would fix it, so shut up and let me fix it!" She hadn't meant to snap at him, but it wasn't like she had all the extra time necessary to control the inflection in her voice. Fortunately, though, Brigham did shut up. It didn't help to feel her cousin's dubious, nearly terrified stare the whole time, but she managed to block everything else out to focus on the only thing that mattered.

She cradled the copper orb in both hands and sent every fiber of her desperate intention toward the magic inside the object she'd created herself and still didn't fully understand.

In seconds, the first signs of success made themselves clear.

Tiny filaments of copper and golden light streamed away from the orb as if it were projecting pieces of itself. The sphere grew incredibly hot in Halsey's hands, but she didn't dare let go. Somehow, despite the blazing pain, she *knew* the thing wouldn't hurt her in the end. Doing this took commitment and dedication, and Halsey had all of it.

With agonizing slowness, the glowing threads of magic snaked their way down toward Brigham's hip and abdomen and the nauseatingly festering wound that had only been there for a few minutes.

Brigham's eyes widened as he watched the process too, and he didn't move a single muscle. His breathing quickened. His mouth opened and closed like he was about to say something, but no words emerged. He was too weak to get up, to scramble away, to tell his cousin to get that psychotic thing away from him. Plus, he badly wanted to believe his best friend actually knew what she was doing. So he let her.

When the threads of the orb's magic reached the rotting gash in Brigham's side, he sucked in a sharp breath through his teeth before letting out a shuddering groan.

Halsey forced herself not to stop the process or check

on him or doubt herself. She couldn't even consider the possibility that she'd been wrong. She couldn't lose her cousin. Not like this.

Not ever.

Then the first traces of the black lines snaking all across Brigham's skin started to fade. They withdrew along his body slowly, moving back toward the source of the barghest's unhealable poison and the nasty gash that started it all. His breath quickened again, but this time, it sounded like it was in relief.

At least, that was what Halsey hoped. Even still, she focused only on what she wanted the copper orb to do.

Heal him. Please. Whatever that monster left inside him, get it out. Fix this.

In another twenty seconds that felt like a lifetime, the alchemized magic Halsey had harnessed did exactly what she intended it to do.

The black streaks were half their previous length, then a quarter, then an eighth. When all the infected lines had disappeared from Brigham's flesh, the copper orb's glowing threads focused on the blackened, dying edges of the slash in his side. Slowly but surely, the evidence of the barghest's poison disappeared the way it should have when he'd taken the potion.

Apparently, nothing about the barghest itself or how to kill it had changed. The real and quite terrifying change with this particular monster, however, was clearly in the way it left its victims half-alive when it was done with them.

Halsey would rather die herself than let that impossibility of a monster take her cousin away from her.

Luckily for both of them, neither of those things had to happen.

The orb was healing him, plain and simple.

It didn't matter that it felt like the thing was zapping all the energy and life force out of Halsey in the process. Despite a rush of dizziness, the burning heat in her hands, and the sudden faintness like she hadn't eaten in days overwhelming her, she maintained her focus.

This had to be done.

It took all her concentration and a lot of Brigham willing himself not to get up and run away screaming. Finally, the tiny filaments of golden light faded from his flesh, leaving nothing but a regular slash across his hip. The color returned to his face. His breath eased and slowed. And it was done.

"There." Halsey closed her eyes and sighed, grateful the searing heat in her palms was gone now and waiting for the wave of dizziness to pass.

As she did, Brigham slowly and experimentally propped himself up on his elbows to look at the slice in his side that was still there and very real. Only it was bleeding now. No longer necrotized by barghest poison. Though it still hurt like hell to move, he sat up further with wide eyes.

"Holy shit." Brigham examined his wound with his fingers, gingerly prodding around the flesh that definitely needed a bandage. He stared at Halsey like *she'd* been the one to put it there. "Hal."

"I told you I'd fix it."

"That was *you*."

"I know."

"It wasn't only the damn ball thing. That was... I felt..."

He urgently scanned her face and swallowed. "It was *your* magic, too. But it wasn't… It wasn't elemental magic at all."

"Brigham, I *know*." She met his gaze and widened her eyes, knowing her cousin was thinking the exact same thing.

Except Brigham was determined to voice the question for both of them.

"Then what the hell was it?"

Get sneak peeks, exclusive giveaways, behind the scenes content, and more. PLUS you'll be notified of special **one day only fan pricing** on new releases.

Sign up today to get free stories.

Visit: https://marthacarr.com/read-free-stories/

AUTHOR NOTES - MARTHA CARR

APRIL 4, 2023

I've started a project answering questions for my son about my life. I realized after last year's fifth round of cancer, and then chemo this time that he was expecting me to die sooner rather than later. It's been a lot for him to deal with and there isn't much I can do to make it better, except tell him stories that I can leave behind – eventually. Hopefully, a long time from now. I'm going to let you guys listen in as well.

My author notes for this year are going to be answers to questions and all of you can get to know me better, too. Maybe inspire, maybe give you a laugh along the way.

Today's question is: What's a small decision you made that ended up having a big impact on your life?

It was in 2017 when I finally got out of my way. I went to therapy, in particular EMDR, and said I was there because I was always getting prestigious and positive reviews about my books, but not a lot of sales. Readers who found the books loved them, but there weren't a lot of them. Was it me?

Of course, we ended up talking about everything else, mostly knotty issues from childhood until we reached a resting place and the therapist said, "For now, you're done. Go back out in the world."

Something shifted inside and I stopped needing to prove I deserved a seat at the table. I stopped inserting what I knew about writing or publishing, or just about anything, where it wasn't really necessary. It became easier to listen and just say yes. No matter what, say yes. Don't predict the future, or wonder why it won't work, or what could go wrong. You don't know anyway. Just go. Trust blindly and step out.

A few months later, I was sitting in a MeetUp in Austin listening to this guy, Michael Anderle, talking about what he had discovered about indie publishing. I went up, asked for his phone number (he won't hand it out anymore, so give that one up - but listen for your opportunities), and kept in touch. I was the only one in that room of about a hundred writers who did that.

When he called a few months later and asked if I wanted to try a new genre, urban fantasy, and create a new universe that would become Oriceran, I said, well, yes. Everything that came after that, even if I was afraid, or worried, or wondered if I knew enough to pull this off, I said yes, let's do it.

Not everything worked out. There's a list of half-assed decisions, or poor timing, or something just happened, but I kept rolling. I didn't second guess myself, or turn back, or spew doubt. I just kept saying yes.

Now, all those positive vibes are adding up to seven

figures and I'm about to launch my first Kickstarter out there on my own.

It changed an attitude inside of me as well that went a lot deeper.

I bought a house, and then sold it and bought a bigger one in an even better spot. Built an amazing garden. Traveled more, went out more. Saying yes cultivated an attitude of being open to the world that's still evolving and revealing itself. I've even gone back for more EMDR to discover more new things.

Life is kind of long and it's meant to be enjoyed. If you're not having fun, start with asking why? Then make some changes. Trust that in the end, it'll be okay and start saying yes more often.

I know that at the end of my life, I'm going to look back and see this wonderful zigzag pattern that was eventually of my own choosing and just got better and better. No regrets because I finally learned how to stand out front and speak up as well as listen, and just keep saying yes. Love you. Love, Mom. More adventures to follow.

AUTHOR NOTES - MICHAEL ANDERLE

APRIL 4, 2023

First, thank you for not only reading this story, but these author notes in the back as well!

Sesame Street and Book Covers

In this exciting adventure, Martha, my indomitable collaborator, and I took our characters on a wild ride. Along the way, we discovered the importance of just one letter – the difference between a monster and a warrior.

Barghest: a mythical monstrous black dog with large teeth and claws.

Barghast: *Not the same thing as a Barghest*.

You see, our story revolves around the fearsome creature, the Barghest, but in a moment of oversight, we received a cover for the book with the title featuring the word "Barghast" instead. It's fascinating how one little E can change everything.

Of course, we all make mistakes, and this was just a minor hiccup in the grand scheme of things. But it does highlight the importance of paying attention to the details, even when you're caught up in the whirlwind of creativity.

Fortunately, we caught the error in time, and the book itself had the correct spelling. However, when it came to supplying the cover to the audio company, we found ourselves in a bit of a pickle. There we were, scrambling to get the E in the right place for our audio listeners.

Thankfully, we managed to resolve the issue, and our monster remained true to its intended form. It just goes to show that even in the world of writing and publishing, sometimes it's the little things that make all the difference.

So, as you dive into our story, know that Martha and I have worked hard to create a world full of rich details and captivating characters. We hope you enjoy every twist and turn along the way. And remember, sometimes the smallest changes can lead to the most significant impacts.

Here's to the power of the letter E and the adventures that lie ahead.

Ad Aeternitatem,

Michael Anderle

MORE STORIES with Michael newsletter HERE: https://michael.beehiiv.com/

BOOKS BY MARTHA CARR

THE LEIRA CHRONICLES
CASE FILES OF AN URBAN WITCH
DIARY OF A DARK MONSTER
THE EVERMORES CHRONICLES
SOUL STONE MAGE
THE KACY CHRONICLES
MIDWEST MAGIC CHRONICLES
THE FAIRHAVEN CHRONICLES
I FEAR NO EVIL
THE DANIEL CODEX SERIES
SCHOOL OF NECESSARY MAGIC
SCHOOL OF NECESSARY MAGIC: RAINE CAMPBELL
ALISON BROWNSTONE
FEDERAL AGENTS OF MAGIC
SCIONS OF MAGIC
THE UNBELIEVABLE MR. BROWNSTONE
DWARF BOUNTY HUNTER
ACADEMY OF NECESSARY MAGIC
MAGIC CITY CHRONICLES
ROGUE AGENTS OF MAGIC
CHRONICLES OF WINLAND UNDERWOOD
WITCH WARRIOR

OTHER BOOKS BY JUDITH BERENS

OTHER BOOKS BY MARTHA CARR

JOIN THE ORICERAN UNIVERSE FAN GROUP ON FACEBOOK!

BOOKS BY MICHAEL ANDERLE

Sign up for the LMBPN email list to be notified of new releases and special deals!

http://lmbpn.com/email/

For a complete list of books by Michael Anderle, please visit:

www.lmbpn.com/ma-books/

CONNECT WITH THE AUTHORS

Martha Carr Social
Website:
http://www.marthacarr.com
Facebook:
https://www.facebook.com/groups/MarthaCarrFans/

Michael Anderle

Website: http://lmbpn.com

Email List: http://lmbpn.com/email/

https://www.facebook.com/LMBPNPublishing

https://twitter.com/MichaelAnderle

https://www.instagram.com/lmbpn_publishing/

https://www.bookbub.com/authors/michael-anderle

www.ingramcontent.com/pod-product-compliance
Lightning Source LLC
LaVergne TN
LVHW091716070526
838199LV00050B/2418